UNCERTAINTY OF REASON

MALCOLM HOLLINGDRAKE

Book Eleven in the Harrogate Crime Series

Also by Malcolm Hollingdrake

Bridging the Gulf

Shadows from the Past – Short Stories for Short Journeys

The Harrogate Crime Series

Only the Dead

Hell's Gate

Flesh Evidence

Game Point

Dying Art

Crossed Out

The Third Breath

Treble Clef

Threadbare

Fragments

The Merseyside Series

Published by Hobeck Books

Catch as Catch Can

Syn

Dedicated to our dear friends

Joan and Mick Neville

Man hands on misery to man.

It deepens like a coastal shelf.

Get out as early as you can,

And don't have any kids yourself.

Philip Larkin

'This be the Verse.

Chapter One

Time does not always heal. Memories sometimes haunt us with a great intensity: we see the place, hear the sounds, smell the smells, and as we relive every detail, we experience again every emotion.

This was exactly how Robin Collier felt when he recalled the crash, in fact, not just the crash but everything that came before it, and after it. When he remembered, he was back at home away from the cold and wet of the East Coast. He was a youth again.

Robin could remember that morning, hearing the engine growl and the distinctive rasp as the old Jaguar started. The sound spurred him to get out of bed and ran downstairs quickly. The usual voices of Radio Four news and the smell of toast suggested today would be like every other day, but the sound of the car promised otherwise.

In his dressing gown he moved out onto the drive, rubbing sleep from his eyes. There it sat, the engine ticking and clicking as it cooled. Robin remembered tentatively putting his hand on the sleek, polished bonnet, fearful it could bite at any moment. He felt the heat; it was alive. The smell was that distinct heady aroma of hot oil and rubber.

In a perfect imitation of Murray Walker he commentated, "the Jaguar is lined up and ready to race, the champion driver, Robin Collier, is well-prepared and keen to begin the gruelling twenty-four hours of Le Mans. The cars are now ready, the drivers waiting … Go! Go! Go! They're off!" He smiled. He had worked hard at perfecting the intonation and his friends at school had been impressed, so too had his father but that was short lived. With a raised voice and a pointed finger Robin's father had always argued that he should cease fooling about to impress his friends, he should stop participating in school concerts and plays, and he should develop greater enthusiasm for mathematics, science and other academic subjects which would be better for his university prospects. Mr Collier did not understand, never mind appreciate, his son's real passion in life – Entertainment. And Robin knew it.

"Your breakfast is on the table, young man. The car's going nowhere without you," Mrs Collier called from the hallway.

Robin had thought to himself that when he could drive, things would be different.

Mr Collier was sitting at the table reading the latest copy of *Motor Sport* which he tossed onto the chair once Robin had sat down.

"Your elbows are on the table, Robin. Remove them." He waited until they were on his lap. "I hate to be the harbinger of bad news but this will be the E-type's last trip with us, son. I've sold her." He casually took a spoonful of boiled egg and rolled it onto his toast soldier. He did not sound sad nor regretful. The words came as easily as if he were saying good morning.

"You promised if I did well at school then you would teach me to drive and race the Jaguar. That it would one day be mine," Robin protested, shocked and confused. Mr

Collier's look conveyed everything, matter of fact as always. After a few moments Robin dared to ask the question. "Why?"

When Mr Collier looked up Robin caught a flash of anger, but it was quickly replaced with a false smile. "We are not using her as she was designed to be treated. She should be winning races in the hands of someone who can afford to spend on development and racing more competitively. I cannot, but I know a man who's keen and he has the funds. It's a swop. At least we've enjoyed a few good years. Remember those special times and we'll move on." It was an instruction to be obeyed. He reached and picked up the magazine again as his wife placed a cup of tea in front of him. "Besides, we need the garage space for your mother's new car."

She immediately rested a hand on her husband's shoulder, bent and kissed his balding head: a rare display of affection. Robin had lost his appetite.

Robin could still remember the knack of closing the Jaguar's aluminium door. It had to be lifted and slammed. The lightweight Perspex in the door's window vibrated with the action. Once in, he had slipped the racing harnesses over each shoulder and fastened them at the waist belt before pulling down, feeling the belts' bite. He had seen racing drivers carry out this procedure before a race.

Mr Collier looked across at his son and smiled. "Sorry son. Let's make it a special trip."

The car roared into life. Mr Collier never fastened his belt unless he was racing, a sign of his arrogant disregard for rules that he had not made to which he would not adhere.

3

"Where to? You may choose." Mr Collier smiled, hoping to appease his son and improve the mood.

Robin could still remember how his senses went into overdrive with the thrill and pleasure of the ride, his heart beating with the pulse of the engine and he knew the road he wanted to take. Trees lined the edge and even when travelling at sixty miles per hour, their proximity to the narrow lane enhanced the sensation of speed. Robin realised his father would drive faster than the legal limit – he always did. Once out of Harrogate and heading along Ripley Road the engine note smoothed as the temperature increased. The next right turn would put them on High Moor Lane, a narrow but straight road that was perfect for a fast run. Robin had felt the car accelerate as soon as the turn was completed. The rear of the car moved out, bringing with it a protesting squeal from the tyres. Glancing at the rev counter Robin knew, as the next gear was selected, that they were approaching the magic of one hundred miles an hour. A ton!

A quick right bend was followed by a sweeping left. The noise was intoxicating. They were now onto Brearton Lane and then would come Robin's favourite track of road, Green Lane. The car growled and the revs increased.

Memory can play through moments as if in slow motion, every detail clear. Robin's memory also returned the guilt to his stomach.

The morning sun hit the driver's side of the speeding car, illuminating the interior. The trees to the right approached and as the car passed, a strobe-like effect was created blurring Robin's peripheral vision, suddenly bringing a palpable confusion and anger. He closed his eyes in protest. The black soon turned to red. Why he did what he next did he would never be sure. He reached out and grabbed at the steering wheel tugging it downwards with as much force as he could muster. The simple tug moved the car quickly off track. Mr Collier fought to bring the vehicle under control but the front wheels were on the grass and the bonnet swiftly made contact with the hedge. Mr Collier's foot moved instinctively onto the brake. The sudden deceleration caused Robin's arms and legs to fly forward but the shoulder straps held him firmly within the racing seat. Mr Collier's chest, however, hit the steering wheel as his face and head connected with the windscreen. His deformed body, rag doll-like, compressed as it was channelled forward through the newly-formed gap between roof and dashboard, before colliding with the upturned, deformed bonnet. The engine screamed momentarily and stopped before steam billowed ghostlike from beneath the fractured metal. From the cacophony of unnatural sounds there was a sudden and eerie silence.

Robin stared at his father's face. He saw him try to move but then watched as bubbles of blood dribbled from his nostrils, blending with the rest of his battered face.

The police inquest into the accident had been speculative. Robin's father never remembered the incident nor did he care. The healing process of his facial scars and disfigurement were of greater concern. Robin had said nothing. His convenient amnesia would remain with him. 'Driving too fast for the road conditions at the time,' was the verdict.

Chapter Two

It was unusual to walk home along the darkening, early evening streets of Scarborough wearing theatrical make-up, a key feature of his trade, but then it was not every day you walked away from the job you loved, the job you believed to be your true vocation. The route from the station to his apartment on Cambridge Street would normally take five or six minutes but on this occasion the journey was a blur. He was in limbo, replaying the earlier part of the day with a fermenting degree of anger and sadness.

After any performance, the silence seemed crushing, it was a direct contrast to the shouts, the music, laughter and songs. Maybe it was the adrenaline release that dissipated too rapidly after the final curtain fell, creating a natural anticlimax. Maybe it was simply relief! Today, however, after this matinee performance, packed with school kids and pensioners, it was treacly thick to the extent it made it difficult to breathe. He had not performed well, he knew that. Something someone had shouted early in the performance seemed to sap his confidence and it did not go unnoticed, he knew it would not and he was proved right.

The Director had soon entered the shared dressing room after the show; that was nothing out of the ordinary. She would breeze in, usually scattering positive words to many of the cast, but also sharing the occasional, more direct, private word to an odd one or two who might not have performed to the best of their ability. The debrief, to her at least, was often classed as director's jewels, constructive criticism, professional encouragement for personal development, but to the cast they all considered it to be a dressing-down. This particular afternoon it was different, the words were neither subtle nor sensitive and to many of the actors watching on, unacceptable. This was particularly significant for the person sitting in front of an illuminated mirror. A made-up face stared back, like a disappointed yet confused Janus. Her words seemed more barbed as they were directed at him. They were neither quiet nor subtle in their delivery. To the man staring back in the mirror they were cutting, cruel and unnecessary. He started to slowly count in his head to calm his growing anger. On completion he had stood, turned to face her and had accidentally fallen towards her. She took hold of him and he held on to her.

"You've not been drinking?"

She released her hold and he straightened. The exaggerated, painted, deep red pout had betrayed his inner emotions throughout the whole dressing-down but in some ways, it conveyed his true disdain. Others turned away embarrassed for their fellow thespian. To the one man, the taller of the two ugly sisters, the words seemed to echo repeatedly within the cavernous blackness that now occupied his headspace; they were sharp hammer blows each finding their target with an unnerving degree of accuracy that slowly crushed him, making him see red. Matters were not improved as she pointed a finger inches from his face. That was to prove the last straw. He saw his father's red face, ugly in anger, appear within his mind's eye.

"What's the bloody matter with you recently? You're supposed to be evil. You're supposed to be booed and hissed at. You're not supposed to be funny and kind and have kids like you. And what's with the voices? If I'd wanted an impressionist, I'd have booked one!" The staccato statements came like blows, one after the other. "To make matters worse you needed too many prompts. Where's your head these days? You were never like this before, never." She shook her head and leaned against the long dressing table that ran down one wall, a shrine filled with good luck and thank you cards, flowers and make-up. "You've had a mixed bag of performances lately. I'm not happy with such poor acting. You're sacked, Stansfield will cover your role."

For a moment he was a child again and he flinched, expecting a clenched fist to crash against his chest. When it did not, he grew in confidence.

"Stansfield! You're replacing me with … Stansfield?" His words spilled from his rouged lips as the thought lingered longer than was healthy. Tearing off his blue bouffant wig he threw it directly into her face.

"We all have bad days, even you. I've been in the acting profession for years and as directors go, you're no Alfred Hitchcock." He mimicked Hitchcock's slow, monotonous voice bringing a few giggles from the others within the room. Her anger flared.

"And remember, no one will die because of the occasional bit of bad acting or directing for that matter. How many curtain calls did we get? Two? Some people are never satisfied."

She left, face flushed, her words ringing from down the corridor. "Make sure you leave what's ours and take what's yours and be gone! Do you hear?"

A silence followed but was soon replaced by giggles and laughter. "Ignore her. We do. Remember we all have a bad performance now and again." Arms wrapped round his shoulders but the anger was still simmering. He opened his closed fist to reveal a key.

"She'll be looking for this when I'm gone."

"From her pocket? Just then? Clever!" Multiple voices asked various questions.

He nodded, changed quickly and left the theatre, refusing offers of coffee or beer and tossed the key in the bin. He put his finger to his lips. "Our secret, the bitch!"

Leaving the stage door, a voice followed him. "See you at the flat."

He raised a hand in acknowledgement as he was met with a chill breeze from the sea that seemed to channel down the street. He needed to get home. Still made up, he walked to the railway station. Being an ugly sister, all green eyeshadow, beauty spot and wrinkles, dressed as a man, sitting opposite surprised travellers for a thirty-five minute journey turned out to be the one bright spot of the late afternoon.

***

Losing the job was a bitter pill to swallow but a temporary position working in the arcade on the seafront presented itself. There was little pressure and it gave him time to reflect. Meeting Jennifer Brown and moving in with her lifted his spirits but in reality, the following few weeks brought the return of his demons. When the mood swings came, solace was found in the bars along the seafront. It was there, gin in hand, alone in a corner surrounded by the disturbing flash of disco lights, that the anger returned. He focused on the loud youth by the bar who appeared drunk and who was arguing whilst poking a finger towards the barman. His father had always pointed before prodding and then lashing out. That was always a precursor to the pain. Closing his eyes, he began to count – 1, 2, 3 – the dark space behind his eyes slowly changed through various colours until he saw red. Within minutes he would be following the youth. He needed to have a strong word.

Chapter Three

As if on cue the now constant flicker of the LED bulb set within the ceiling brought his reminiscence to a sudden halt. It became an annoying distraction making concentration difficult drawing his eyes from the television. It had been a while since he had paused the film as the Lamborghini struck the bulldozer. It was a favourite scene from the film and one he liked to watch whenever he was alone. He played it repeatedly in slow motion but on this occasion the flickering annoyance of the light had become too intrusive, too real. "The crash and the light – déjà bloody vu." He mumbled.

The flicker had started quite suddenly earlier in the evening and for no reason – intermittent initially but over the course of an hour it settled into a disturbing and infuriating rhythm, a strobe-like blinking that seemed to illuminate even the darkest corners of the room. Within minutes he kicked off his shoes, stood on the settee and unscrewed the offending bulb.

"Nothing annoys me more than flashing light." Robin laughed, a piercing, unnatural scream as if in contradiction. He studied the surface of the bulb but could only see the small LED circles set in the round beneath the glass covering. *In the old days the fractured filament would be within the glass bowl – a broken and blackened cat-like whisker, easily seen*, he thought to himself.

He shook the bulb close to his ear before tapping it with his finger. There was no sound. It was something his father would have done before crashing it against the nearest wall and allowing it to scatter across the four corners of the room. There it would remain for days until he allowed Mother to clear it. He remembered the irrational anger and its consequences. Looking at the bulb the memories flooded back and his hand shook. He stared at the nearest wall and then the empty socket above his head. He fought the urge to launch it.

Sense won and he took a deep breath before replacing it. Leaning over he put down the light switch; it flickered now with an even greater intensity. With a curse beneath his breath, he removed it before launching it towards the wall, careful not to hit one of the framed posters. Miraculously it did not shatter but rebounded before falling to land intact at his feet. The frustration built. He wanted to lift his foot and crush it with all the strength of his resentment and anger that had suddenly ballooned from nowhere. He closed his eyes. "You've fucked me up!" he mumbled, wrapping his arms tightly around himself as if he were in a straightjacket. A low, extended growl erupted and tears ran down his cheeks. "Count, count!" he ordered as he heard the numbers climb in his head. Initially coloured black they slowly changed along with his breathing. "It mustn't turn red, it mustn't. Not now, please not now!" The brighter colours began to fade back to black and then grey as the count was decreased.

Opening his eyes, he deliberately collected the bulb and moved through to the kitchen, depositing the offending article in the bin before turning to open the fridge door. Everything was neat and orderly and the smell from the *fridge fresh* was immediate. He removed a bottle of tonic. The interior light flickered momentarily. "Don't you bloody dare!" he instructed, venom returning to his voice. With a similar anger and force, he slammed the fridge door shut, the remaining bottles set within rattled in protest.

"Gin. I just need gin. 'We'll always have Paris if we don't have a … bulb!'" The voice accurately mimicked that of Ingrid Bergman before the words of Bogart filled his head and he mumbled perfectly, "'Of all the gin joints …'" He did not finish the quote. The cabinet holding the bottle held his full attention. It took him back to Scarborough all those years ago. Jennifer liked his Bogart impersonation. He settled back onto the settee and ejected the film. He had had enough for one day.

Chapter Four

DCI Cyril Bennett pulled into the square and parked next to the needlesharp Feversham monument. It was rare that he managed to get the morning away from work mid-week but the attraction of buying a small oil painting by Reginald Brundrit brought about a rescheduling of his time. For eight in the morning Helmsley was quiet. A number of workers were pulling onto the square to buy breakfast from the bakers. For Cyril it was time to stretch his legs and reacquaint himself with the castle ruins. The half-destroyed building reminded him of a split nut, the yellow-golden stone illuminated by the low sun made even more unique and spectacular. There was a peace that always seemed to be present whenever he paid a visit to the market town and sadly, that was not often enough. On crossing back over the stone bridge, he glanced at the beck that flowed briskly beneath. It ran whispering over the stones, delicate and clear, the submerged gossamer reed appearing to wave at his stare. He checked his watch. He needed to be in Kirkbymoorside by nine to view the painting. He would not wait for the auction proper. Police work had always been a thief of his time and he could not afford the luxury of a full day.

The auction house was set back behind a garage and next to a garden centre. The car park was quiet. It was his first visit. He always got a tingle of excitement the moments before viewing. He hoped it would match the condition report as he had been disappointed in the past on more than one occasion. He was not today. It was as expected. After consultation with the auctioneer, he booked a telephone call to bid and noted the approximate time the lot would go through the following day. It was now about getting back to Harrogate and the police station. The excitement of the chase would have to be suppressed for twenty-four hours.

Chapter Five

It had become apparent to Tom for the first time that week the days were growing longer. It was only marginal but noticeable. He always took the daily walk to and from the office in the dark. Apart from the artificial light which leached from buildings and streetlights, bleaching the immediate surroundings, bringing myriad shadows and shapes, the chiaroscuro of narrow streets and open areas seemed so familiar at this time of year. He worked in the light and lived in the dark. He felt nocturnal. Tom's early morning route to work was always the same but over the last few days there had been a noticeable but subtle change; a marked and distinct lightening across the eastern sky was growing evident, a clarion call for the dark, long days to slowly wane and ebb. To those not familiar with this time of day it would be unnoticeable, but to Tom it was the beginning of a change of season, the early birth of spring. Without pausing he looked at the distant church spire, needle-like, its vague silhouette just visible. *That would not have been visible a week ago.* His thoughts brought a smile yet there was still a sharp nip to the air and a slight frost coating on the exposed dark green skin of The Stray.

He had taken to walking to work for nearly twelve months, same time, the same direction, the same pavements, same shops; even stranger to him, he seemed to see the same people. Like him, they appeared to be programmed. Up, coffee and out. Not only were those walking familiar but so too were the cars he noticed on certain parts of his route. They had become recognisable; one in particular, a red Fiesta, hazard lights flashing, was usually seen most days, illegally parked, engine running, outside the newsagents. He had even named it – Lester – and often wished it a good morning as he passed. The silliness made him chuckle. It was, he thought, as if Harrogate ran by clockwork, everyone and everything had a designated moment, it was as if the town were the stage, its inhabitants, players, each acting out a certain role. However, as in real life, there was the occasional aberration. This town was a busy commercial hub, constantly striving to attract businesses for conferences and festivals, encouraging tourists from every geographical area and all walks of life to visit whilst enticing them to spend their time and more importantly their money during their stay.

As he walked, he sometimes received a fleeting greeting or a smile, a nod, a clear sign these were touring actors, stand-ins who did not know, understand nor follow the set script. It often seemed false and improvised. They were the strangers, the interlopers. Tom's planned journey always seemed calm and timely until the odd insomniac, the curious tourist or the early morning runner jarred his daily smooth-running routine, therefore interrupting the movement of the clockwork's cogs and gears. Fortunately, any interruption to his morning progress, was usually momentary and although an unnecessary hiatus, it did not bring the imaginary mechanism to a total, grinding halt.

What did bring this particular day to a standstill was the sky, that same eastern sky in which he had witnessed change. Usually at this hour it was a blanket of grey-black but not today. Tom stared at a deep red line that ran like a fine, blood-wet blade slicing the horizon open and making silhouettes of anything standing before. It was at that precise moment, as he compared the red to that of a bleeding wound, that he sensed a presence. To another observer, standing now not too far away, the red sky held a greater significance.

***

Despite knowing the alarm would soon be pulsating its annoying morning greeting, Cyril struggled to release his hand from beneath the quilt. Julie slept on with the minimum amount of movement, curled foetus-like and hidden beneath the bed coverings. He collected his watch, held it at arm's length and checked the time before shaking it and slipping it on to his wrist. He had beaten the alarm three days on the trot and for some perverse reason, felt a tingle of elation. He pressed the 'off' button with a victor's swagger. It would be a further ten minutes before he woke Julie. He had brewed a pot of tea, slipped the cosy over the pot before popping bread under the grill. He moved the tray containing all the accoutrements to the table. He had just started pouring his tea.

"Conquering hero again this morning and it's still dark. Excited about the auction?" Julie appeared rather bleary-eyed as she tied her dressing gown and moved into the kitchen. She kissed him. "You need a shave."

"Hat trick. Only by ten minutes today but a challenge is a challenge and yes, as always, very excited. It's a lovely painting. Tea?"

She yawned and nodded whilst pulling up a chair.

"How's Hannah coping with the bump? Owen's like a cat on hot bricks. Says he's going to attend the antenatal classes. Now there's an image to conjure with." Cyril paused and pulled a face. "He has that baby book you gave him permanently on his desk with various coloured Post-it notes protruding from the pages. I keep telling him it's not an exam he's about to sit." The smell of the toast stirred him and he immediately stood and turned the bread under the grill whilst managing to burn the back of his hand.

Julie chuckled. "Not laughing at you." She took his hand and kissed it. "You'll be fine just put some butter on it. No, I was thinking about Owen. For such a big chap he's a special softy. She'll be coming up to her thirty-six weeks before we can turn round. Chris will be taking her place soon and he's like a kid at Christmas. Hannah's excited for him too and offering all the support she can." Julie poured her own tea as Cyril buttered the toast. She noticed him add a small dot onto the burn as instructed.

"How come ordinary bread becomes so good with just a bit of heat? The smell, the flavour. Heat transforms something so basic into ..." He took a bite and a small yellow globule of molten butter trickled from the side of his mouth before he stopped its downward track with his finger.

"Just like my diamond, all pressure and heat, I believe." She looked at her engagement ring before kissing his hand.

***

The feeling intensified. Staring at the red and growing light

19

brought a discomfort Tom had experienced before but not in his new everyday life – it was a sudden stabbing, intrusive feeling and at that moment seemed irrational bringing with it an uncertainty. It was as if he were suddenly being scrutinised. A tingling sensation ran along the nape of his neck. It was neither warm nor cold, just discomforting, bringing with it an enhanced awareness from all of his senses. The cars' engines seemed louder, the shrill song from what he thought to be a robin, perched in some obscure roost high up and to his left near one of the streetlights, was now amplified. Tom moved the shoulder strap of the laptop bag he carried to bring it closer to him, therefore making it more secure. As it came to his chest, he wrapped it with both arms like a mother protecting a newborn.

Slowing his breathing allowed him to control his sudden anxiety. It was then his training kicked in. Instinct. He made his whole body turn slowly through three hundred and sixty degrees; his eyes, lingering momentarily at every one of those degrees of the circle, turned whilst he searched his surroundings, the buildings, the openings, the gaps and the crevices until he saw it. His eyes immediately focused on a face staring back and he paused. A warm flush of fear ran through his whole being before he realised, he was staring at his own reflection in a dark, empty shop window; a cruel trick of the light. Continuing the rotation there was nothing else to see. Even upon the realisation he had been disturbed by his own reflection, the feelings still seemed so real. He checked again, this time taking his gaze higher, stopping at the upper windows and roof edges. There was still nothing out of the ordinary.

From behind he suddenly heard approaching footsteps, rapid and eager to cover ground. He turned whilst taking a step backwards and clutched the bag more firmly. The runner, head down, suddenly crashed into him. Strange arms enveloped him and clung to his jacket in an attempt to straighten. Tom gave a short, involuntary shout as he stood his ground and maintained his balance. The runner, regaining his equilibrium, pulled away before raising one hand and offering an apology, a slow drawling voice that did not befit the stranger. Tom took another step back. The runner turned away and was soon putting distance between them. Tom straightened his clothing. His anxiety dissipated as quickly as it had appeared. Checking his watch, he was surprised at the time. He would be late. He had another ten minutes to get to the office but he knew that would be impossible unless he ran too.

"Not like you, Tom, to be a minute late. Watch stopped?" Michael Stockwell sipped his coffee as he perched on the edge of his desk whilst pointing at the large clock on the wall. "But ten minutes, that's a record." It was clear from his build and his confidence that he too was ex-forces.

Tom glanced at his watch and shook his head. "Make me a brew, Mike. Strange experience this morning. Two sugars and I'll tell all."

***

Turning the key in the front door, Cyril watched as Julie unlocked her car.

"I can drop you." She looked back to see Cyril raise a hand. "You sure? I'll see you tonight. Home about six if all

21

goes to plan. Give Owen a kiss from me." She chuckled as Cyril screwed up his face at the thought.

Crossing West Park, Cyril followed the footpath that dissected The Stray. The crocuses carpeted the area between the trees and also lined the edges to each pathway, a phalanx of protective, multi-coloured tightly packed rows. Their vivid ranks would bring the tourists and the photographers to what was now an annual pilgrimage that seemed to grow more popular year on year. His mind flicked to the tasks of the day and the long walk to and from work allowed him the luxury of focusing on the day's targets and order them into a manageable structure. It was something he had always done. He cherished this time even though the journey seemed to take him longer these days.

He had a court appearance followed by a meeting with his superior all before he could think about lunch. Then there was the auction – he focused briefly on that. He slipped his hand into his coat pocket and retrieved one of the mints stashed there. He unwrapped it. Since quitting vaping these had been his saving grace. It was a substitute for the menthol and it took away the constant yearning. His phone rang.

"Bennett." The call was from DC Brian Smirthwaite.

"Brian, sir. Morning." He did not wait for an answer. "I'm sending you a car. You need to see this for yourself. And sir, it's not pretty."

Cyril checked his watch before responding. He gave his location. "Where?"

"Lock-up garage just off Ripon Road. Crime scene personnel are on site. Discovered early this morning by a milkman."

***

Mike handed Tom his usual mug. He did not say anything but looked at his colleague expecting a joke or a feeble excuse. However, there was an expression in Tom's eyes that made Mike draw up a chair. He had experienced this look on occasion whilst on tour, particularly when under threat. "Take your time. What was so strange?"

Tom continued to sip his coffee, both hands wrapping around the mug. He stared directly ahead for a few moments before turning. "I walk the same route every day, five, sometimes six days a week. As you know it's through town, fairly well lit, apart from a couple of the streets near the park and the edge of The Stray. Always felt comfortable even when in winter, the dark is ..." he searched for words, "... Dark but friendly if you understand me." His voice faded slightly before taking a further sip. "Mike, today I felt fear, real fear. Not for the whole journey. It was when I turned out of Crown Place, the cobbled street next to the Royal Pump Room. It started not long after, just by the roundabout. I'd stopped to look at the fantastic red in the sky and suddenly I knew or maybe I just thought that someone was watching me closely, scrutinising me." Pausing for a moment as if to collect his thoughts, he continued. "Remember when on patrol you could get a strong sense at certain times that you were being watched?"

Mike nodded. "Never forgotten it."

"It was not dissimilar to that but equally as strong." He shook his head. "Sorry, this sounds like twaddle. We're in Harrogate for goodness' sake!"

Mike put his mug onto his desk and leaned forward. He

could see that there was genuine fear in his friend and colleague's eyes. "I stopped to look at the sky too. Blood red. First time I've seen it this year." He thought immediately about the ancient rhyme 'red sky in the morning shepherd's warning' and wanted to quote it but thought it inappropriate. "Did you see anyone?"

"My own bloody reflection staring back at me from an empty shop. It didn't look like me at first and took my breath away. It was only when I finally brought it into focus. I did a full sweep as we were taught when on foot patrol. My senses were so alert. You know the feeling. You've done tours into hostile places. You just get this sixth sense, usually before all hell fire is let loose."

"Been there, my friend, been there." Mike tapped the lower portion of his leg and the metal of his prosthetic gave out a dull, metallic note. "We had no warning but the team knew something was imminent. You needed eyes in your arse sometimes."

"Strangely, a jogger crashed into me at that moment. He appeared from the same direction in which I'd come. I only clocked him when he collided with me. He apologised and strangely enough was soon gone. His voice sounded so familiar but then my senses were so heightened. I was probably confused."

"Whose voice did you hear?" Mike asked curiously.

"That's the thing, I don't know. I quickly realised it wasn't someone I know personally. I've heard the voice on TV or in a film. I know it didn't fit the runner."

"Change your route tomorrow." Mike put his hand on Tom's arm. "Precaution that's all. It's what we were taught. Remember? If in doubt, make changes."

"Do you know what was bizarre?" Tom finished his coffee.

"The feeling went as quickly as it came?" Mike muttered recalling his own experience.

"You're right. It did for me today. One minute I was tense and ready and then the next, there was nothing apart from an urgency to get into work."

"Your runner couldn't have followed you from home, could he?"

Tom shrugged his shoulders.

"Remember what I've said. Change your route each day for a few days at least or drive in."

Chapter Six

Turning right off Ripon Road it was soon evident by the number of police vehicles they were at the location. Four lock-up garages stood in front of a block of apartments. Other similar garages were situated both higher and lower on the road. As always, the limp police tape, secured to any available surface, blocked the way. Temporary lights blazed behind screening that had been erected to block the lower area and the gaping aperture of the structure from prying eyes.

Dawn had taken a strong hold on the day and the eastern sky was turning a duck-egg blue, bringing with it greater visibility to the town's streets and roads. The temporary lights were still on behind the screen piercing the enclosed space of the second garage within the row. Cyril stood and made time to inspect the surrounds of the crime scene, taking in the finer details, something he had always done since his early days as a detective. He had been advised by his then boss that this simple action would help arrange things in order, to get a sense of the place. It had been wise advice. The Crime Scene Manager approached and nodded to Cyril before the gesture turned to a spontaneous shake of the head.

"Worst I've ever witnessed, sir. Poor bugger survived but God only knows how. It's up to the surgeons now but what they'll do I don't know."

"Maybe his God was on his side today." Cyril's tone was flat and without any real feeling. "Do we have an identity?"

"Male. Shane Coffrey, nineteen. He's known to us. Been trouble since he was a kid. One of the many feral, petty criminals that infest the darker corners of our streets. We believe he now deals in the hard stuff but as yet we have no evidence. He's thought to be staying at a temporary address in Knaresborough which is yet to be confirmed but has a grandparent, his nan. She lives here in Harrogate and when we've confronted her in the past, she's been very defensive, thinks he's still an angelic six-year-old and that the sun shines out of his arse. The details came from the latest report they had on him. He's due in court in July for riding a dirt bike, no documents and no helmet, through the centre of town. Not a bright lad. He believed we wouldn't chase him. That bike was confiscated but we also confiscated another bike from his nan's house about two months ago. Wasn't registered, neither tax nor insurance. It's been scrapped. As I said, his details are within the system. We assume he was either brought here or lured." He handed Cyril an iPad. "These images show what the poor bastard went through."

Cyril flicked the cover from the pad and watched the video showing the discovery of Coffrey from the body cam of the first responder at the scene. Pausing it occasionally he spread his fingers to enlarge parts of the static image. Smirthwaite, who had driven Cyril to the crime scene, moved away after the first few minutes.

"He's crossed the line and gone into someone else's patch I bet." Cyril realised he was talking to himself as he turned to see Smithwaite returning, beads of sweat having broken out across his forehead. "You, okay?"

Smirthwaite nodded. "Usually, I cope well in these circumstances but today …"

"Only his face from what I can see. Nowhere else on the head or body?" The question was lost and received no answer.

Cyril noted from the video that Coffrey was curled naked in a foetal position, his left hand stretched beyond his head. Blood covered mainly the upper frontal part of his body and as if in contrast, what appeared to be faeces smeared the lower rear half of the torso. In the artificial light they both seemed to be of a similar colour. A limited amount of blood spatter was evident on the nearby walls, fine arcs of what appeared to be black marks that contrasted with the lighter grey of the walls and ceiling.

"The milkman heard a banging on the metal door and he opened it thinking someone had locked themselves inside. According to Forensics, the internal handle had been removed recently. Anyway, when the milkman opened the door, he was greeted with what you can see there." The CSM tapped the pad. "He rang emergency services immediately. He too was in one hell of a state and is also at the hospital. Shock can be a dreadful thing. I've someone waiting to take a full statement when he's fit. The first responder took these images. We've posted a watch on the lad as I'm sure they wanted him dead."

Cyril looked around for a milk float or van. "Milk van?"

"The milk company sent someone for it. I don't think our chap will be returning to dark mornings for a while. Not what you'd expect to find. The initial medical reports on Coffrey suggest his whole face is fractured and I mean whole. Every bone was deliberately targeted. Eyes punctured too. A miracle he survived. I doubt that's how a lad of his age would want to survive." He pulled a face that was a cocktail of sadness and fear. "The crime scene people suggest he may have been held kneeling and methodically attacked at the far end of the garage where his clothes are still dumped in the corner. They're checking for marks. If he was held against his will ..." He did not finish. He had correctly interpreted Cyril's look which told him he was stating the obvious.

Cyril handed back the pad. "Thanks." He moved to the car and checked his watch again. "Brian, I want April and Owen on this immediately but it will be my case. I also need to be in court in an hour." He noticed Smirthwaite's frown. "Two Inspectors and a DCI on one case? I can read your thoughts, Brian. I'll get the clearance from upstairs you see if I don't. I'll stress that the victim could have been his child." Cyril raised an eyebrow and climbed into the car.

Chapter Seven

The court case had been a success. The verdict had removed two more dealers of class A drugs from the streets of Harrogate and some families could feel a little more secure. However, the meeting with his Chief Constable had not been as smooth as he had hoped owing to the latest case with the potential for drug related links. It seemed to him that as they removed some of the criminal fraternity from circulation, others immediately filled their places. Sitting in front of the Chief's desk, an area always covered with a small mountain of horizontally filed paper and files held in place by pebbles and stones, never gave Cyril a feeling of confidence in his boss's organisational ability even though he was constantly reminded by his superior that a tidy desk was the sign of a sick mind.

Cyril found it hard to concentrate on finances and procedural fiscal matters. His thoughts kept returning to images of the lad in the garage. Whoever had done that had a sick mind and he doubted it had anything to do with a particular tidy desk.

"Like a fucking vacuum, Cyril, push them out of the system and others are waiting to squeeze straight back in. The cost on resources is simply unacceptable but for the moment I'm afraid it's a necessary evil."

This part of Cyril's position, justifying spending and the

use of manpower, was not the part of the role he relished. He knew it to be essential and he knew it needed to be done well, but the task was the least palatable of his job description and it drew him away from what he believed to be real policing. Even delegating had been a struggle, but now with the team he had developed, it came a little more easily. There was, however, a rewarding moment within the meeting when it was stressed just how important and valued Cyril and his team were and that he, as Chief Constable, would always have Cyril's back.

"I've seen a brief on the lock-up and the video footage. These people are the lowest of the low. Find who did this, Cyril, and find them bloody quickly. The accounts and therefore the bloody budget, for the moment at least, can balance themselves."

The last sentence was like music to Cyril's ears.

***

Flicking the lanyard over his head, Cyril covered the lock with his pass and opened the door from the Police Station entrance. He progressed with a new found enthusiasm only stopping at Owen's desk on the way to his office. It was still where it had always been.

"There's an office if you want one, Inspector Owen, you know that?"

Owen shook his head. "That would mean I'd have to leave this collection of gargoyles." He waved his hand in the direction of the other desks set within the large space. "I'm better off here. They watch me, I watch them." He grinned.

"It's your call. Tea, Owen, tea is required. In five if you'd be so kind. We need to chat. You've heard about the lock-up I take it?"

31

Owen stood. "Seen it, heard about it, repulsed by it and want to get hold of the bastards who did it as fast as possible but tea comes first, sir." There was a sarcastic edge to his voice but it was lost as Cyril walked away before swiftly turning back to ask.

"I need to see April too. Do we have a weapon?"

"Medical evidence seems to support some kind of pein hammer but nothing yet from the scene. Everything's here." Owen pointed to the computer.

"Tea, Owen."

He slipped his overcoat on the hanger, an instinctive part of the routine before usually removing his electronic cigarette. This, however, had now gone. He fumbled instead for another mint; there was none.

Cyril had experienced difficulty in clearing his mind that morning. Seeing the images of the youth brought back memories of the worst ever day he had experienced in the force. It was scratched deep into his psyche. His emotional stability wavered when he allowed the images to focus fully in his mind's eye. On occasion his reserves of patience had, like they were at this moment, been pushed to the limit since he had, casually and regrettably, tossed his electronic cigarette and the various vaping accoutrements into the waste bin – the very bin that now seemed to stare back empty in open-mouthed shock at the implied complicity in his rash act. Since ceasing vaping, he had formed two habits to overcome the yearning, mints and restless fingers. Today he had foolishly run out of mints.

DCI Cyril Bennett ran his finger around the rim of the empty cup as it sat on the contrasting saucer, harsh white pot against floral design china. The contrast was visually jarring and annoying. Why it proved so difficult for Owen to match one item of crockery with another, unless he had been reminded, Cyril would never know. However, that was not the cause of his distant gaze, this stare removed him from the present and took him into the past. It was something far deeper that drew him away from the here and now, it was an emotional scar that although not raw, still could be seen, but only in his mind's eye.

The partly open top drawer of the filing cabinet, positioned a couple of metres across the room, filled his vision and his focus. It was that stare that contrived to rub the mental scar until it became raw and disturbing. That drawer, normally left locked, was gaping slightly like the entrance to the garage he had witnessed earlier. This space was a forbidden other world, a place private and hidden from the everyday, normal workings of his office, the station and his personal life.

Moving from behind his desk he crossed towards the cabinet as if attracted magnetically. He paused. His fingers rolled over the drawer's cold lip. He breathed deeply like a diver preparing to launch himself into the void before he pulled gently with a degree of uncertainty. The drawer protested with a slight squeak as it was drawn open exposing the dark interior to the electric light.

It was still there just where he had reverently left it. He knew it would be, face down, resting on the grey metal where it was stored, entombed and laid to rest – buried alone just as the memories were in one section of his mind.

Dropping his glasses from his head to his nose he lifted and turned the picture frame to reveal a smiling face. Liz Graydon stared back. Hers was not the stare of sadness or reflection but one of optimism and excitement. A moment in time, captured and frozen for posterity. A demeanour that would never alter or be sullied. He remembered that very moment the photograph was taken. It demonstrated the importance of someone's face: it was their identity. He thought immediately that the person or persons who attacked Coffrey had stolen that.

Liz Graydon had been a key member of his team, an officer targeted, kidnapped and murdered in revenge for Cyril's success in an earlier case. Seeing her body propped against the gravestone had nearly broken him. His future policing was dedicated to the memory of Liz. He felt he owed her that. Moments like this, in the present, triggered the hurt from the past, they were hurdles he knew he would have to overcome.

"Liz, sir?" Owen's voice broke the ice that encapsulated his thoughts and startled Cyril as if caught in flagrante delicto. Owen placed the cup and saucer on his desk and collected the other. "Remembered to find a match, sir," his voice was soft and sympathetic.

Cyril turned the photograph to face Owen as if in answer but said nothing himself only managing to force a guilty smile as his face flushed a little. Owen had seen the guilt before, it was clear to see in his expression. Owen smiled back and nodded. A reassuring gesture that allowed Cyril to nod too.

"When I was a nipper, sir, I had a pet rat. Lovely it was too. Clever creatures, rats, but maybe I've mentioned this to you before. If so, you'll recall I even kept it when it was dead. I kept it in a box under my bed until everyone knew it was there by the stink. After some persuasion we buried it in the small garden we had and my gran told me when I got upset about the death of a friend or loved one, to look back and smile at the memories but never to stare. I didn't fully understand what she meant then but when we lost Liz those simple words came back to me. Suddenly they seemed relevant and they seemed mine, private like, given to me by a special woman. They helped me. You can have them if you want, sir, if you think they'll help. I know you think about her often and sometimes you feel guilty but that's not right. We all know that, even Liz knows that. You got the bastard and without you, I don't think we would have." Owen turned to go.

"Owen? Those are wise words from your gran. Thanks. I'll keep them safe. I hear Liz's voice sometimes. I know it's not real. Her laugh too. People often ask how humans can harm others, like in this Coffrey case. I could have done that to the person who harmed Liz, Owen, just with these." He held up his hands. "And have no regrets."

Owen stared at Cyril. He said nothing as he remembered that he had felt the same.

"Just ignore me. It passes. How's Hannah?" Cyril slipped the photo frame back into drawer, pushed it closed and turned the key.

"Blooming, sir, like all the crocuses on The Stray, a tad moody, but she's beautiful all the same." He winked at Cyril and it brought a smile. "As you know, she's still working with Julie but maybe not for much longer. I find it hard focusing on things as the baby seems to fill my thoughts. Funny how something hidden can have such a strong effect on you."

Cyril lifted his glasses onto the top of his head before glancing at the cabinet. "Indeed, Owen. Indeed. Do you have any of those mints?"

"An Uncle Joe's? I'll get you one. Your tea's there." Smiling he turned and left. Light seemed to reappear from the now vacant door space and the mood in the room immediately changed for the better.

Cyril looked at the images of the broken and destroyed face. It was a total contrast to that of Liz as he had seen her propped against the grave stone. Having a face when she died meant she was still Liz. He swore then that for her he, DCI Cyril Bennett, would find who had done this to Shane Coffrey. Owen returned, dropped a mint on the table and pulled up a chair. "Last one. I'd give you my last Rolo too if I had one."

Cyril's phone rang.

"Mr Bennett? Good afternoon. Ryedale Auctions. We're two away from your lot."

In all the turmoil, Cyril had forgotten about the painting and he was quickly brought back to the present as he felt the nerves of anticipation squeeze his stomach tightly.

"Here we are. The Brundrit, lot 1097. I'll bring you in after the room and internet bids stop."

Cyril's heart fluttered as he heard the auction faintly in the background. The price climbed incrementally.

"It's at £500, Mr Bennett. Will you go £550?"

Cyril bid until it was at £700. There was a pause and he heard the gavel drop.

"It's yours, sir. Congratulations."

After a brief conversation about collection, he put the phone down and he waited until his stomach settled. He raised a thumb to Owen who immediately sensed the ghost of Liz had been temporarily laid to rest.

***

The Westminster Arcade was quiet. The first two shops had recently moved out leaving an air of desperation to the Victorian entrance. Upstairs, the Harrogate Tea Room was busy. Tom sat in in the corner. His morning had improved beyond all hope. As a Court Enforcement Officer, formally known as a bailiff, he had worked for Northwind Legal for just under two years and had been rewarded with positive work reviews over that time. From commencing his new career, he had believed his role should be to guide and support rather than cause upset, make threats and bring fear. People in debt, not knowing about how and where to seek help, were to him as vulnerable as the homeless and needed to be given as much support and professional guidance as possible. Not everyone understood the complexity of the law. *Giving as much help*, had been his mantra since taking the job. Many entering the profession came from a forces or police background and it had to be said that one or two could give the profession a poor reputation, particularly those working within the private sector. However, there were strict rules and he knew them by heart.

On returning to his desk, he found an envelope propped against the computer screen marked, *T Craig – By Hand.* Slipping his coat on the back of his chair he scrutinised the handwritten mail. Mike was not in the building and the two other officers were busy behind their computer screens.

"Anyone see this get delivered?" Tom looked across at his colleagues. Their faces popped out from hiding before focusing on the waving envelope. Both heads shook in unison and they mumbled in the negative. Picking up the letter knife he slid it along the top. Opening the cut, he extracted the contents. They comprised two images printed on plain paper and a note. One image was of the morning's red line – the sky he had paused to witness earlier in the day – the other was of the Ford Fiesta parked half on the pavement and half on the road. Tom felt the same flush of nerves rush through his body. He read the note in a whisper. "'The town has a thousand eyes.' What the fuck!"

At that moment, Mike returned, a coffee and sandwich in hand. He smiled. "Okay? Good lunch?"

Tom waved the images. "Your idea of a practical joke?" As soon as the words left his mouth, he knew from Mike's face that he was not responsible. Mike dropped his lunch onto his desk and came over grabbing the images.

"No." The expression on his face reconfirmed he knew nothing of this. "Have you been threatened this week? The case on Tuesday where you had to itemise belongings to cover the debt? You said, if I recall correctly, there was trouble."

"Nothing. Everything went smoothly in the end. People's nerves got frayed that's all. Shouting and some body contact."

"You must take this upstairs. The last thing you need is some nutter on your tail seeking vengeance for a five-grand debt. You hearing me? If you don't, I will."

***

The tap on the door diverted Cyril's attention from the screen. He peered over his glasses to see April and he did not give her a moment to speak. "What do we have?"

"Just when you think you've witnessed it all we find ourselves with this. Have you seen the state they left him in, sir?"

Cyril nodded. "How and with what?"

"Considering the number of strikes to the facial area they believe it to be one of these." She handed him a photograph. "A ball pein hammer. Specialist and an expensive tool. All fourteen facial bones were broken and shattered with some areas being struck multiple times. There seemed to be a concentration on the eye sockets. Both were splintered, resulting in fragmented bone puncturing both eyes and causing the dislodging of the retinas. Blinded."

Cyril frowned before lowering his glasses onto his nose. He studied the photograph of the hammer.

"The pein, the rounded end, was measured at that." She pointed to the sizes added below. "They believe it's probably an embossing hammer of some kind." April folded her arms.

"Probably? Embossing what? Do we know?" He peered over the rims. "Are you telling me it's not been found from the close search of the immediate area?"

"Yes. More tests are being done but until we find the actual weapon." She moved back to the front of his desk. "You wouldn't have to hit a person very hard to achieve the desired results especially when striking twice in the same place. Both parts of the hammer's head have a different sized ball. Your standard hammer would be too big. So, like stiletto shoes on sand, this smaller size would concentrate greater impact to the targeted area with the least amount of force. Whoever did this, sir, knew the damage and pain a single strike would cause. It would be significant, particularly if repeated, and as I've said, there's evidence to suggest areas of his face were struck a number of times but apparently always in a controlled manner. Interestingly, I spoke initially to the doctor and surgeon who reminded me about the fragility of the facial structure. The bones in places, as you know, comprise cavities. I tried to chat to Dr Julie but unfortunately got Caner on the phone. He informed me the facial bone structure has developed over time to have weak areas where fractures occur to prevent damage to the harder skull and therefore to protect the brain. It is believed, and feasible, that the perpetrator didn't want to kill our man, just destroy him." She paused. "We await toxicology."

Cyril could see from her demeanour there was something wrong. "Problem?"

"Why is Caner so intent on treating me like a child?" Dr Isaac Caner was one of the pathologists working in the north-east.

Cyril found his manner too brusque and understood what she implied. "Because, April, you allow him to. Stand up to him. He'll respect that. And remember, they're not always right. Forensics?"

She was taken aback as his words resounded with a degree of truth. Taking a deep breath, she continued. "They're looking at the blood spatter patterns. They believe from those and the position of the victim during the attack, they will be able to offer a judgement on the perpetrator's height, providing only a single person carried out the hammer attack, and in which hand the hammer was held.

There was serious bleeding from eyes, ears, mouth and nose as you can imagine."

"What state is he in now?"

"Critical. In ICU. They've put him in an induced coma to protect his brain."

"What about the immediate crime scene area?"

"Blood trail found to a specific point at the beginning of the entrance to the neighbouring play area. It's mainly footpaths, grass and surrounded by trees and shrubs but the trail stopped there. We've organised a fingertip search of the immediate area. More officers have been drafted in as speed is of the essence."

Cyril opened Google maps and focused on the garage's location. April stood to his right shoulder and indicated with the pen she held.

"There, sir. The playground area is quite extensive and the perpetrators could have gone in either direction, but you have to ask why you'd go back to Hampsthwaite Road. Speaking to Owen and Smirthwaite, we think the quietest route would have been to Coppice Drive."

Cyril followed the tip of the pen and nodded. "There are also exits on Portland Crescent, Osborne Gardens and St Luke's Close. What if they went in different directions? Have the dogs been involved yet?"

"Sir, yes but nothing."

"Who owns the garage?"

April flicked through the file she was carrying. "Belongs to flat 6. Owned as a second home since 2008. A Philip Ashton."

. "Is it let?"

"Not according to his neighbours. We're trying to contact

him. Lives in France and it's believed he only uses it for holidays. He pays a neighbour to check it and retrieve mail. They don't have a key to the garage, only the flat."

"Do we have more details on Ashton?"

"Businessman. Late sixties. Owns four garage come petrol stations and is or was in partnership. Divorced and I believe that's in the final stages. They lease buildings on the sites to other small business, usually for car repairs. We're gathering more info."

Cyril twiddled with the pen allowing it to bounce between his finger and thumb. "They use hammers, these car repair places," he mumbled to himself before immediately changing tack. "CCTV and house to house being checked I take it?"

"In progress."

"You wouldn't happen to have a mint, would you?"

April retrieved a tube from her pocket and popped it on his desk. "Keep them."

"Thanks. You said 'perpetrators' earlier. Do we know if we are looking for more than one?" He popped a mint into his mouth. "Open mind, April, open mind."

Chapter Eight

As she spoke, Tom looked at his hands and felt as though he were making a mountain out of a mole hill. His boss casually leaned one elbow on her desk as she made careful notes. She was aware of the possible risks associated with the job and she never took threats made to her staff or concerns from them lightly.

"This is the first time this has happened, Tom. You're sure?" Gail Wilson-North looked directly at him; there was genuine concern in her voice. Although they were in her office they were sitting informally at the same side of the desk.

"I've had experiences like it in the past but those were understandable considering the place, position and the circumstances." He paused briefly as if to give further thought to her question. "I've walked this route to work daily and nothing has ever happened before. It was just today." He looked at her and summoned a smile that was obviously strained. "I thought it might be the result of too much cheese before bed maybe!" His expression did not falter.

She smiled back but was neither convinced nor comfortable with his show of bravado and he knew it.

"Then I received the note."

"Do you have it with you?"

Tom removed the envelope from his inner jacket pocket

and handed it to Gail. She read it before folding a clean piece of A4 and popping it within the fold. "We'll keep it safe just in case. It could be vital evidence."

Tom was startled. "Just in case I don't come in one morning?"

Gail shook her head. "No, Tom. Just in case."

There was another long pause in the discussion before Tom tapped a finger on the desk as if to break the spell that trapped his thoughts.

"As a matter of course, Gail, we've checked the CCTV images at the entrance to see who might have delivered it, but you know the foot traffic we have sharing the building with other businesses. Anyone of those people could have popped it on the Reception desk when passing in or out. It was after that, I assume, it was brought up with the mail."

"Right. I know you work in teams but I'm going to review your folders, your warrant book and your bailiff's notebook for the last month. I want you to do the same. Anything, anything at all you feel is out of the ordinary, no matter how insignificant it seems, make a note and I'll do the same." She could see from his face he was not happy with her suggestion. "Anything that nags check your badge cam footage for the appropriate date and action. You're familiar with the procedure."

"I'm professional, caring, understanding and sensitive to clients' circumstances as is the team. We don't back people into corners. I know some working in this profession can be aggressive but that's why, I hope, we are no longer called bailiffs. *Civil enforcement agents,* still sounds official, if not a little James Bond, but the title has a less threatening ring to it. I want to achieve a result that helps all parties and that's how I conduct my professional duties."

"You are all very professional, Tom, I make sure of that but we still receive complaints, that's human nature. People are in a difficult place when you appear in their lives, many will act irrationally but there will always be some, I know from my experience, who can seem unfazed. They demonstrate an understanding and are most apologetic. They are usually the ones to be more cautious about. Still waters, Tom, still waters. I know how dedicated you are and you know what I think of your professionalism from your regular reviews."

Tom forced a smile to appear and mouthed a quiet word of thanks.

"What about outside your working day, or something from the past, a previous life shall we say and what about any recent relationships?"

That thought concerned him even more. "As you said, Gail, let's go through my files and if it happens again ..."

There was a long and uncomfortable pause from both.

"If you're happy with that."

Tom stood. "Thanks."

On returning to his office, Mike peered from around his computer screen. He checked his watch. "Sorted? Owt or nowt, matey?"

A long sigh was the immediate answer before he went to the filing cabinet and withdrew two ring bound folders and other documents. The European log of cases was almost empty and he returned that immediately. "Have I upset anyone enough this last month is the question to which we need to find answers." He dropped the files onto his desk and released another sigh as his shoulders sagged in unison.

"We're not exactly man's best friend when we turn up on the doorstep. We usually bring a reality check that can trigger even the mildest mannered of our society. Debt and the many problems that go with it can be a cruel reaper. Remember that. Remember too that some people never forget!"

Tom looked up. "A real Job's comforter you are."

***

Cyril stared at the x-ray images and scan results for Coffrey that were now on file. He awaited toxicology results on the victim but knew they would not be forthcoming for a while. The clothing found within the lock-up had at least yielded some forensic evidence: He read it out loud to himself.

Considering the spatter, we can, at this stage, make a presumption that the perpetrator was right-handed and standing at approximately five foot ten inches tall. The shoe print patterns have been sent for analysis but we know our victim was barefoot, his shoes were located at the rear of the garage. The remaining shoe impressions are size nine and size ten. We are still unsure if there were two people with the victim. Expect further analysis and identification of the footwear within twenty-four hours. The milkman did go into the garage and we had the first responder and the other paramedics so you can imagine the number of prints we are dealing with.

Interestingly there were two T-shirts. One had the words 'The Dark Knight' printed over the silhouetted image of Batman that filled the front. This garment had not been worn but was mixed with the rest of the clothing. It could prove to be significant.

Evidence of Class A drug residue was traced to two areas of the clothing found. It is likely the victim was an addict. Further to follow.

Cyril read through the information again and jotted down key words as Owen knocked on the open door.

"We have an address, sir. For the victim, Coffrey. It's now on file."

Cyril moved the mouse on the mat until he located the information on screen. "What about the grandmother?"

"Police liaison and a signer, that's a sign language interpre ..." He did not finish as he saw the look on Cyril's face. "Anyway, they've been and taken a statement as she's as deaf as this wood." He tapped the architrave. "Funny, according to the report she showed little emotion on being informed that her precious nephew was in ICU. She just returned her stare back to the silent television and shrugged her shoulders. "Internally, the house was neat and tidy. She has carers in three times a day. However, you couldn't say the same for the garden and the garage. Unkempt might be the polite term."

Cyril focused on his own screen. "I read your report, Owen."

"Coffrey's always been a problem kid. Exclusions from various schools, plural, sir. Parent, mother single. We don't believe she married the father although the boy took his name. Coffrey senior died after a drug and alcohol binge two years ago. She continued to have numerous partners, and according to Social Services, she'd had enough of

Shane at this point and chucked him out onto the streets when he was sixteen. He then came to live briefly at his nan's. We're not sure when or why he stopped living there but we know he stayed for quite some time. Neighbours told of their seeing him on a number of occasions. Some of his clothes are still there too. She also confirmed that he still calls to check up on her and borrow a quid or two but she insists he's a good lad with a heart of gold and that people just can't see it. To quote, 'He's been labelled and he can't shake that off.'"

"I bet he borrows too and our records show he's neither good nor golden. Check how often he's been in trouble since living with her. Have you done a full check on the property, garden, garage?" Cyril took an extra strong mint from his top drawer and popped it into his mouth.

"When the bike was removed, the officers had a quick look but it was full of crap. Paint tins, some furniture. Like many suburban garages, no car. If cobwebs were drugs, he'd be a wealthy lad."

"If she's as deaf as you say what's to stop him using the garage without her knowledge?"

Owen watched as Cyril returned the mints to the drawer. He shrugged his shoulders. "He'd have to go past the lounge window to get to the drive and the garage. According to one of her carers, she misses nothing. Sees all but hears nowt!" He also wanted to ask if his boss could peel an orange in his pocket having not been offered a mint but thought better of it.

"Neighbours?"

"Other than seeing him about, we've had a few complaints detailing his riding the dirt bike in the area without a helmet. Some believe he's been dealing in drugs as they see a group of youths in a passageway on the estate and he's usually not far away. He should have been in court this July."

"I want the house and the garage checking. I'll sort the warrant. Anything from the CCTV cameras on the night he was attacked?"

"Three lads seen walking along Montpellier Road before heading up Ripon Road. At this stage we're assuming they were heading for the lock-up. No sign of a struggle. Timing fits too. House to house reported a parcel was left at an address close by. Delivered at 02.10 and it was legit, a battery for a hand vacuum according to the owner. He was amazed by the time it was left."

Cyril frowned. "Find the delivery driver. Check if he saw anything or whether he had a dash cam. Right, what about 4, Brewster Street? Interesting house that." Cyril looked on Google Street View. "He lives there? With whom?"

Owen shrugged his shoulders again. "According to the records a John Fletcher and Janice Blackledge. Rented. Problems in the past. Rent arrears and non-conformity of the tenancy agreement as well as other nonpayments, some were fines – not having a television licence being just one. They've had visits, warnings and final demands."

"Bailiffs?"

Owen nodded.

"Why does the pathway we seek to travel always get muddier the further we go?"

Owen stared back. He did not have an answer. It was ever thus.

***

Owen turned onto Brewster Street and slowed until locating number four. Cyril looked at both sides of the road assimilating as much as he could for reference. What he saw was neither unexpected nor shocking. It was clear that the occupants showed little respect for the garden or the property. A child had chalked on either side of the front door, illegible multi-coloured squiggles. Toys and an upturned pram were discarded on what once was a lawn. The left curtain hung limply, obviously missing a number of curtain rings, giving the window to the left of the front door the look of a semi-closed eye.

Cyril avoided a puddle of oil that surrounded a road drain where someone had emptied the waste after servicing a car. He frowned. Owen knocked. A dog barked frantically from within and Cyril stood on the pavement watching for any movement of the yellowing net curtains in either of the upstairs windows. There was none. The barking stopped as the dangling curtain moved and a child's face appeared just above the sill before being moved quickly out of view. A scream followed and the barking, more subdued this time, began again.

"Quiet, both of you!" The voice, loud but stressed, was clearly heard. It quelled all noise.

Owen knocked again. The door opened on a chain.

"Mrs Blackledge. Police." Owen held up his ID. A child's face appeared in the gap before she was pulled away and a further cry echoed from within. The door closed briefly to be opened fully seconds later. A warm, stale aroma flooded out, a cocktail of wet dog, stale chips and damp.

"Fletch isn't here. Hasn't been for a couple of days. Just buggers off without a word. Thought you might be the council. Bailiffs again."

The child clung to the mother's leg. "And this little madam has been a pain in the arse too. You can take her and lock her up but don't forget to throw away the bloody key!" She placed a gentle hand on the child's head, a gesture which contradicted her tone and request.

"May we come in? It will only take a minute or two."

Janice moved away and went inside taking the child with her. Owen noticed a cot in the corner. The baby was awake and fascinated by a mobile dangling above and oblivious to all else. Owen moved to look and it brought a pang and a smile.

"You can have that one too. Two for the price of one! A bloody bargain and then I can sit in peace and quiet."

Owen stood back before glancing around the room. A large TV attached to the wall seemed to fill the space. The wires dangled, ill-disciplined across the mantelpiece before disappearing to the side of the chimney breast. It was on but the volume was low.

"Sorry for the mess. Kids, who'd have 'em? Me, sadly." She answered her own question. "I also have a big kid who's usually missing when you need him for domestic stuff." She started to move items of clothing from the settee, the child still clinging to her leg. "Just never seem to have time. If Fletch did more it might help but he's hardly here."

"So, it's just you, your partner and the two children?" Owen asked helping her to move some toys from the floor. The dog barked from the other room and scratched on the closed door but went quiet after another screamed order was relayed.

"First time a man's lifted a finger in my house, officer.

51

What are you doing later?"

Owen blushed slightly and tossed the objects on the side along with the others. Cyril had entered and he could immediately feel his shoes sticking to the carpet. He said nothing but looked around the room.

"Yes, as you see, usually just us three unless he comes home."

"Have you had anyone staying recently, Mrs Blackledge?" Owen's tone was light and unthreatening. He bobbed down in the hope of being at eye level with the child but she moved behind her mother.

There was a pause and Janice flushed slightly. "It's Miss and no. Has someone told you they have?"

Owen retrieved a copy of the latest photograph of Coffrey he had copied from police records. "This young man?"

She took it only giving the image a cursory glance. "No. Who is he?"

Owen was about to put the photograph in his pocket when he bobbed down again and showed the child.

"Shane, mummy. I like Shane. He tickles and cuddles me."

Owen saw Janice pull firmly at the child's arm and a cry immediately followed.

"Fletch brought him home. Said he needed a place to stay for a few days."

"And?"

"Few days my arse. He was here for a bloody month. I told him he couldn't stay owing to the tenancy agreement, no paying guests, but our Fletch does what our Fletch wants. Rules don't exist if they don't suit." She picked up the child from the cot and positioned its nappy close to her nose before popping him back. "And there's another job to do unless either of you gents wants to break the mould."

Neither responded to her request.

"Thought not, but I can't blame you."

"When did you last see Shane?" Cyril spoke for the first time eager to get to the truth but also eager to conclude the interview and move into the fresh air.

"What day is it?" She paused. "The days just mash together with these two. The day before yesterday whatever that was."

"How was he when he left, and did he leave with Fletch?" Cyril did not move from the spot he was on but focused his attention on Janice.

"Shane could never get up. Slept here on the settee." She pointed to a sleeping bag screwed up in the corner. "I brought him a brew. He didn't have anything to eat. Fletch had gone out earlier, before he was up, the day before yesterday. Work he said. When Shane eventually got up and left, he said he had errands to run and might not be back. I was relieved to be honest although he was a help with the kids."

"What does Fletch do work wise?" Cyril knew from his earlier checks that neither worked and were supported by benefits.

"It's not paid work as in real employment. He helps a mate who has a recycling business. Disappears and doesn't come home on occasion." The pause was palpable.

"You have a name of this mate and the business?"

"He has a van, a truck thing and he collects scrap. You know, goes round the streets. My parents called them rag and bone men; now they recycle," she added in what she considered a posh voice. "Fletch says he'd go bloody daft if he stayed home all day and don't I know it. You're allowed to help mates. It's not breaking any laws. What we'll do when this next is born ..." She patted her belly. There was hardly any sign of pregnancy.

"I'll ask again. A name for this mate?" Cyril's patience was slowly diminishing and it reflected in his tone.

"He called him Steptoe but I don't think that's his real name."

Owen looked towards Cyril but neither continued on that tack. Cyril quickly changed the questioning. "Fletch does what Fletch wants to do as you said. Did Shane Coffrey pay for his stay?"

"For him staying cost the same as a well-known stately home as far as I was concerned."

Owen frowned.

"That's bugger all to you and me. Ate little mind and occupied Olivia when I needed help. He wasn't all bad. But he might have had an arrangement with Fletch."

"Did you leave Olivia with Shane alone ... when you weren't here?" Cyril asked, not concealing the concern within the question.

"Sometimes. He appeared to enjoy her toys more than she did. He always seemed a bit sad. Loved to help at bath time too."

"Thank you, Janice. We'll not delay you any longer. What time are you expecting your partner home?"

"I don't know. It varies. I expected him last night but then ..."

"And Shane?"

"I'm not. Fletch called and said he'd moved on and not to let him back into the house. It's all guess work living here. I just cook, clean and look after the kids." She spread her hands in sheer frustration. "My life is all excitement and surrounded by surprises!"

Chapter Nine

The Incident Room was light and quiet. Some handwritten notes and a greater number of photographs adorned the whiteboards. In the centre of one was an enlarged street map of Harrogate. Magnetic markers were positioned to illustrate key locations relevant to the case.

Cyril, Owen and April adjusted the files and notes before them. The large illuminated screen attached to the far wall gave a blue hue to the surroundings, the North Yorkshire Police Badge clearly displayed. It was all very clinical.

"We have four more matching CCTV images of the three people spotted on Montpellier Road. As you can see, all three people are wearing hooded and dark jackets. These were sent to Forensics in Wakefield for enhancement to get a clearer look at their footwear and see if there's a possible link to what we have already. Unfortunately, even with our latest enhancing technology, there's little chance of making out their features. We have height and build. The experts suggest the middle chap is likely to be Coffrey. Piggy in the middle. In all these shots he's always placed centrally but whether that's a deliberate act or coincidental we don't know."

Cyril pulled out a file and he pushed back his sleeves a few centimetres. Owen noticed the immaculate crease down his sleeve and then the cufflinks. Each was a small silver aircraft. He checked his own but remembered he had folded them back as he had a button missing.

"What about the nocturnal delivery driver, Owen?" Cyril did not lift his head.

"Traced him but he saw nothing. The company supports night delivery. No dash cam either."

April spoke. "Did some more digging on the victim. We know that he's been in trouble a number of times but I went back further. We know he was thrown out of the family home but there is some evidence from psychology reports during his schooling to suggest that as well as regularly suffering parental physical harm, he might have been the victim of domestic sexual abuse. It's only a suggestion and was never established as according to psychological play therapy reports, he was an un-cooperative child when very young and as a youth, stubborn as well. Link that with a reluctant, alcoholic mother and the long ago disappearance of his birth father, you'll find it's not a recipe for a child's developing mental stability. Coffrey lived in a house where the male role models were only consistent in probably delivering drunken abuse and therefore, they were anything but. Mother failed to meet appointments on a number of occasions and he apparently slipped through the child psychologist's net. If there had been inappropriate behaviours at home, there's a report from his school suggesting the child was witnessing domestic prostitution. If this were the case, the mother would not be too happy at having the details discovered." She quickly scanned the rest of the page. "That's how it will have to remain unless he's able to tell us differently."

57

Owen tapped the table with his finger. "'He tickles and cuddles me.' Those were the words she used. It seemed strange to me too, sir. That's what the child immediately said about Coffrey when she saw the photograph."

"Two and two, Owen, well done. If there has been any inappropriate sexual contact has our Fletch tried and punished the lad?" He looked at April and Owen before sliding the said report to each of them. "Speculation only and we don't work on speculation but we do store it. I need to chat with 'Our Fletch' and I need to do it sooner rather than later. Arrange a watch on Brewster Street and as soon as he's back I want him interviewed and if needs be, brought in."

***

Tom Craig had finished his search of the files. He had checked bodycam footage of two incidents where the home owner had proved to be unduly verbally aggressive and threatened physical harm to either himself or his colleague. He had noted the dates and times as well as the location. His phone rang.

"Tom. If you've concluded your reviews, I'd like a chat. Ten minutes."

Gail Wilson-North was looking out of her office window when he arrived. She held a small bottle of water and two glasses. "Sorry it's not stronger." Knocking the glasses together she popped them on the desk and poured. "Well?"

"I have three. Two occupants were particularly aggressive and one if you recall very intimidating at the serving of the warrant. None could or would pay what was demanded from the court. I checked the bodycam footage and I've taken still images from that."

58

Opening the folder he had brought, he put the contents on the desk along with the case notes.

Gail checked the file numbers. "I also looked at these with interest, Tom. All have since paid what was owing but it took further persuasion with the first chap."

"It was the woman who was the most difficult." He tapped one of the pictures. "She ripped her own clothing and then accused us of trying to rape her!" It had been the first incident of that nature he had witnessed and he sincerely hoped it would be the last. "Then there was Constance Hartley-Lowe, nonpayment of a large court imposed debt to do with her house. She was with a chap who was armed, possibly a game keeper. Later she told the police some tale. They checked the video footage and nothing was done."

"So, Tom, now you've had time to reflect on the incidents and refresh your memory, what do you want to do? We need to assess the risk and that might include police involvement. If you've been labelled and possibly targeted, we need to formulate an action plan. You must feel comfortable at work and in your private life. You wouldn't be the first enforcement officer to be the victim of a vigilante and you will not, I'm sad to say, Tom, be the last."

The word 'vigilante' brought a flutter of anxiety to his stomach. His army training had taught him the power of being incognito, invisible within the everyday crowd. The hidden enemy in Afghanistan had done that so well. You could never separate friend from foe, knowing just whom you could trust was always difficult and that uncertainty brought with it a great deal of stress. The thought of living in Harrogate in the present and wondering if there was some member of the public waiting to reap revenge for doing his job effectively and efficiently, made him suddenly feel quite nauseous. He sipped some water.

"There's nothing I can do other than my job. I'll take a different route to work."

"Drive I would suggest. You have my personal number so call if you remember anything else." Gail smiled.

"If there really is, a …" he paused momentarily, "… a vigilante who will wait, pick their moment. Maybe, Gail, it was just my being oversensitive. A bit of PTSD. It happens in my dreams. Not as much as it once did. I don't think you ever truly recover. I need to focus on work and be with my colleagues." He drained the glass. "Thanks. Appreciate your concern and I'll be alert and keep you fully posted."

Gail smiled but did not reply. She somehow knew that neither she nor Tom could chase ghosts. After all, the note he had received remained securely locked in her desk.

***

DC Stuart Park and DC Shakti Misra sat in the car looking towards 4, Brewster Street. The dashboard clock showed 5.47. Even though the day's light was beginning to fade quickly, Shakti saw the man first in the rear-view mirror. He climbed from the cab of a large, caged flat-bed truck. She observed him wave to the driver before walking towards them. She nudged Stuart.

"This could well be our man."

They watched as he approached the house. He was carrying two plastic shopping bags. Kicking open the gate, he approached the door and then kicked that too to announce his arrival. Shakti saw a woman look from the downstairs window and moments later the door opened.

"Give him a few minutes to settle and then we'll ..." Before he had finished the sentence, Shakti saw John Fletcher's face appear at the downstairs window and he looked directly across at the car. A second or two later the door opened and he approached.

Park got out of the car and removed his ID. "John Fletcher?"

Fletcher stopped. "My partner said you'd been there for a while. Wondered who you were, like. Consider me a member of our neighbourhood watch, like."

Park smiled. "Right! Police, and we need a word with you. Either here in the car, at the station or in the house. Believe you've got two kids. Your choice at this stage."

"What's it about?"

"Your choice, Mr Fletcher."

"The car."

Park opened the rear door and Fletcher climbed in. A smell of stale sweat soon permeated the confined space. Shakti turned on the ignition to open the front windows. Park went round the other side and entered.

"What's going on. Janice said you'd been today. I put two and two together when she told me about the car."

"First, I need to caution you. This doesn't mean you are being arrested but what you say now or don't say may have a bearing on our future inquiries."

"I understand, just get on with it."

"Where have you been for the last two days?" Shakti asked from the front driver's seat.

"Helping out a mate. Can you not do that or is it that you can't have mates if you have a criminal record?" His tone was defensive, bitter and arrogant. "You'll know I don't work. There aren't the jobs for the likes of me. As I've just said, criminal record for what I did in my younger days. Tends to stick like shit to a blanket. Makes people pass your name on the list at interview no matter what the job."

"What were those offences?"

"Don't piss me about. I need my tea and I certainly need a shower. You know what's on my record."

Shakti chipped in quickly. "Indeed, we do. GBH, aggravated assault, theft … Do I need to go on?"

"I only threatened. The GBH was a bloody set up. It was either me or them. I got six months but served three. I was good."

"Away two days. Long job?"

"Collecting down the coast. Scarborough and Brid. His old stomping ground. He has a caravan there. That's where we stay."

"How do you know Shane Coffrey?"

"Through a mate. Asked if I could help him out. Needed somewhere to stay."

"Same mate or another?"

Fletcher pulled a face and Park saw him clench his fists as if to control his anger. "Another. You might not like this officer but I have quite a few friends. Funny that, a criminal having pals."

"I'll need a name."

Shakti showed her notebook.

"Why?" Fletcher turned in the seat to be square on and to face Park.

"Let's try another tack. When was the last time you saw Coffrey?"

"He was snoring his bloody head off on my settee the other day when I left for wor ..." He did not finish the word. "He wasn't there when I went in a few minutes ago and Janice says he's gone."

"You didn't know him at all and yet you left him in the house with your partner and your kids. Furthermore, Janice left him alone looking after the children on occasion. Was that not a concern? After all ..."

There was a pause and Shakti realised they had hit a nerve as Fletcher tensed.

***

The same emotions he had experienced over the recent years as a child entertainer crept back as he closed the estate car's boot. He always believed he had missed the true opportunities for someone of his talent. Some days those regrets weighed heavily but on others, like today when things went well, he could quickly put them behind him. The props he had used were stored neatly and orderly. The children's party would continue for another hour or more but his work was done. The clown make-up would remain but the huge flat shoes, the wig, made with a bald patch at the top and orange, straggly locks to the side and the large false red nose were removed as they made driving a little difficult, especially the shoes. The old overcoat he slipped on would conceal the costume and keep out the cold. After the tension and warmth of a performance, once outside loading the car he soon felt the chill. He had rarely been stopped whilst driving home in all the years he had been in the job and when he had been it brought smiles from the police, especially when he produced the artificial flowers from up his sleeve or unbeknownst to them removed a part of their equipment.

Counting the money he had just received, he returned it to the brown envelope before popping it into the glove box. The children had had a wonderful time and relished their eagerness to participate, laugh and applaud. This is what always attracted him to the role of the actor, the entertainer and the all-round fun person. There was one child, however, who had been distressed from the beginning. Her mother defended her by confessing she was afraid of clowns but that was not unusual. There had been many such incidents and not only the children – many accompanying adults admitted to feelings of discomfort. Once the balloons appeared and the live rabbit was produced from the top hat, the tears subsided and the timid child had crept ever closer. This was the real reward, their faces. If he could be paid in happy faces then that would be all the remuneration he would need. He closed his eyes and imagined each and every one and that in turn brought a smile to his own exaggerated red mouth.

Once home, he unloaded the car and the props were secured in the shed. He poured a small gin and topped up the glass with tonic. He had no lemon or ice but then life in general was never perfect. He sat, slipped off his shoes and popped his feet on the coffee table before checking his watch. The two keys sat next to a magazine. He had all the time in the world. Maybe he would watch a film. He knew the perfect title.

***

For Tom, the thought of going straight home and staying home alone in splendid isolation, with only the television for company, brought with it a degree of despair after the day he had so far experienced. It lingered heavily on his mind as the working hours seemed never-ending. His reassuring daily routine had been disturbed and this had brought an imbalance to his normal equilibrium.

Tom had no alternative but to eat alone. He had decided to eat out and not box himself in. It would be too easy to hide. The two friends he had called had other commitments. He would go to his usual restaurant. The familiarity and the food would be comforting and more importantly reassuring even though it was often busy. A pizza, Hawaiian with extra pineapple, was what he fancied. Going to a familiar place and eating a favourite meal might just bring a return to normality to conclude the day. Hopefully a corner table would be available which would be just perfect. It would suit his mood. After all, when you are on your own you can at least people watch!

Chapter Ten

"I saw him with Oli, Olivia. He didn't know I was watching and I didn't like what I saw so I had a strong word with him and told him not to come back."

Stuart Park glanced briefly at Shakti. "I take it from what you've said Olivia is your daughter?"

Fletcher shook his head. "Janice's. Olivia is not mine. Only Lucas. She's pregnant too." He pulled a face as if to show disapproval. "I just seem to have to throw my jeans on the bed and she's …"

"Go on. What exactly did you witness, Mr Fletcher?"

Fletcher began to fidget as he opened and closed his fists, now seemingly reluctant to speak. "I came home and there was nobody downstairs, I could hear voices and laughter upstairs so I went up thinking Janice was bathing one of the kids. Olivia liked to help her mum. I could hear her giggling, squealing, it was Oli. I call her Oli. It was her in the bath. Janice wasn't there only Shane. He had her standing in the water in front of him and he was running his fingers, insect-like, up her leg, her inner thigh really, whilst saying the spider nursery rhyme … Incy Wincy ... You know the one?" Fletcher stopped speaking trying to control a recurring anger and he waited for acknowledgement. The two officers both nodded. His face reddened and small flecks of saliva began to form and coat his lips. "The shit stopped when he saw me and immediately stood and backed away. He must have seen the look on my face. I saw his mobile phone on the chair. I thought he might be …" Fletcher banged the back of the passenger seat before lowering his head. All went silent.

Shakti and Park allowed the silence to grow, to become uncomfortable. They wanted him to speak, to continue whilst still incensed but he clammed up.

"Did you hurt Shane, Mr Fletcher?"

Fletcher turned to Park. "I could have fucking killed him to be honest, smashed his fucking face in."

"And did you?"

Fletcher leaned away and frowned. "No. I said nothing then as it would have upset Oli. I could see she wasn't comfortable when she saw my face. I lifted her out of the bath and wrapped her quickly in a towel. I then waited a few minutes and as if by magic Janice came in – she'd been to the shop. I think she could tell there was something wrong by Shane's face. Oli could too, she started to cry. I made an excuse that I needed Shane to help me with something, I can't remember what I said and we went into the back yard. I told him I needed to see his mobile. I checked the images but it wasn't what I thought. I told him that I wanted him out the following day and if I saw him with Oli on his own before he went, I'd …" He looked at both Shakti and Park. "I said I'd castrate him."

"But you left him the next day. He was with Janice and the kids and even when you suspected he was acting inappropriately towards Olivia you still left?"

"I told him to leave as soon as but I told him that he should also thank Janice, she'd been like a mother to him, have something to eat and never return. I rang Janice in the day to see if he'd gone. I also told her that should he come back, she should call me straight away."

"You believe he was interfering in a sexual way with your child and you didn't report it?"

Fletcher looked directly at Shakti and a slight grunt came from his constrained lips. "In the yard I had him by the neck. He swore it was a game, the spider game. He told me it was played on him when he was a child by some of his mother's friends. To be honest I could not only see fear in his eyes but sadness, maybe even regret if that's the right word. I suddenly felt sorry for him. When I raised my hand he said, 'No Dad.' It stopped me in my tracks. We've all made mistakes, we've all been there. I guess, even you. It was then that the extent of his being abused as a child came out. Believe me I felt sick. He was still a kid in a way, liked playing with Oli's toys. Work that out if you can. I know he's got a shit load of baggage in his head and I guess he didn't spill all the beans. I guess he must be too embarrassed."

"You felt so sorry you allowed him to stay on?"

"I'm no soft bastard. I can hold my own with the best, Christ, I've had a belly of it throughout my time and so has Janice. We're trying to make some kind of life out of the shit hands of cards we were both dealt and I guess so is he. Let's hope he's learned a lesson."

Shakti turned to address Fletcher and there was clearly a confused look on her face. "Remember, Mr Fletcher, you've been cautioned. I'm going to ask one question. Have you seen Shane Coffrey since that morning?"

Fletcher shook his head. "No, and that's the truth."

"Do you have his mobile number?"

"No. What exactly is all this about?"

***

Tom's optimism was rewarded and he was shown to a table in the corner. He had a clear view of the restaurant as well as an outlook on to James Street. He ordered a glass of red wine and as the menu was popped onto his table his phone pinged, the tone signalling a received text. It was Mike.

Sorry I couldn't make tonight. Had a long-standing arrangement and that's not easy with one good leg! ;) Hope a meal out will help you feel better. See you tomorrow. Call if you need me, don't worry about the time.

Behave!

He smiled and shook his head, before picking up the menu. He was a good mate.

The waitress paused, electronic pad in hand ready for his order.

"Medium Hawaiian, please, with extra pineapple."

Even though his mind was clear, the trawl into the file had instigated a concern, a worry that he had deliberately failed to share with Gail. He began to reflect in more detail as he waited to be served. The words 'property rich and cash poor' seemed to run around in his head like a persistent echo. He closed his eyes and pictured the driveway to the house, remembering the satisfying crunch of the fine gravel as the car moved towards the elegant front door. One yellow and one portly brown Labrador retriever barked momentarily as he and his colleague climbed out from the van. It was then he saw her for the first time. She was quite diminutive, smartly dressed but with a powerful voice that had the two dogs return to her side and sit without hesitation. Constance Hartley-Lowe. How could he forget that name? *That was a cross to bear in itself*, he remembered thinking on reading the name on the warrant before he had even seen her. The waitress returned. The thought brought a smile.

"Medium Ham and Pineapple. Can I get you anything else? More wine?"

Tom looked at the offering and then at the waitress. "Wine, yes, please."

"Enjoy!"

"I'll let you know if I don't," he muttered beneath his breath.

"Anomalous," he said to himself as he cut the first slice. There he was looking at the most beautiful house set in its own grounds, located a few miles from Easingwold, and he, a bailiff, was there to collect a debt. It was company policy for bailiffs not to work on their home territory. The debt was for nonpayment for building work carried out over eight months previously. Two vehicles, both expensive, were parked in front of a row of matching garages and yet in his hand, he recalled clearly, he held the paperwork, a Court demand for the collection of payment for an outstanding debt that amounted to over thirty thousand pounds. The removal of one of the cars would have settled the debt but it had quickly become apparent that nothing was as it seemed and the word *lease* kept finding its way into the conversation. It was there that he heard again the words 'property rich but cash poor,' and on this occasion it made sense to him. Hartley-Lowe's ensuing statement, however, stuck with him. 'Your parents' legacy can become not only a form of abuse but also your worst nightmare.' She had continued explaining that inheriting the family home, the heritage, and the death duties that accompanied that privilege were akin to a prison sentence. It was at that point a young man had appeared from the side of the house. He carried an open shotgun resting over the crook of his arm. Within a few seconds he had positioned himself a short distance behind but to the side of her so that they resembled the armorial lions they had seen on the gate posts as they had entered the driveway. The man did not speak. The gun remained broken.

Tom remembered the one-sided conversation as she stood her ground, she seemed neither fazed nor intimidated, just angry and frustrated by the circumstances in which she found herself. It clearly seemed to support her argument. He tried to recall her exact words.

I'm now asking you politely, Tom, is it? I want you and your colleague to leave my property. I find you and your cameras, your black, military clothing both frightening and intimidating. Your surname might make you believe you are James Bond but I know you for what you are, bullies and leeches representing a builder who does not fulfil his promises. Raising money is hard and estates have had to be sold or given to the National Trust in lieu of the extortionate tax system we have in this country. We've done what we can with that and believe me it's been difficult. Forty percent is what you pay in inheritance tax, can you believe that? Bloody robbery on savings you've already paid tax on! So, the outstanding monies you demand will be paid when the builder finishes the roof.

We're still suffering leaks, more than we had before he started! You've seen the letters we've sent? It clearly states that outstanding monies owed will be paid when the leaks stop.

May I remind you that you've not been invited here, I've received no formal notification of your visit and therefore you are breaking the law of trespass. He recalled how she lifted her hands and pointed to the man to her side. *He has witnessed what has gone on just as your body cameras have. I will telephone the police should you not follow my polite request and be gone or show me the warrant that allows forced access.*

A group of girls broke the relative silence of the restaurant with a round of high-pitched laughter; the joke had obviously been good. It also broke off his thoughts. He sipped more wine. Her words were as clear as if it were yesterday. She had said his name, not in full but she had cleverly made it known that she had read and noted his ID. It brought back a slight flutter of excitement in his stomach. He recalled how his colleague had challenged him once back in the van.

She was a bit of all right for her age. You had the warrant but didn't act. We should have at least looked at taking control of goods. It's not like you, Tom. Going soft? Old enough to be your mum. Jim had chuckled and nudged him. *Feel sorry for her or did you fancy giving her one?*

With Jim it always came down to sex. He remembered asking if he had ever faced a gun before but was told in reply that it was, *Fucking broken over his arm. Young lad. No bottle.*

Tom had returned the warrant and as far as he recalled,

it had been served and arrangements had been made to have an independent inspection of the disputed work on the property. His second visit, in a private capacity, would remain informal and personal.

Removing his phone, he dialled the office. There was always somebody there, always somebody collating work for the following day.

"Christian, it's Tom. I want you to confirm for me the outcome of a case. I'm certain I know the answer but I'd be grateful if you could just clarify."

Within two minutes he had the answer.

***

The call from Stuart Park came as Cyril walked home.

"Leave him there if you're sure of his story. He's hardly going to do a runner with two kids and one on the way. I trust your instinct. Sensitive policing is what our leaders preach. Well done! I'll read the full report in the morning. I've heard Coffrey is making some progress but is still in ICU."

A post on the police website had requested dash cam footage of the three people seen on Ripon Road giving times and approximate route. House to house enquires were proving tedious and without results. It was strange that there was no CCTV footage of either of the remaining two after the event. It was as if they had been whisked away. Cyril made a mental note to look at the routes that could have been taken from the garage without coming into contact with the town's CCTV. If this had been planned, such knowledge would be crucial but then why be seen at all? With all of his expertise and experience and just when he thought he was beginning to understand the criminal mind, he discovered he was still as bewildered.

As he entered the passageway leading to Robert Street and home there was a marked strengthening of the wind.

***

Tom collected his receipt, drained the wine from his glass and left. Station Parade was busy, it was already dark as the rush hour was drawing to a close. *Constance Hartley-Lowe*, the name tumbled in his thoughts. There was a ring to it, a gilt edge as if you could tell the colour of the spoon you would have found in her mouth at birth. From where he was standing, if he had read the strength of her anger, she would have preferred it to have been plastic! He pulled up his collar. His job brought him face to face with a cross section of society but many were the less fortunate, the unfortunates who find themselves trapped and barely keeping head above water. There were also the players, those who thought the law and the courts would never catch up with them and even when they did, fought tooth and nail to make wrongs right. For those people he had little sympathy.

A lonely meal can sometimes be just the fillip one needed. He would collect a bottle of wine on the way home, settle in front of the TV and try to put the day behind him. Already he was feeling more positive.

Chapter Eleven

Although dark, it was not yet nine. Within fifteen minutes Tom approached his flat, a stone-built, Victorian villa on a quiet road. Not all the houses along the road had been converted into apartments. Two were now open for bed and breakfast and some were still private homes. Fishing in his pocket for his keys, he started to tap his clothing above the numerous pockets of his jacket, *the key dance* as his colleagues had called it. It followed the same routine. He found a single key on a ring, not what he was looking for and neither was it familiar. His were missing. Had he picked up somebody else's at the office by mistake? He could not remember removing his keys any time during the day.

He pushed open the outside door to be faced with another. The hall light brought myriad colours from the stained-glass panel that filled the upper area and sides of the porch door and frame. He checked his pockets again. Nothing. He tried to recall the last time he had had them, seen them. He had locked the flat and closed the door that morning, the door at which he now stared, the vestibule entrance, he had heard it close, locking itself.

He looked at the intercom to his right and pressed the button for flat 4.

The speaker crackled briefly before the elderly voice could be heard. "Hello."

75

"Miss Johnson, it's Tom from flat 2. Sorry to trouble you but I might have left my key in my flat door this morning."

"Thought I heard you earlier." There was a long pause. "Must be hearing things in my old age. You're late tonight, Tom. Busy day?"

"And how. Been for a meal." He did not want to get too involved as she could natter for an age.

"I'm sure that they weren't there when I went out today but what does an old fool like me know?"

He laughed. Fortunately, he heard the door open with a click and he propped it ajar with his shoulder. "Thank you. Hope all is well." He did not wait for the response.

Closing the door, he walked up the stairs to the first landing. A fire door was positioned for the next flight of stairs. His flat door was to the left. The keys were still in the lock. He remembered that he had stopped to tie his shoe lace after closing the door. It must have been then he had been distracted. It seemed to be the perfect end to the day.

Opening the door, he removed the keys from the lock and tossed them into the bowl containing some odd coins that was nestled on the narrow hall table, before fumbling for the light. He also tossed in the newly found key after giving it a closer inspection. The familiar smell of home was never more appreciated. Throwing his coat over the back of the chair, he flicked on the television before moving through to the kitchen for a glass. The bottle, a screw top, was never more inviting. Once settled, he grabbed his mobile. It rang a while and a female voice answered.

"Thought you were never going to ring."

"You'd never believe the day I've had. Sorry you couldn't get over."

"Me too. Tell all."

***

Fletcher had showered and eaten. Janice could cook and she was fastidious about Olivia eating well even if it meant their going without. He listened as she was reading a story before bed. She had not been best pleased to hear he was going out. They had rowed about Coffrey. Each had blamed the other, she him for bringing him home and he her for allowing him to supervise the kids. The silence between them was the only victor. She had watched as he looked out at the motorbike covered with a tarpaulin. There was no tax or MOT and it had never been insured. That was another problem that had brought one of the bailiffs to their door for nonpayment of a fine on a previous occasion. He had been lucky it had not been confiscated and scrapped or confiscated for payment of outstanding debt. He had Steptoe to thank for saving them on both occasions. On leaving he had slammed the door to make a point and walked down Brewster Street. She had watched him for a while. He checked his watch. Turning from the window she settled on the chair and wept.

***

The sound of voices swam into his consciousness as Tom opened his eyes and waited for them to fully focus on the television. His head felt thick and sticky and his mouth dry; the empty red wine bottle confirmed the reason. He closed his eyes again and the voices briefly faded. He quickly opened them again. Apart from the illumination from the screen, the other lights in the room were off. He was confused as they had been on, he had switched them on when he came home. The same anxious flutter that he had experienced earlier in the day expanded in his stomach. He lifted his head and leaned back over the arm of the settee to scan the now inverted room. There was nothing, only the movement of the light projected from the television screen. He closed his eyes before rubbing them with the heels of his hands. He gently cupped them. Many tiny coloured lights seem to flash within the trapped private darkness. He allowed himself to enjoy the peace and he finally relaxed.

"Get a grip and go to bed," he said out loud. His eyes were still closed, his head on the cushion of the settee's arm and his fingers were linked and folded on his head.

"You'll get all the sleep you need when you're dead."

The voice came from nowhere. It was deep and languid but Tom knew that it was real, the same voice he had heard that morning. An involuntary, guttural expletive erupted from his throat drowning the other sounds within the room. It was a cross between a strangulated scream and a yell. It continued as he rolled, semi-conscious off the settee and onto the floor. His head quickly followed the direction of the intruding voice, his eyes wide as his constrained scream faltered and the hot, prickling sensation of fear smothered his skin and quickly took hold, paralysing his body.

The shape was above him, looming. It looked human and real but confusingly without human facial features. Tom's instinct, suddenly fuelled by the fear and adrenalin, brought an immediate reaction as he forced his legs to push his body up. His hands, clumsily sinking into the settee's cushions, failed to help. It was in vain. The movement was too slow and too late. Whatever struck him just above the eyes in the centre of the forehead was immediate and his evening ended there.

***

"So, what would be your prognosis of Shane Coffrey's future having seen the scans and x-rays as well as the reports?" Cyril sipped his Black Sheep Ale before rotating the glass in his hand. "Cheers!" He looked directly at Julie.

"I couldn't comprehend that one person could do that to another and Cyril, I've seen some horrendous and deliberate injuries in my time but then, my patients stopped breathing long before I saw them. The question revolves around his survival. If he pulls through this then they'll rebuild his face at best but it will need to be plated and reformed. Teeth are relatively easy to sort once the main structure is repaired, providing the muscles to the jaw regain function. It's the damage to the nerves that will give most cause for concern. This sounds cynical and possibly clinical, Cyril, but he'll not see the results of the work they perform."

"They can rebuild?"

"A chap in Alaska had his face ripped off by a bear he was chasing on a snowmobile, and although he's not the man he was, the reconstructive surgery was marvellous. After seeing the images and the x-rays, I contacted an old colleague, a maxillofacial surgeon, to determine the time scale and the amount of work that will be required."

Cyril sipped more beer and was beginning to feel uncomfortable as the conversation progressed. "And?"

"'How long is a piece of string?' was his answer. It's apparently to do with the amount of scar tissue you make. He regaled me with some of the birth deformities he had witnessed being corrected as well as those seriously injured in motor accidents and through domestic carelessness; one chap hurt badly by a chainsaw kicking back sounded dreadful. However, as he says, we can rebuild the physical but it's the psychological damage that's hard to address."

Cyril thought about the photograph in his office cabinet and understood immediately the amount of counselling Coffrey would need to go through if he stood a chance of a return to any sort of emotional normality.

Julie moved closer to Cyril. "We often take what we have for granted. We've worked hard for our successes but ..." She wanted to mention the stability of their upbringing, their hard work to succeed and the deep down support of loved ones but knowing the complexity of Cyril's childhood made her hold back and he immediately sensed her reticence.

He raised her hand and kissed it. "We're all dealt cards in this life, Julie, and it's how we play those cards that's key to how we progress educationally, emotionally and therefore socially. Knowing how to play the hand is the key and that skill often comes from the parental guidance and the example we are set from an early age. My parents, even my father, initiated the fundamental characteristics that helped me build and shape my life for the better and maybe possibly the worse. Who said, 'Give me the child until he is seven and I'll give you the man'?"

"Aristotle, I think."

"Correct. Some people chuck in their hand too soon whilst others either bluff their way through or play life's game with care and skill. I deal with people who, in most cases at least, expect something for nothing. You and me and the people who surround us work bloody hard with what we've been given. My childhood was difficult but I knew I was loved and that they'd do anything for me just as your parents did for you. It's knowing someone loves you. Some nippers don't have that, the parents are too involved with drink or drugs or not even present. Remember the Larkin poem: 'They fuck you up your mum and dad'?"

Julie nodded. "A minority, let's get some perspective."

"Like I've said, the family unit has been diminishing for years, not just with the destruction of whole communities that began with ridding towns of terraced rows and placing people vertically and not horizontally, but also the TV, the idiot's lantern that now glows in all rooms so kids and parents live separate lives. They no longer sit and eat at a table and goodness only knows what some kids are watching. In many ways, Larkin was right. There's less and less rigour required."

Julie blew out a sigh. "You'll suffer vertigo one day whilst standing on that soap box of yours."

"I know because of my past. I have a degree of empathy, as I know you do too. That's what makes us human and that's what makes the difference, makes us better at what we do both socially and professionally. We can see the grey and not just the black and white. In some ways, I've been through what they are going through and therefore I can see their side, not take their side, but understand it. Am I making sense?"

There was an immediate silence as Julie leaned further towards Cyril. *The words he used, we and I, are all confused,* she thought but said nothing. She understood. She had believed from their first meeting that he was a special man and each day she had a clear affirmation that she had made a wise decision in marrying him. He was kind and generous but there was a hidden fragility deep beneath the surface.

Chapter Twelve

Gail Wilson-North flicked through Tom Craig's files for the second time and cross-referenced a visit he had made regarding collection of monies owed to HMRC. There was an anomaly in the recording of the report. Picking up the phone she dialled Tom's internal number. The call went unanswered. She dialled Reception. Lynn Burnes the receptionist answered in her usual breezy manner.

"Hello, Mrs G, how can I help?" Gail had asked her to refer to her as Mrs G when in the office.

"Has Tom arrived this morning? He's scheduled in for the first part of the day but he's not at his desk."

"He's not checked in and his ID pass is still with me so as yet, no." Gail glanced at the clock on her computer screen and frowned. It was rare for Tom to be late and yesterday was the first occasion she could recall for many months if at all before.

"Put me through to Mike, please. He's out all day according to the schedule."

Immediately she heard it connect to Mike's mobile. It rang a while.

"Hello." He was abrupt and breathless.

"It's Gail. Sorry to ring when you're with clients but Tom hasn't arrived in this morning. Have you seen him?"

"I left the office early and he was due at eight."

She heard the muffled words, 'Oh shit!' and imagined he had covered the phone with his hand.

"You've tried his mobile?" Mike asked, anxious for her answer.

Gail felt foolish. She had not, only his internal extension. "No, sorry, I'll do that now."

"Let me know if there's a problem. Hopefully we're just finalising payment arrangements here. We've had full co-operation. I'll be free in ten minutes. Let me know either way."

Gail hung up, checked the file for Tom's number and dialled. It went immediately to answerphone. A wave of anxiety flushed through her body and she rang Lynn asking her to try his number every five minutes. Gail checked her watch. She would give him fifteen minutes to answer the calls aware of Mike's growing concern. There was nothing.

"Mike. We can't contact Tom. Can you go round to his apartment? I know he was a little shaken yesterday. You know him best. You can pick up the rest of your visits later." Gail was clearly concerned and it was reflected in her voice.

Within forty minutes the white van was parked outside the building that housed Tom's apartment. Mike glanced up at the bow window on the second floor. The curtains were still drawn. Mike knew instinctively something was amiss. Tom was fastidious in his timekeeping. He would not be still in bed.

The wrought iron gate protested feebly as he pushed it open before allowing it to swing back with a clatter. A face appeared from behind lace curtains in the lower window and watched as he approached. Mike raised a hand and smiled but received nothing in return. He pressed the button next to Flat 2. There was no surname just the capital letters 'TC' for Top Cat, his nickname when in the forces Tom had told him. "Nine bloody lives, Craig," he mumbled as he waited, remembering the conversation. After the third attempt he selected the flat he thought belonged to the woman, the sentinel, who had observed his arrival. The intercom crackled.

"Hello."

"Hi, I'm a friend and work colleague of Tom from flat 2. He's not come into work today. He wasn't well yesterday and we wondered if he was okay. Have you seen or heard him this morning?"

There was a pause. More crackling. "No. I believe he lost his keys yesterday and the lady from number four let him in."

"What time would that have been?"

"I'd just fed my cat so maybe about nine o'clock when I heard him on the stairs."

"I need to check. Could you let me in and I can knock? He might have overslept."

"I'll go and knock. You can't be too careful these days, young man." The crackling stopped. He noticed movement in the hallway. The figure was diffused with the coloured, pattered glass. Moments later the intercom crackled again.

"His keys are in his door. He must be in."

"Please let me in as he might be unwell."

The electronic lock clicked and the door opened slightly. Mike pushed with his shoulder. The lady was waiting in the hallway.

"I do hope he's alright. Up the stairs to the left."

Mike mounted the stairs. For a man with a prosthetic

leg, he was very agile. The keys hung from the Yale lock. He paused, removed a pair of nitrile gloves, stock equipment for a bailiff when entering some of the houses to collect items to be sold to pay off a debt. He also switched on his body cam knowing it was being monitored back at the office. He gave a short explanation.

"Attending as requested. At Tom's apartment. Time is 09.47. The keys are in the door. I'm entering."

The key turned easily and dropping the lower handle the door opened silently. The room was dark apart from the light from the television. Strangely, there was no sound.

"Tom, it's Mike." His voice was clear and seemed to echo within the room. The Victorian high ceilings helping to amplify the sound. There was no response. He reached for the light switch and noticed the bowl on the narrow table, containing a few coins, another pair of similar keys and a single key on a ring. He then saw the coat and moved over towards the chair. The foot protruding from the front of the settee immediately caused him to halt. He called Tom's name but there was no response. He talked to the body cam as he approached. "Oh shit. Get the emergency services. If you're monitoring this, get an ambulance."

The face he stared at was unrecognisable, swollen and bloodied. His military training immediately kicked in and he felt for a pulse. There was one, irregular and shallow. Removing his mobile and pulling off a glove he dialled 999. Gently, he turned Tom into the recovery position and constantly monitored his breathing.

The sirens could be heard minutes before the first responder entered the building. Mike, standing at the top of the stairs after going to prop open the outer door, urged him to move quickly. As the paramedic climbed the stairs Mike's phone rang.

"It's Gail, I've seen the body cam footage. Bloody hell. What's going on?"

"He's been attacked in his own home. They're attending to him now. The room's being sealed. It's hard to say but it's now a crime scene. He was scared yesterday, bloody scared and I did nothing."

A few moments later more sirens shrieked and more vehicles blocked the road. Two more medics were in attendance along with two police officers. Mike paced the bottom corridor with growing concern that they were taking too long.

"What's happening now, Mike?" Gail asked.

"They're taking too long. We should have done more for him."

"We did what we could considering what we knew. Now we need to do more, we need to dig more deeply. You should go home when you can. Take some time."

There was a brief silence. "They're taking him out."

Gail could hear the numerous voices. It was clear Mike was asking how Tom was.

"'He's been stabilised,' that's all they said. I have to go. The police want a word."

Chapter Thirteen

Owen and Cyril were in the Incident Room studying the photographs of the outdoor play area close to Coffrey's crime scene. House to house enquiries were still in progress but possible routes thought to have been taken by the perpetrators had now been dismissed as unlikely. Smirthwaite entered. They both turned.

He walked to the boards and pointed to the CCTV images of the three possible suspects taken on the night. "We know who they are. They came forward after seeing the social media posts. We can discount them."

Cyril looked at Owen and then back at Smirthwaite. "And you've checked their stories?"

"All legit. They saw nothing unusual either."

Cyril shook his head. "Go through the images for the area again. I want stills of anyone, any couple seen in that general location from eight in the evening to – " he looked at the time Coffrey was found " – to six a.m. We're concentrating on multiple possible perpetrators rather than keeping an open mind. If he were coaxed or lured there it could involve drugs but it could be sex with either gender. There's a chance he was given the location or he was escorted."

"Or Coffrey invited someone back there." Owen's tone was unconvincing as he moved the images and attached them to the 'out' board using coloured magnets. Evidence was never totally discarded. Cyril moved over and straightened the photographs. "It's straight or it's not, Owen. You've probably hit the nail on the head if that's not an inappropriate metaphor. Coffrey might have had a key. We presumed differently and that, my friend, is a fundamental error in our line of work."

Owen smiled.

"Did we ever locate his mobile?" Cyril asked, turning to look at the boards again. "We know that he had one from the interview with Fletcher. Here, it's here in this report."

"It wasn't in the clothes left in the garage and nothing has been found in the searches. Tracking records now but it might not even be registered if it were used for dealing."

"Owen, what makes someone go to a strange place at night to meet someone who might do them harm, maybe even to meet with a total stranger?"

"Let's presume for drugs. This might not be the first time the garage area has been used. Nobody can even tell us whether it was ever securely locked. According to Philip Ashton's neighbour, he hasn't been back to Harrogate for over six months. Empty garage, quiet place, perfect rendezvous site. What if Coffrey knew the person he was meeting there? What if he used the garage? Maybe he had no place to stay and he stumbled across something he shouldn't have or someone stumbled across him?"

Cyril looked at Owen and raised an eyebrow. He picked up a whiteboard marker and wrote, *What if?*

Owen put his hand in his pocket and pulled out a wrapped mint. "You look as though it's time for a mint, sir. What if he stumbled across something he shouldn't have

89

found?"

Cyril took the mint. "Or seen, Owen, or seen."

The phone rang. Owen answered. Cyril watched as he allowed the menthol flavour to fill his mouth whilst crushing the yearning to vape.

"Where? And he's in ICU? Thanks, Shakti." Owen hung up and looked at Cyril. "We have another. Severe facial injuries but alive. An enforcement officer, bailiff. We have his colleague downstairs, a Michael Stockwell. He found him and gave life-saving treatment. Ex-forces. Shakti is at the apartment now with Harry Nixon and CSI are at the scene. They sent Stockwell to us as he seemed emotional at the flat but was keen to describe what he had discovered. His finding the victim is recorded on his bodycam."

"Who's the victim?"

"Tom Craig, thirty-seven, works for Northwind Legal. Enforcement Agent."

Cyril turned back to the boards and flipped through Shakti's report detailing the interview with Fletcher and Blackledge. "We have a common denominator. They were visited by bailiffs collecting a fine for not having a TV licence along with other fines and of course they are linked with Coffrey. It would be too much to hope that the visit was carried out by Tom Craig, I suppose. Contact Northwind and find out and I'll see Stockwell. Join me when you have the info."

***

Shakti and Nixon sat opposite Miss Johnson in Flat 4.

"He's a quiet chap. Been here about a year. Sent me a Christmas card. Why would someone hurt him?"

"That's what we need to discover, Miss Johnson. Does he have many visitors?" Nixon asked.

"The odd one or two I've seen come up the path. Some I see leave but others, the odd lady friend or two seem to just disappear." She frowned disapprovingly. "I think they stay. He has a new one, older than the rest but attractive. Has a fancy car too. Never ceases to amaze me why men would like soiled goods. My parents insisted I wait until I had a wedding ring on my finger. Now they stay overnight at the drop of a hat."

"Have you been married?" Shakti asked whilst noticing there was no wedding ring.

"No, never met Mr Right."

Nixon looked at Shakti knowing just what she was thinking.

"Do you have security cameras in the building?" Shakti quizzed, swiftly changing the subject from men as it seemed to cause her some distress.

Johnson frowned as if insulted by the question. "This is a respectable house, officer, with caring and honest folk living here. This is also a good neighbourhood. Why would we need cameras?"

The fact that someone in the same building had been bludgeoned to within an inch of his life had apparently not yet registered with her.

"What about last night apart from when you let him in. Did you see anyone else?"

"No. I take a tablet to help me sleep and once my head hits the pillow ..."

"There were no occupants in Flat 3 at the moment," Shakti asked.

"They're away, working abroad. Don't recall where. Then there's Mrs Nosey Britches downstairs. She's the eyes and ears of the place. I suppose another reason we don't need a camera."

Standing, Shakti and Nixon thanked Johnson and turned to leave.

"You'll let me know how he is?" She asked, surprised by their sudden movement.

Shakti nodded. "When we know." They quickly approached the front door. The building was still busy with CSI operatives and a police officer was standing at the entrance when Miss Johnson called down the stairs.

"This might be nothing but ..."

Nixon turned to look at Shakti who returned to Johnson's room. Nixon called on Flat 1.

Within fifteen minutes he had received a statement from 'Nosey Britches' as well as collecting the contact details of Flat 3; the owner would be approached once Nixon was back at the station. He waited, chatting to the officer by the front door until he was re-joined by Shakti.

"Anything?" Nixon looked at her, patted the officer's arm and headed for the car.

"She heard someone on the step when she got up for a pee. The fifth step creaks apparently and she heard it. She said it would usually creak if the person was heavy, like a man."

Nixon laughed. "Right. She weighs more than me! Did she give a time?"

"Thought somewhere after midnight but couldn't be sure. I've added that to her statement and uplifted it. Good internet signal from there."

***

Mike Stockwell sat nursing a coffee in the station entrance hall and felt as though he had not had a moment to reflect since leaving for work that morning. He disregarded the ringing phones and the chattering from those hidden from view behind the Harrogate Police Station front desk. Closing his eyes, he reran the moment he had found Tom. It seemed slow and not in real time but vividly sharp and clear. It was the image of his distorted facial features that seemed to bring the memories to a complete standstill.

"Mr Stockwell?" Owen held open the far door and tightened his lips. It was neither a smile nor a sympathetic gesture, but it did have an implication that suggested the seriousness of their meeting. "Please, bring your drink with you."

Stockwell stood and moved across to Owen who offered his hand.

"Inspector Owen, Mr Stockwell. Thanks for coming over. Sorry about your friend. DCI Bennett is waiting to see you."

"A Detective Chief Inspector no less." It was uttered without an edge.

Bennett stood when Stockwell was brought to the door of the Interview Room and introduced to him.

"I'm sorry to receive the news of your friend and colleague, Mr Stockwell. Firstly, I need to inform you that we will be recording this interview." He pointed to the smoked domed covered cameras in the corners of the room. "This is for your benefit as much as ours. Being in the military I'm sure you're aware of amnesia. You may also be aware of dissociative amnesia, a condition that stems from emotional trauma, such as being the victim of a violent crime or witnessing the results."

"It's not a problem. My memory is clear and it's not the first trauma I've been through." Mike lifted his trouser leg and exposed the metal of his prosthetic leg.

"Now that's clear, may I compliment you on the professional way you dealt with the discovery of your colleague, Tom Craig. Your speedy intervention may have given the medical teams the necessary time to prevent further cerebral injuries. I believe you managed to enhance his airways. The latest news is that his condition is now stable and he has been put into an induced coma."

Mike nodded. "You never forget your training. My buddies, after I clumsily stumbled across an IED, didn't and that's why I'm still here."

Cyril continued. "However, the fact we can't yet interview him brings additional complications for the investigation. We have no eyewitness accounts other than from a Miss Johnson who lives in the flat near his. From that time, until you found him, we have a vacuum to fill."

"There was no sign of a break in as the keys were in the door to the flat and another set was inside in a bowl—"

"I was about to ask you to describe your attendance from leaving your vehicle to finding the body."

Mike Stockwell went through what he had seen and heard.

"We know that there are two keys to enter a flat. The first is the inner door. That can also be opened from each flat, and then the individual flat key. You know Tom well. Would he leave his keys in the door? I have to admit to doing it myself on more than one occasion and my door faces the street!" Cyril frowned. "I put it down to thinking ahead."

"Last night? I don't think so after the morning he'd had." Mike explained the concerns Tom had confided in him and that Gail had expressed her worries in the office.

Cyril's expression demonstrated concern.

"It was like a sixth sense. He knew someone was watching him. The runner who crashed into him. He felt he recognised the voice but couldn't place it. He thought it was an actor, TV or film but he wasn't sure who."

Moving to the door, Cyril requested a street map be brought and within minutes both men were leaning over the desk, Mike showed them the route he believed Tom took each morning.

"It was about here where he stopped and where he and the runner collided."

Cyril marked the route adding a cross at the strategic points indicated.

"Has he ever discussed this type of concern before?"

"Not in all the time we've worked together. I don't know him that well, a friend from work you might say and being both ex-forces we seemed to get on. I advised he change his route from the regular journey he made each morning. We would do that naturally if stationed, let's say, in an unsympathetic posting."

"What about going home last night?"

"He asked me to go for a meal. He didn't want to spend the whole evening on his own but I had other commitments. I sent him a text to see if all was well. He was going to have a pizza and then go home. The lady in the lower flat said he'd arrived home about nine. I didn't speak to the lady on his floor although I did see her when the emergency services arrived."

"Did you call again?"

"My boss called his work's mobile but it went straight to answerphone."

Cyril made a note to see if Tom's mobile had been located during the search. "Did he have a personal phone?"

"If he did, I didn't have the number. We were work friends."

"You mentioned you sent a text."

"Work's phone."

"Why were these concerns he had not reported to the police?"

"Have you tried ringing 101? If everyone who had a panic attack reported it to the police … Need I say more?"

Cyril knew the system was flawed but said nothing.

***

Owen was checking the computer to see if the early results from Forensics regarding the garage incident had arrived. He was not disappointed. He wrote on a scrap piece of paper the word *naked* and tagged on a question mark before tapping the paper with his pen, short staccato beats with no particular pattern.

"Morse code, Owen, or is it the latest tune that's become an earworm?" Nixon queried as he approached the desk.

"If bloody only! We now have two who've had their faces kicked in within twenty-four hours of each other give or take, but neither has suffered any other injuries. You'd think there would be self-defence related damage. If someone came at you with a weapon, you'd stick your hands up."

"Indeed." Nixon's expression changed. He demonstrated where the damage might occur.

"One victim is in his flat, the other in a garage. One is fully clothed whilst the other was naked. They're arse about face to me. I could understand the chap in the flat being in the buff but that's not the case. Neither weapon was left at the scene. I like consistency, Harry, consistency in all areas."

"That's fine if the perpetrator is the same person but there's another 'c' word you need to consider and that's coincidence. The kicking in of both faces, as you so delicately but inaccurately put it, might just be that. Don't forget though, they're both alive. If it's the same person who's carried out these attacks, they could have easily killed the victims; they didn't and is that luck, planning or circumstance?"

"But then they both still could succumb, let's not forget that. If they didn't want them dead what could that be telling us, Harry?"

Harry raised his shoulders. "We have a potential killer out there selecting people because of the way they walk, the colour of their hair or their sexual proclivity and he just wants to destroy their faces?"

Owen swivelled in his chair. "Like they've annoyed him or her. Why the face?"

"It takes away their identity. They cease to become human beings if they are faceless."

"Too deep for me. Maybe some people don't need an excuse for violence. Remember the line that's the precursor for pub fights? *Who are you staring at?* There are also the folks who bear a grudge for ever and patiently wait for the

97

opportunity to right what they thought was a wrong. Even more strange, and I've thought about this often, criminals and murderers could be having tea and cakes on the next table to you in a café and you'd never know."

"I've said it before, Owen, these people breathe the same air and they're not all locked up!"

Chapter Fourteen

The smooth surface of bright aluminium bodywork bounced a diffused glow from the strip lights hanging above the workshop in neat rows, reflecting and detailing the slight distortions within the metal finish. Running his hand along the flank of the re-formed body panel gave him as much feedback as his experienced visual critique of the area. As always, the senses were key to the task of reforming the damage to old cars. The sound of the strike of the flat-faced, metal hammer beating against the hollow of the aluminium panel, echoed within the workshop. It was neither heavy nor uncontrolled but subtle and deliberate, each strike almost a kiss. Adrian's ungloved fingertips caressed the result, feeling for an accurate outcome after each strike, a skill that had been acquired over the many years of applying similar blows and touches. This action was quickly followed by a squinting eye, focusing along the shapely coachline.

He sat back on the low wheeled stool and viewed the car's naked shell. It had once been a sad Ferrari 250 GTE 2+2 and time had not been kind to the car. Quantities of filler over the aluminium bodywork had concealed the damage, not only to the outer skin, but also the lightweight, tubular chassis. Years ago, the car would have been deemed valueless, too old and would probably have been scrapped, its twelve-cylinder engine moved to a kit car but today, with the increased value of the marque, it would be saved. This rise in monetary value had seen the resurrection of many such wrecks and therefore an increase in Adrian's workload.

"Vanity, Adrian, to admire your own work!" The voice broke out into a chuckle as a hand tapped his elbow. "Bloody good reforming and patching that, my son. You can't see the join as one comedian said to another." Greg, a Geordie, still had the strong accent even though he had lived in Yorkshire more than ten years and sounded like Brian Johnson from ACDC. He even wore a similar cap.

"Squint down the swage line and let me know what you think, Greg, and less of the bloody cheek. From that end first." Adrian pointed to the front of the car.

Greg obeyed and crouched, tilted back his cap, closed one eye and moved his head slowly from side to side before going to view from the other direction. He put his finger and thumb together to form a circle. "Bloody belting, that. You're making a cracking job of it I have to say, bonny lad."

Adrian looked down at the flat faced hammer. A few of his tools had been a gift from his father many years ago. His name was stamped in capital letters on the wooden shaft.

"Good tools mean good jobs. I'm having a brew and then I have to repair two wheel arch edge splits before heat shrinking the rear quarter panel." He pointed to the area in question. "Drink?"

"Coffee as always." Greg moved over towards the spray booth. "Joe will have what he gets. Young apprentices don't get no choice in my book." He winked. They knew he always drank coffee.

Collecting the hammer, he popped it into his tool rack along with the variety of hammers stored there, each one a different design and shape, made for a specific task. He returned to the car and ran his hand over the recently completed area. A nod of appreciation quickly followed before he went to the kitchen.

Adrian sat on a plastic chair, his hands wrapped around the mug of tea, his feet on an upturned crate and stared out at the workshop. To the left, the spray booth doors gaped. Joe was placing a bonnet onto a frame ready for the finishing colour coats of paint. He had worked on that panel the day before; a straightforward shape apart from six holes set in two banks of three near the nose. The car to which it belonged sat in yellow-green etching primer in a corner of the shop. He admired the base colour. To his eye it enhanced the car's shape. He mouthed the word *Dino* with a degree of reverence followed by *Ferrari* adding a perfect, if not exaggerated Italian accent.

***

Fletcher had been alone in the interview room for fifteen minutes before Cyril entered. He introduced himself at the same moment Park came into the room. Fletcher had risen to his feet and looked at both men. It was a cold welcome.

"You know DC Park, I believe. Please sit. You've been here before, Mr Fletcher. Not this nick, I know, but you're familiar with these proceedings so we don't have to go over the formalities unless you wish me to do so?" He left the question open and received a shake of the head in response.

"We've had two serious incidents occurring and both coincidentally are linked to you in some way. We need some clarity regarding Coffrey and an enforcement agent, a bailiff. Both are now in a serious condition in hospital and both incidents happened when you were not at home. You might now appreciate the logic as to why you were brought here today."

Fletcher did not move. He remained motionless, his arms folded and looked directly at Cyril. "I know one of the people for sure, Coffrey. We talked about that in the back of your car last night." He turned to look at Park. "I've met a few bailiffs too, more than my fair share. You know where I've been. We both told you everything yesterday."

"Where were you last night?" Cyril stepped in immediately.

"Are you spying on me? I went for a drink with Steptoe, Ian Tempest."

"Where?"

"Cold Bath Brewing on King's Road."

"Long way from home."

Fletcher laughed. "Right, it might be the other side of the world to you men but it's ten minutes from my house. Ian picked me up and before you ask, he doesn't drink. Been sober quite some time. I had a few, mind."

"I believe you were home when the enforcement officers came. According to the report there was some trouble." Cyril opened a slim file that he had placed on the table.

For the first time Fletcher laughed. "A warrant to enter my home and take possessions to cover an outstanding fine for not having a television licence. He had a warrant and wanted access. As you can imagine, with having kids in the house, I told him to bugger off. I have it on video. Janice took it. You know they're not allowed to enter a house if kids are present. The fine has been paid now as I was allowed to pay on the drip. He wasn't the first to visit us and he may not be the last. We're not bad people, Janice and me. Also paid the extortionate fee from the bailiff's company. I know it's a job and we all need to work but hell, I'd rather insert wasps up my arse than hound folk who are struggling."

"We have the details of the enforcement agents' visits on file here."

"We're trying. It's just that we might not have had the upbringing and guidance you two have had when we were younger but I'm telling you straight on my kids' lives, I protect my family and if it means standing up to bullies then I will. People make mistakes in life and are punished. I did but I'll not go back inside. I believe there should be a degree of tolerance from society especially when people are at a low point in their lives. I don't want charity. I want fairness and from where I stand, I haven't had too much of that."

Cyril was impressed by his vocabulary as well as his confidence and his moral conviction. Reflecting on the conversation which had taken place with Julie the previous evening, he glanced at Park.

"That's why I helped Shane when asked and I'll help anyone in genuine need until they take it for granted or abuse my hospitality. People look at my amateur tattoos and immediately draw their own conclusions, usually wrong ones but I can't blame them for socially stereotyping me as a yob. All these demonstrate is a misguidance in youth." He held out his hands. The tattoos were simple. "I try to be kind. You might not believe that. I do try."

"How kind are you to Steptoe?" Park asked with a degree of cynicism in his voice.

"I've told you when you asked in the car, he's a mate and when a mate asks for help, if it's possible and legal, I'll give it. He reciprocates with buying me a beer or two."

Cyril raised another eyebrow.

"Do you have anything to link me to these two crimes? You have my DNA on file and my prints. If not, I'd like to go or I'd like a duty solicitor."

"No, there's no need. As I said, Mr Fletcher, coincidences only and as Agatha Christie said, 'Any coincidence is worth noticing. You can throw it away later if it is only a coincidence.'"

Fletcher pulled a face. "If you say so."

"We just needed to clarify your whereabouts at the times we believe the incidents took place. I'd like to thank you for your time. I'll get someone to drive you home."

Cyril stood and leaned across the table with an outstretched hand, not something he would usually do in such circumstances. There was a reluctant pause on Fletcher's part but he took it. "As long as it's cleared up. I'm sorry to hear about Shane. One thing. It may not be relevant ..."

Cyril knew that people who saved things to the end of a meeting were anxious about asking for or giving information. He smiled. "Please, anything might just be the key we need."

"Ian, Steptoe, told me that the last time he saw Shane he was trying to do an impression of Donald Duck but not very well. Shane told him that he'd met a chap who made him laugh. He mimicked people. Shane's favourites were Donald Duck and The Joker from Batman. He'd tried to teach him to mimic both and obviously failed but he also told him this chap could do those meercats from the TV and some magic tricks. He didn't share that sort of information easily, in fact, he didn't usually talk about any friends as we don't believe he made friends easily unless they were kids. When he was doing the Incy Wincy game I told you about, he put on a baby voice, a bit like the duck."

"Did he give the name of this friend?"

"No, sorry. Not that I recall. It's probably nothing. I shouldn't have said."

As Fletcher left, Cyril sat and played with the pencil rotating it in his fingers. The link with the T-shirt located in the lock-up had immediately been flagged as a link with the word Joker. Cyril closed his eyes in order to collate mentally the pieces of evidence that were being revealed. They were there, dots on a page just needing to be joined in the correct way.

"It's about voices, Cyril," he said to himself. "The answer is there for the taking."

***

Adrian folded his overalls neatly and placed them into the holdall before collecting his brown checked jacket from his locker. He cast another glance towards the metal skinned skeleton of the car on which he had spent the day working. Dark blue heat marks now spotted the car's aluminium rear flank where the panel had been heated and shrunk – hammered and reshaped into the perfect form. It was free of undulations, now level, with only the smallest variation but experience told him the sprayed polyester filler coat and the guide coat would rectify those and he could relax. It had been a rewarding day. He had two days off but the car would be there on his return. Going to the tool rack, he selected three panel beating hammers of his own; nobody else used them in the workshop and they had enough tools to finish whilst he was away.

The three men stood ready to leave and the alarm code was entered. The audible scream was activated giving them time to leave and close the door before bringing down the roller shutter. Adrian handed the keys to Greg. Joe was glued to his phone having just retrieved it from his locker.

"Enjoy your days off, bonny lad. Can I give you a lift?"

Adrian laughed. "Right! Days off you say? I promised to finish some work. Joint venture with a friend or have you forgotten that? So, it's not really a holiday as such just a break from being with you two!" He winked and patted Greg's arm. "A lift? Kind offer, as usual but I've seen you drive that bloody death trap and I know who reformed the chassis so no thanks. As you should know by now, the walk is my therapy. Don't forget to lock his phone away during working hours!"

Greg laughed and Joe ignored the comment. The banter was always the same.

"I've told him if I see it, I'll surgically remove it with the gas axe." They both laughed but Joe pulled a face and walked towards the car. He had heard it all before and never thought it amusing.

The sun was still just above the houses and the sky was clear. Adrian stood and breathed the fresh, cool air. Checking his watch, it would normally take twenty minutes before he would arrive home but this evening the pub was calling. Greg passed giving a single blast on his horn and a wave. The engine of the old Porsche echoed against the sides of the confined, small industrial units that backed onto the railway line away from the road.

Chapter Fifteen

He paused before entering the passageway and mumbled, "Lights. Camera, action," out loud to himself before walking down the passageway. It was always a challenge when the sun was getting low as the tight railings conspired and formed a strobe effect within his peripheral vision, a flashing that he had never been able to cope with and yet it attracted him. He raised a hand to the side of his eye in the form of a blinker and moved more quickly. Coming this way, when the conditions were right, was a siren's call that lured him, a personal dare of self-harm to see if he could ignore the effect; in some ways, if he were honest, he derived a degree of masochistic pleasure from the discomforting experience. He hoped that there would be an outcome that would lead to an uncontrollable urge, the consequences of which he would regret at some time in the near future. It was then he thought of the last victim, Tom, according to the business card, his face inverted, his head on the arm of the settee. *Faces are funny when upside down,* he thought. *The eyes blink the wrong way. Did Anthony Hopkins ever blink in 'The Silence of the Lambs'? No. Maybe you shouldn't have done Tom. Blink! Blink! Bang!* He could hear Hopkins's voice fill his mind. It was one of his favourites. He had mastered the accent and wondered if any of his ancestors were Welsh. *Our Tom, never knew I'd followed him.*

He dropped his hand and walked on allowing the regularity of flashing light to hurt until a feeling of nausea flushed through him. Within minutes he was out of the passageway and standing on the pavement. His voice changed to mimic perfectly that of Richard Burton,

"'And all should cry, Beware! Beware!

His flashing eyes, his floating hair!

Weave a circle round him thrice,

And close your eyes with holy dread.'"

It was almost reverent and trance-like. Closing his eyes brought blackness. "Count, count don't let the black change. Don't let the colours come. Not red, not red!" Opening his eyes he stared ahead and walked on. The colours in his mind's eye slowly changed until he saw the red of the man's coat. He focused on the new-found target; the lone figure sitting on the bench.

Moving quickly, he approached the grassed area, pausing by a tree. The anger the light had distilled in his mind seeped through his whole body; to him it was uncontrollable and for no reason. He knew it was triggered by the flashing light. The person before him was now a threat. He studied the victim's every feature from his shoes to his red coat and finally, the most important part, the face. For a second, he saw the face of his father, red and full of anger before it changed to flowing with blood, the face that stared back from the deformed car bonnet. He smiled. "You never forget the first time. Never!" he whispered as he stared at the red coat.

***

Across the grass Peter Whittle stood up from the bench,

109

stretched, then rubbed his backside. The bench was too hard and too uncomfortable for a longer stay. He began to walk down Skipton Road unaware that he was being scrutinised. Within five minutes he was on Dragon Road. Home was just around the corner. The stone-built terrace house had an air of neglect about it. It had not always been that way but now he only existed. Since the death of his wife of forty years he had become lost, rudderless and without focus. His sadness was evident in the lack of maintenance to his home: maybe it was the lack of a woman's touch.

Popping the key into the lock Peter turned and saw a man approaching his property before stopping suddenly, clumsily and unnaturally. Most people walking along the terrace were local – few tourists or strangers came this way – but this was not someone he knew. He resisted enquiring if he needed directions. The stranger's manner made him uneasy and he quickly pushed open the door. Closing it he checked it was locked, and went into the front room; he was curious to see if the strange man had gone. Peter did not move the net curtains but stood away from them and glanced up the road in the direction from which he had come but there was no one there. He was just about to turn away when he spotted him, further down the road now, motionless and staring at Peter's window.

There was something unnerving about his posture, his intense focus, and Peter took a step back hoping the darkness of the room and the curtains would have concealed his presence. Nerves fluttered in his stomach. He had lived here all of his married life and he had never experienced anything like this. Then he suddenly gasped as the stranger raised a hand and waved, a slow and deliberate movement. Peter could see the stranger's lips moving as if he were talking, the action visible and exaggerated. Then he turned and walked away.

Peter watched him leave. He moved closer to the window the further down the road the stranger walked and observed until he rounded the bend. Peter anxiously moved upstairs and entered the back bedroom, now full of boxes that contained his wife's clothes. He tentatively looked out onto the back yard and the narrow ginnel that separated the two rows of terraced houses. He was there, standing at the end. A moment later he was gone.

***

Adrian rubbed his forehead and then his temples before finishing the pint he had looked forward to since leaving work. The local newspaper he had collected from the rack remained open as he went back to the bar.

"Two in a week's not going to be good for the town. I take it you've read about the men." She pulled the pint concentrating on Adrian and still automatically stopping as the beer reached the top. She allowed the froth to dribble down the glass.

Adrian nodded as she checked the pint. "Both in ICU. Must have been one hell of a beating."

Adrian strummed his fingers on the bar's mahogany surface and then straightened the towelling cover advertising a local beer.

She placed the pint before him. "Wonder what they'd done to deserve that? Mr Christianson, who comes in here regularly, ex-police officer I'm told, says it's all drug-related. County lines stuff whatever that is. The first one, I think his name's Coffey, says he's known for it, bit of a dealer but you hear a lot of bullshit behind the bar. Some nights there so much talk I'm up to my knees in it! I should have been called Rose!"

Adrian chuckled at the thought before returning to his table. He flicked the pages of the paper back until finding the article. "You're nearly right, Jenny. It's Coffrey. Only nineteen." He read the article again.

"Finished our car yet? Must have if you're in here boozing and enjoying the latest Harrogate rag," Stephen Firth enquired.

Adrian looked up. "Miracles take longer than you think. I have a couple of days off and even though it will be a busman's holiday it will be sorted. When's the auction date?" He did not lift his head but pushed out a chair with his foot. "Hope you've got deep pockets. There was more to do than you thought. Get a drink. I've opened a tab."

"The auction? Sooner than you think and earlier than we both would like."

Stephen Firth sipped the beer as he made his way back to the table, his upper lip briefly sporting a froth moustache. The back of his hand quickly sorted that.

"Just talking to Jenny about the two poor bastards who've been attacked. Isn't your boss's lock-up and property near there?" He tapped the relevant part of the article.

Firth took another long drink. "It's his place, the garage, that is. I had a brief chat with the police as we hold the key. It's left empty as you bloody well know and we use it to store stuff on the odd occasion. You've used it once or twice but for goodness' sake say nothing to anyone. I shouldn't have let you if the truth be known." He finished his pint. "Another?"

"No, thanks. I have to work on the car tonight for an hour or so and need to be sober, the thing's crooked enough as it is." Adrian looked up and grinned. "Tomorrow at mine before tea. Let's say five and I'll show you the progress made."

Chapter Sixteen

Cyril finished his risotto, carefully placed his cutlery into the bowl and wiped his mouth with his napkin. Julie had only eaten melon and ham and had finished before him.

"You enjoyed that." She slid her hand across the table to his.

"It would be my final meal if I'm ever lucky enough to get that chance in life." He raised his eyebrows before sipping some wine. "When I called you today you commented on the latest case, something about reason when I mentioned the two victims being in ICU after they'd suffered a severe but controlled beating."

"I actually said, Cyril, the uncertainty of reason." She watched as Cyril frowned, a signal that he did not understand. "I'd been thinking about it and there appears to be no reason, no motive when you consider there's no link between the two victims, other than a coincidental one from what I understand. Having two victims with similar but not identical facial injuries, you feel there's a need to draw comparisons but the victims are as different as chalk and cheese. The facial injury is the common denominator only if I discount the thin thread of evidence that binds both to the discordant family you mentioned. However, the motive to carry out the violence might, just might, be the reason but that brings with it a degree of uncertainty and so, Cyril, this was the reason for the comment – uncertainty of reason."

Cyril scratched his head and pulled a face as if he were trying to comprehend the logic.

"A justification for an action is the description of the noun – reason. So, the reason is uncertain. You've nothing evidential to justify the reason," Julie pointed out.

Cyril was quick to respond. "Verb – to persuade someone with a rational argument – maybe even if the persuasive element is a hammer?"

The question went unanswered.

***

April was the first into the Incident Room. The news she had received from the hospital had suddenly given the case greater urgency. Coffrey had succumbed to his injuries and passed away in the early hours. She had duly noted the time and along with the date, added the facts to the board. Owen entered, his left trouser leg running with coffee that had dribbled from his overfilled mug. April pointed to the offending article.

"Shit! Bloody just had them cleaned too." He removed a handkerchief and bent, trying to brush off the liquid only to cause a small wave of coffee to flood over the rim of the mug.

April moved and took it from him. "As a man, Owen, and a clumsy one at that, you should know your limitations. Men can only do one job at once and only if supervised by a woman. That's now two items of soiled clothing. Hannah's going to be thrilled with you!"

Owen frowned as he looked at the staining on the handkerchief before shrugging his shoulders.

"We're now looking for a murderer." She handed back

his coffee and pointed to the board. "This morning. In some small way it's a blessing for the lad."

The still photographs taken from the body cam belonging to the first responder clearly supported her judgement.

"What about the second victim, Tom Craig?" Owen looked away from the board. He had seen enough.

"Still in ICU but improving. The induced coma has been lightened as he's responding well. The doctors want him out as soon as possible and to bring him to a semi-conscious state."

"Does the boss know?" Owen sipped his coffee as Cyril walked in.

Owen turned and whispered to April, "Speak of the devil."

"And he doth appear, Owen." Cyril picked up a marker pen and added the words, *Uncertainty of reason,* to an empty board but said nothing in support of his action. He paused before adding:

REASON – NOUN – justification for action. VERB – to persuade someone.

He tapped the board with the pen.

"Which of those is the more relevant to this case do you think?"

Owen looked at April, unsure.

"At this stage we've neither rhyme nor reason based on the evidence we have, as far as I can see."

Cyril tapped the board again and then read April's notes on Coffrey's death. "The devil, Owen, looks after his own. Remember that." He tapped the note. "Anything from toxicology regarding both victims?"

116

"Still waiting."

"He has a relative, grandmother, nan, here in Harrogate. You were organising a warrant to search the place if you remember, sir."

Cyril chewed his lip and looked at Owen. "Mmm, consider it sorted, Owen. Organise a visit. You might need one of the family support team. How old is she?"

April checked the records. "Fifty-eight. Fairly young for a grandmother of a nineteen-year-old."

"Not the youngest I've met in my time in the force but they're definitely getting younger."

Cyril picked up the phone. "Can you please get Dr Pritchett to call me at her convenience. Thanks."

"Owen. I want you to interview Coffrey's grandmother. Take Shakti. You may also need a signer if my memory serves me correctly as a while back you mentioned that she suffers from severe deafness. I want names of any friends Coffrey might have had. Then look for links with known or suspected traffickers and also check to see if any of those are guilty of nonpayment of fines, particularly where bailiffs, sorry, enforcement agents have been involved. Any connections may prove vital. There's nothing from HOLMES?"

"Not as yet." Owen looked at April and received the same response.

"We've been a bit slow with this line of investigation. My fault." Cyril frowned. Such a slip was unusual and he admonished himself for it. "See her today if you can. I want as much info on that lad as possible and on her. Don't forget the mother. The full works. I also want Forensics at hers and in particular focus on his room if he still had one there. Garage, garden and any shed."

The phone rang as Owen left. It was Julie. "Thanks for getting back so quickly. Coffrey's dead and the details are with the coroner. I wondered who would do the post-mortem? I'm hoping to have toxicology results soon but it seems clear he was a drug user."

***

Philip Ashton pulled his Aston Martin Vantage up to the front of the hotel. He sat leaning his head back on the headrest and closed his eyes as he briefly listened to the indiscriminate sounds of the cooling engine.

As usual, the Eurotunnel Channel crossing had been effortless which was more than could be said for negotiating the roadworks at Alconbury on the A1M. He had decided not to stay in the flat and booked the hotel. It was his hope not to remain any longer than necessary. He would also, he believed, have enough to do meeting with the police and then securing the site providing it had been released. Rain drops began to pepper the windscreen. It reconfirmed his reason for moving to France. As he had grown older, the finer climate, the improvement in communications for his businesses, the general ambience and the space away from people had attracted him to the Bordeaux region. It had been reconfirmed on receiving the information about the crime committed on his property that his decision had been a wise one. It was not the Harrogate he once knew. He was not averse to change but from what he read and saw on the news, the crimes within the towns situated in the north of England would soon catch up with those seen in the capital. From a distance, that place seemed lawless with a mayor more concerned with stopping central London traffic than getting to grips with the ever-increasing young deaths from knife crime.

As requested, Ashton called the station to inform DCI Bennett that he had checked into the Hotel Du Vin, and he quickly made arrangements to meet later that afternoon. As it was close to home, Cyril could kill two birds with one stone.

Philip Ashton stood in his room and stared out across Prospect Place and the main road towards The Stray. The rain had stopped. He admired the carpet of coloured crocuses spread beneath the trees that followed the route of the road. There was one consolation: the police had wasted little time in arranging a meeting. He now needed to get a firm understanding of what had taken place during his absence. His phone rang. There was someone to see him at Reception.

Stephen Firth had made himself comfortable in one of the armchairs and was reading a broadsheet, his face hidden, when Philip entered. The Receptionist pointed to the chair and he approached. With a flick of his hand, he tapped the back of the newspaper.

"Hiding from the boss?" For the first time since his arrival, Philip had a positive lilt to his voice that was accompanied by a smile.

Firth stood, dropping the paper onto the chair. "Like bloody smoke creeping up like that. Good to see you. You can buy me lunch if it's not too late."

Philip made a point of looking at Firth's pockets. "Been a while since I was in Yorkshire and you've still not found your wallet."

"My boss doesn't pay too well if the truth be known,"

Stephen mumbled.

They both laughed as Philip threw an arm around his shoulders and led him through to the rear garden. "We can eat out here under one of the heaters and imagine we're in France."

"My imagination's not that good. How was the drive?"

"The return will be much better once this bloody mess is sorted, of that I can assure you."

Once the food was ordered the mood changed and with it, a more uncertain tone was evident in Stephen's voice.

"So, what's happening now, Philip? I've seen the news and had a phone conversation with the police but it's patchy. Knowing you were due today they asked me very few questions."

Philip said nothing for a few moments and then lifted his gaze. The stare was cold. "You fucking tell me. You have the only original key in the UK to the lock-up. If I recall correctly, it was your responsibility as my manager to look after the place and ensure its security at all times. That's your job title and you receive remuneration commensurate with that role. Right?" Philip left no wriggle room and he watched as Stephen's head nodded feebly.

"We needed to store the odd car there, out of the way like but only company and legitimate business." The lack of conviction within Firth's voice did not reassure.

"You needed to store the odd car or equipment on occasion you told me a few months ago. They found no car, just some poor kid beaten to buggery. When did you last use it?"

"A couple of weeks ago. We stored one of the vans for a few days. I sent the lad to collect it and to ensure it was locked up."

"Which lad would this be?" Philip moved his face closer as if he knew the answer before Stephen spoke. "Are you sure only company and legit storage?"

Stephen was momentarily lost for words but quickly regained his confidence. "Yes, really! His name? Latham, Paul Latham. Temp we hired. No longer works for us. Became a bit of a pain in the arse."

"So, what you're telling me is that you trusted some no-mark, some pain in your rear with the key to my personal garage and more importantly one of my vehicles?"

"He had a reference, headed paper. He'd wanted to be in the army and attended the Army Foundation College for a while. He said he was on the longer course but he'd decided it wasn't for him. Couldn't cope with the discipline. He told me straight the reason. He was a big lad, broad but smart and polite. I put him on a month's trial as we do."

"Officially?"

Stephen shook his head.

"You trusted him with the cars and the key to my place?"

"He brought the key back and the van was in one piece. That was his job, collecting and delivering the odd car from clients and returning them after the service but only when we were pushed for staff so he didn't do many. Remember, that's all part of our customer care package, a service you insisted upon, Philip. His main job was washing cars and he had a keen eye for the finer detail. He was hired primarily for that mainly owing to his age." He paused and Philip relaxed a little. Stephen knew the next news would be the bête noire of the conversation. He took a breath before

121

continuing. "Only issue we had with him was his funny turns. Said he suffered from migraine and would call in. Didn't make the full month. Some of the lads thought he was on weed and that they suggested it might be the trigger for the headaches. When I heard that, I made some enquiries at the College but for data protection they couldn't give me the information so I asked some other junior soldiers who were in town. One hundred quid lighter I had the answer. He'd been kicked out for testing positive for drugs. However, that's not all, he hadn't used his real name with us. He'd obviously written the reference himself or got someone to do it. Correct initials but the lad kicked out of the college was a Paul Lattimer. Who'd have known they test the lads for drugs? Strangely, he may have been tipped off as he didn't return. Had he done so I think I'd have smacked him."

Philip sat back and looked at the sky. The cumulus cloud sat high and the sun coloured yellow along the fine deckle edge.

"My lock-up should have been just that but according to what I know there was no sign of a break in. Pardon my pun here but the key, Stephen, is key here!" Philip grinned but Stephen's face remained straight. "Let's imagine your lad had a key cut. That doesn't take much brain power. Most supermarkets have a machine that cuts them for you. You don't have to interact with another person. You don't leave any trace. Now let's imagine he knew from chatting at work that my garage was rarely used and on cold, wet nights would make a perfect place to sleep or for moving and storing drugs. Doesn't take a genius to work that one. He comes in the dark and goes in the dark. Tell me if this is too far-fetched for you and I'll simplify it as the police will put two and two together fairly quickly."

"It's an empty lock-up not your apartment." Stephen's voice reflected he was on uncertain ground.

Philip curled up his lip. "It's a bloody crime scene now and I left you in charge. I want his details and I want them in my hand before five as I've a meeting with the police, a DCI no less and if that doesn't make the hairs stand up on your neck, I don't know what will. It's serious shit and I'm not sitting there, empty-handed and red-faced. I'm a business man and should know who works for my business." Philip paused and read the expression on his friend and manager's face. "Fuck!" He lifted his face skyward again as if seeking divine help. "You present me with a catalogue of errors. If this doesn't get sorted swiftly, you'll be searching for references yourself and they'll not be coming from me."

Stephen shook his head. "He didn't really work for us. Paid in pound notes. Like we always did. You knew of it in the past and promoted it. 'Saves in the long run,' you always preached."

The food arrived but neither man had an appetite. Each picked at the contents of their plate.

"Leave it with me and I'll check with the other lads and get a message to you with all the details. He'll be on our CCTV system so you can give that to the police." Firth stood and left.

***

Owen stared down the short driveway of the bungalow and the black garage door. A badly painted wrought iron table was to one side opposite what he assumed to be the kitchen door. A matching chair was leaning against it. Grass

123

and horsetail weed grew through the joints of the paving flags. It had not seen a car for years.

"That takes some shifting." He flicked the tallest piece that resembled a small conifer with his shoe. "Deep rooted these, Shak, like the bloody criminal fraternity that's spreading its tentacles out from the major cities."

Shakti was too busy watching the curtain twitch in the front window and tapped Owen's elbow to draw his attention. "They were correct, she misses nothing." Moving to the door Shakti rang the bell. The tune 'A Wandering Minstrel' seemed to fill the hall. It was shrill and tinny but effective as the door soon opened. Shakti held up her ID. "Mrs Carefoot?"

Leaning forward she looked at the proffered card. There was no warmth in the welcome. "Come in."

Her words were pronounced and rounded. Shakti and the signer followed as Owen brought up the rear. Once settled in the lounge Shakti introduced each officer and the signer supported her speech.

"I can hear fairly well when we are this close and I can read your lips so she's redundant." She nodded towards the signer. "I thought you'd come back. He's died I've heard. Is that right?"

"Sorry. Yes."

"He was a good boy really, you know. He just had a bad start in life. Some mothers can cope with their offspring, whilst others, and my daughter fits into that category I'm ashamed to say, can't. Never took responsibilities seriously. Always wanted a good time. Liked the booze too much and that brought the men ..." She clasped her hands on her lap. "His real father left because he couldn't compete with her drinking. Violent man but he kept them together somehow. When he'd gone the family crumbled. It was only a matter of time before she finally kicked Shane out. I felt for the lad. As you can imagine he'd failed at most things but wanted to be loved and quickly fell in with the wrong crowd. The silly boy thought they were real friends. That's when I took him in, thought it best. I couldn't see him homeless. He loved his nan. He told me often."

Owen watched and her body language did not seem to reflect her words. He had heard enough lies during interviews to have a gut feeling when things were not right. He felt it here.

"Mrs Carefoot." He waited until she faced him. "When did you last see him and when did he last stay here?"

"He hasn't stayed for a while. Said he was staying with a mate. A few weeks maybe but I couldn't give you an exact date. I saw him, however, the day before your people came to tell me he was poorly."

Owen raised an eyebrow at her description of his hospitalisation and condition. "For how long?"

A smile turned into a short laugh. "Minutes. He didn't see me. He does this you see. He thinks I don't know. He gets whoever he's with to park up the road and then he nips down the drive and into the garage. The door is an up and over and one of the springs has broken but you can still get in. To be honest I watched as the car went and the driver looked like a woman." She chuckled. "Fancy our Shane having a girlfriend. I bet that's why he didn't stay here."

"Why would he go into the garage?" Owen leaned forward.

"'Them that asks no questions isn't told a lie.'" She

spoke directly as she studied Owen's face and saw the frown appear. "That's Mr Kipling."

Owen could only picture cakes and looked quizzically at Shakti who quickly moved the interview on.

"Why do you think he came sneaking in and out, Mrs Carefoot?"

"I don't know and I don't want to know. I asked many questions of my daughter when she was a teenager and all I received were lies. I'd search her out, quiz and confront her knowing she was lying and all it did was drive a wedge between us. I was determined not to do the same again, not with Shane. He'd seen enough watching his family fall apart. Men came and went after his father left and he had suffered enough beatings and whatever else. He needed love not someone always pestering and asking questions." She paused. "Anyway, what could it be that he had in there?" The question was shrouded in innocence.

"Drugs?" Shakti and Owen spoke almost in unison.

The nan moved a hand to her mouth. "Never, not our Shane!"

It appeared to be a genuine reaction but neither Shakti nor Owen was convinced.

Owen continued. "You might not have grasped the full consequences of Shane's murder. I'm afraid it is now a murder enquiry but it's strange that he was found in a garage not too dissimilar to yours. Could he have moved whatever he stored there to a different location to spare you from involvement?"

For the first time since their arrival all three people facing the woman saw an immediate change in her demeanour as she looked down at her tightly clasped hands. Owen immediately thought of his own gran. How she had sheltered him, brought him up and cherished him. He recalled how he had often tried to pull the wool over her eyes and only later did he realise she had been aware of his misdemeanours but had said nothing. She had enabled him to make mistakes and to learn. He also protected her wherever possible. Like Coffrey, he had loved his own gran and without her he would not have been the man he was. He felt a sudden pride and yet sadness at the circumstances in which this lady found herself.

"I'm sorry. There's something you should know. On that day he pushed a note through the door. That's how I knew he was here and that's how I saw the driver. Normally, I hear nothing. I thought I knew him but ..." She took the note from between the pages of a magazine positioned on the coffee table next to her chair.

Shakti swiftly looked at Owen and she could see a sadness in his eyes. He moved over to Mrs Carefoot and rested his hands on hers.

"Some youngsters have never been allowed to show their true feelings and they keep them trapped within. Some words like 'I love you' can mean little these days. To write that note took guts. He knew what he was doing was wrong but he was brave enough to show his feelings in the note he sent. Having what he thought to be a real friend, one who trusted him was probably special and unique even though he knew in his heart of hearts what he was doing was wrong. Probably, Nan, he didn't know right from wrong with the confusion of emotions created as he developed new-found, personal relationships. All I can assure you now and it's little comfort, is that we will catch whoever is responsible."

A tear ran down her cheek and she clutched Owen's hands. "Bless you. Thank you for your understanding."

Shakti stood and turned. She also was moved by Owen's sensitivity.

Chapter Seventeen

The face stared back from the mirror. The make-up was finished apart from the lipstick. A smile appeared just before the voice mimicked that of Marilyn Monroe, "If you're gonna be two-faced at least make one of them pretty." He pulled a face, contorting his features, creating a distorted rictus before blowing himself a kiss. "Not too bad that voice but it could do with more work." He repeated the quote but this time more slowly. He was no happier. His annoyance immediately made his thoughts turn to the man he had followed and he pictured him in the window hiding behind the net curtains. Monroe's voice returned "I know you were watching. I waved but you didn't return the courtesy and that's just not polite. I spoke but you failed to listen. I was good too. Morgan Freeman is so difficult to get right. 'Get busy living or get busy dying.' Such a good line from a wonderful film and so appropriate even if I say so myself. I'll make that wrong right, you'll see. Not long now."

***

Owen and Shakti stood by the front door and watched as the Crime Scene Investigators moved into the house and two entered the garage after propping open the broken door. Owen had taken a photograph of the note and sent it to Cyril before it was bagged and added to the evidence now being collated.

"You were very kind, Owen. At first I thought you didn't believe her."

"I didn't and I don't but I do feel sorry for her." He suddenly looked puzzled. "That reminds me. What on earth was she on about? Mr Kipling and lies? All I could think of were his exceedingly good cakes."

Shakti chuckled but knew from the way he spoke he was now distancing himself from the final emotional part of the interview.

"Not that Kipling, Owen, Rudyard. The poem *The Smugglers*. She knew Shane was up to no good but thought it wise to say nothing. Bit like society in general. They look the other way these days and you did too."

Owen chewed his lip as he thought of his own grandmother. "When my gran was young, she told me that adults often gave kids a clip round the ear if they saw them doing something wrong as did the local copper. If they didn't clout them, they gave them a bollocking. Too frightened nowadays and you can't blame them. If they did, we might not have the problems in society that we do."

"You were a good copper in there, Owen. The CSI will investigate his room, then the garage and garden. I couldn't believe how relaxed she was about it all. Probably relieved that the truth will out in the end as they say." Shakti looked at the front window and saw her staring towards the road. "In some ways, Owen, she's lost everything. Her daughter and now her grandson. Life can be bloody tragic. You saw that though and she was grateful."

One of the CSI came from the garage holding a specimen bag. It was a single key on a ring.

"This is relatively new and is not for this garage.

Thought you should see it."

***

Regent Parade was awash with sunshine. It spilled from behind cloud allowing the budding trees growing on the central reservation that separated Skipton Road from Regent Parade to shadow the pavement and buildings with long, dark fingers. For a man walking in a public place wearing make-up, he only attracted the occasional stare even though it clearly contradicted his general attire. It was of little consequence to either party. He allowed himself a cheeky smile if a stranger's gaze lingered for too long and that often made them avert their eyes. Adjusting the parcel under his arm he continued to walk briskly, enjoying the sun's warmth and occasionally looking in the shop windows. He was in no hurry. A smile came to his lips as he paused and read the sign above the small building linked to the bakery announcing he was standing in front of *Stephen King – Auto Services*.

"Beep, beep, Richie," he whispered mimicking the voice of Pennywise from the Stephen King film, *It*. "Fancy Mr King, my creator, living in Harrogate and mending motors. Who'd have thought it?" A high-pitched laugh followed. "I might just kill you all … I might!" The voice faded as he quickly looked around. He had not brought anyone to a standstill, no one was staring even though the laugh had been loud. "Beep, Beep, Richie. Beep, Beep!" He moved on.

Within five minutes he was looking at the terraced house. The same net curtains, now appearing more yellow than off-white in colour, were set within the bay window. They concealed the room from the street. Moving slowly, he crossed the road and pushed open the gate. He slid his hand into his pocket.

"Is that a hammer in your pocket or are you just happy to see me?" The voice of Mae West, accurate and clear spoke to no one but him. It brought a smile. He moved the parcel to his right so as to be in full view of the window. The word FRAGILE was clearly visible, picked out in bold, red letters. After all, there had to be a reason for a stranger calling and who can resist a parcel? Taking a deep breath, he knocked on the door. The blows were firm and deliberate. Turning his face from the window and his ear to the door, he listened.

***

"How did it go, Owen?" Cyril spoke without looking up.

"If I said to you the name Kipling, what would come to mind, sir?"

Cyril lifted his glasses onto his head and focused on his colleague. "Poet, Rudyard, *The Jungle Book*, *Rikki,Tikki Tarvi*, *The Smugglers*. Do I need to go on?" He watched as Owen pulled a face.

"Not cakes then?"

Cyril shook his head. "The relevance of this bizarre conversation is what?"

"Coffrey's gran quoted from that poem. The reason she didn't question him about things. She'd been lied to before and it had brought a rift between her and Coffrey's mum, her daughter."

"And the father is?"

Owen looked back and said nothing.

Cyril continued. "Nan is Carefoot, the daughter is Carefoot or did she marry and become Coffrey. Basic stuff.

132

I sincerely hope that we have the answer to that at this stage of the investigation as we were late collecting evidence from there."

"It was in the report but more has now come to light after today's chat. Took the father's name at birth. Father lived at the family home briefly, the address is on file although they are no longer linked, but then left owing to mother's alcohol addiction. Nan told us he was a bit of a bully, hit him a lot. Thought it would make him read and write better. It didn't. Mother often got a good hiding too from all accounts. As I've said, heavy drinker, the mother. When the father left, she managed the child for a while as best she could but from all accounts wasn't good for either. She regularly brought men home and Nan suspected prostitution and that during this time he was physically and possibly sexually abused. Mother then kicked the lad out when he went off the rails. Probably started fighting against things. She moved to Spain, bar work, can you believe? A fox in a chicken house you might say. We're awaiting information from the Spanish police."

Owen immediately thought of the woman as if she were an echo from his own past. What made him take the path he did when he was left with his gran he would never know. He had been a bad lad at times too but considering everything, his life had turned out well. He knew that both women had tried their best. However, they had failed as Shane had continued to take the wrong path.

Cyril could see from Owen's expression something was troubling him and he had an idea what.

"Remember too, Owen, and try to understand it. Another quote from Mr Kipling. 'If you can meet with

Triumph and Disaster And treat those two impostors just the same.' Note it down as the meaning is worth thinking about, particularly in our job and especially with this case. Maybe that's what his nan is doing. Maybe it's what you are trying to come to terms with. You decide." Cyril watched the look of anxiety bleed across Owen's face before picking up the paper on which the note Owen had sent had been printed. "But don't worry now, my friend, not now!" He began to read the note out loud:

Sorry for not comeing round offen – I've found a friend who likes me. Makes me laff a lot. I help him with stuff. He has loads of voices. He makes me happy. I help him. I cant upset him as hes good to me like you – hes kind.
Love you loads, nan. Xx Keep safe.

"It had been screwed up. She'd straightened it before she showed us, she kept it within the pages of a magazine. I think receiving that note had made her cross. The fact that he'd shoved it through the letterbox and not talked to her. She told us that she believed the person driving the car was female." Owen pointed to the word 'him'.

"Do we know if Janice Blackledge had a car or can drive?"

"Easy to find out if she has a licence." Owen made a call and put the phone down. Within two minutes it rang. "Nope, no licence and no vehicle registered to her or her partner."

"I guess some motorists today believe driving legally means nothing!"

Cyril scribbled *loads of voices* on the note pad in front of him. He went on to the screen report of his interview with Fletcher and then the earlier report regarding Tom Craig's attack.

"Familiar voice, probably from a film or TV. Shane's favourite was Donald Duck but also The Joker. It's been staring us in the face, Owen. A mimic, an actor."

"Someone hiding behind a voice? An impressionist, impersonator, maybe?" Owen asked.

"Maybe and maybe not but a person who uses his voice for effect. Get someone checking local theatres, green rooms, agents for mimics initially. Post the idea in the Incident Room."

"Children's entertainer, sir. They're popular."

"That might be the link with Coffrey. He would be easily enticed by a character who could impress, make him laugh." Cyril tapped Coffrey's note. "Check the internet for local entertainers. Don't disregard the element of drugs, however. Keep all avenues open."

An email popped up on screen. Cyril looked at Owen. "We have a DNA link connecting the flat to the garage but it's also on the national database. It's linked to two unsolved crimes, both committed in 2010 within the Scarborough area, both serious assaults, both murders." He took a tube of mints from the top drawer before offering one to Owen.

"Like buses. You wait ages and then two come along at the same time. I'll get the info on those." Owen popped the mint into his mouth.

"They were murders though. Let's not forget we have only one. The other's still in ICU." Cyril sucked the mint as he read the file. "Both single males. Twenty and twenty-seven. Both badly beaten and found late at night ...

Malcolm Hollingdrake

locations ..." He skimmed through the information. "First one found near a public toilet, the second in his apartment. Here's the pathology reports. In layman's terms they died through delayed medical intervention and not the severity of the trauma. I'll get Julie to take a look. Get someone to go through these and double check to see if there are any similarities within HOLMES, now we have the link to do with voices."

"Shane was found by chance, Tom Craig because he had people looking out for him. Without his colleague's swift intervention, he may well have died too. Craig may have had a greater chance because of his general fitness. Squaddies tend to maintain a certain discipline unless they hit the booze or drugs to cope with their experiences," Owen commented as Cyril drummed the table as the sentence was ending.

"Scarborough! Well, well, who would have thought? Steptoe, our own Ian Tempest's old stomping ground. The day Fletcher didn't come home he was collecting in Scarborough and Brid and according to Fletch it was where he was brought up. Fletch was with him on both occasions we found ourselves with a victim. I'd like him in. And Owen, a full background check. Even down to income tax." Cyril grinned. "Certain information can be a marvellous bartering tool."

"Nearly forgot. CSI found a newish key at Coffrey's garage. It was hanging from an old bracket. It wasn't from the house or his nan's garage. They'll keep us informed."

***

There had been no sound of anyone approaching to open the door but it was clear that someone was watching

136

through the lace curtains. They were standing well back but they were there. That sense made him look in the opposite direction but he ensured the parcel was visible. He rehearsed in his head the line from a film, the line he would quote when the door opened – *This is for you to give me when you apologise.* He had tried to mimic Keanu Reeves but he had failed miserably and felt the anger fester. He would use a voice that came to him on the spur of the moment if the door opened.

The sound of someone turning the inner lock carried as only a faint click but it was enough to make him step back slightly in anticipation of the door finally opening a little. He now positioned the parcel at chest height, both gloved hands holding either side, thumbs around the back to give maximum force when he moved forwards. He needed to time the push perfectly. His nerves now on edge, he felt the excitement build and he squealed a little. He took a swift look round to see if anyone was close by; there was nobody. He moved his right leg back in readiness for his planned move as the door began to open.

"What do you want? I've not ordered a parcel." Whittle's voice was aggressive and yet at the same time the second statement carried a degree of curiosity.

"I have a parcel for you." The sentence was only just finished when the door opened more fully. It was then that the box with the body weight behind it made contact with the door, forcing it open. Peter Whittle was thrust backwards making him lose his balance. He began to fall. His arms windmilled, knocking a picture from the wall. It would now be a race whether it or Peter would hit the floor first. Peter won. Using his foot, he quickly closed the door as the parcel was thrown at the head of the now prostrate figure.

"This is for you to give me when you apologise." He had chosen Richard Burton's voice but was disappointed with the rendition. Quickly he negotiated the dazed body of Whittle who lay totally confused, trying to come to terms with what was happening. Swiftly grabbing Whittle's raised arm, he dragged him down the hallway and into the back room. This action lifted Whittle's shirt, separating it from the waistband of his trousers and his exposed skin rubbed against the carpet. The resulting friction quickly burned his exposed flesh. Whittle tried to turn and grab the leg of a small hall table to stop himself from being propelled unwillingly backwards but he merely caused it and the objects on it to crash to the floor.

"You didn't wave. I waved. Do you remember? You simply didn't wave back! Now see, you're spoiling things here. Breaking things. Be nice and relax. I just want to be your friend. You look like a kind man but I bet you don't have a lot of friends." The voice was back to that of Pennywise and the laugh that followed made Whittle's eyes bulge.

"I know that voice. Stop! Stop!" As they passed through the door, Whittle's free hand grabbed the framework bringing the movement to a sudden halt.

"No, no!" A firm kick removed the hand and the dragging continued a moment or two longer.

Once in the room, the motion stopped and the stranger's face came closer to Whittle's. The laughter stopped too. The intruder spoke in the same familiar voice inches from his face. It was persuasive and true to character. Whittle felt the warmth of the breath on his skin and inhaled the smell it carried.

What was that smell? Garlic. It was garlic. But it was the voice … He knew the voice but the make-up was not right – it was feminine, confusing, incongruous and frightening. This was a man's voice, familiar but he was wearing woman's make-up. Whittle's senses were bombarded into a confused maelstrom as all the information flooded in. He tried to speak but nothing came, only a low guttural moan. *I must move,* he thought. *I must stand and run – escape this nightmare.*

Peter felt the first deliberate, painful blow as the hammer struck the centre of his forehead. It was direct and firm driving his head back onto the carpet and for a moment there was nothing but momentary darkness. Instinctively, he raised a hand and waved it in front of his face, a feeble, pointless defence.

"Ha ha! You can wave." The hand not holding the hammer waved back. "See how easy it is. Polite too. Reciprocating makes the world go round." The hammer struck a second time, on this occasion just above the right eye socket. The sound from the breaking bone as the small round metal ball struck was that of a dull thud. Whittle's head fell back onto the carpet. The broken skin wept jewel-like, small bloody beads that had all the appearance of pomegranate seeds. They rolled in quick succession down the side of his head before disappearing into his white hair turning it a dark pink. The contusion that followed seemed to inflate like a small red balloon.

"Why?" The feeble words breaking from Whittle's lips were quickly met with a sharp, direct hammer blow that crashed through his front teeth. He would not speak again. Tooth fragments, stained by pink-red froth bubbled and dribbled onto his chin as his breathing became more laboured.

"Bubbles and balloons. Red ones too. How did you know it was my favourite colour?"

He raised the hammer again.

Chapter Eighteen

Cyril did not need to resist the temptation of nipping into his favourite pub, The Coach and Horses, even though he could have killed a pint and a moment's solitude, as it had been closed for quite some time. He continued down West Park until the Cenotaph came into view. The area was busy as usual.

Mounting the steps, he entered the hotel. It was a place he knew well. The Receptionist was all smiles. "Detective Chief Inspector, it is our pleasure. How is your lovely wife?"

Cyril felt his mood immediately lift. "She's fine thank" – he swiftly glanced at her lapel badge noting her name – "you, Fiona. You look well and your greeting is a tonic after a difficult day, a day that's not quite over yet. I'm here to see Philip Ashton."

"He's in the garden area probably under one of the heaters. He said he was expecting a guest. May I bring you a coffee?"

Ashton was reading, the table spread with notes and photographs when Cyril emerged. The lights were already on. He immediately looked up, stood and nodded. "DCI Bennett?"

"Indeed." Cyril proffered a hand. Both men sat. "Thank you for meeting me and I'm grateful you've travelled from France so swiftly. I'm sorry the circumstances have become so grave."

Ashton's initial reaction was to smile but his expression quickly changed on hearing the word 'grave'. "Yes, grave. I believe the young man has passed away. I was sorry to hear that. I've had a word with my staff who are responsible for the garage when I'm away and we have some information for you." He pointed to the table. At that moment the coffee arrived. Another table was brought.

Ashton explained the reason the location was used by the business on occasion.

Cyril made a mental note of the words 'overflow, sensitive and convenient'. It was the term 'cock-up' that brought a greater focus.

"We occasionally employ young people who make an approach for work experience. We expect a reference, of course, and we give them a trial. This lad came to us." Ashton pushed a photograph towards Cyril. It was clearly an image taken from CCTV. "His name was Paul Latham."

"Was?" Cyril was quick to respond.

"I'm coming to that, Chief Inspector. Latham was good; smart, efficient, a careful driver I'm told even for one with a limited amount of experience owing to his age. He needed our trust to develop his driving ability – none of us improves without practice wouldn't you say?"

Cyril said nothing. It felt as though bad news was being wrapped in yesterday's papers. He patiently waited for the answer to his question.

"We check that. There is, however, an issue. He would ring in to say he was suffering from a migraine. According to my manager, one or two of the workshop lads believed he was a drug user."

"You mentioned references."

"Reference in this case, from the Army Foundation College. He said the experience wasn't as he'd expected and he had requested to be released. The reference referred to an additional medical condition."

"How old was Paul Latham?" Cyril sipped his coffee and took the biscuit that came with it.

"We discovered that his name was in fact Paul Lattimer."

"Age? You said he drove for you. To be a junior soldier in the College you must be between fifteen years and seven months and seventeen and five months when you start one of the two courses. So, Mr Ashton, he must have been over seventeen to hold a driver's licence would you agree? We must also remember that under-eighteens are not subject to a notice period when they sign up which means they can leave at any time. You knew that, didn't you?"

Ashton flushed. He had known about the college for years but had little understanding of the finer details. "Indeed," he lied.

"Then surely you'd checked his driver's licence?" There was an extended pause.

"No, they didn't and they've had a reprimand for the error. So, as I said, a cock-up and not the first. When drug use was suspected, and I think it's quite prevalent in people of his age, recreational, I believe they term it, my manager contacted the college but data protection prevented their disclosure of private details. However, he was able to discover, from let us say, chatting with junior soldiers in town, that a Paul Lattimer and one other had been excluded for drug use. They randomly test them and he was sent packing. From all accounts it doesn't matter where they are on the course."

Cyril looked at the photograph again and his experience warned him. He felt as if a deliberate smoke screen were gradually being laid down. His gut instinct was beginning to tingle and he felt uncomfortable. "From where this conversation is heading, Mr Ashton, you're next going to tell me that Lattimer here," he held up the photograph, "was in some way linked to the lock-up?"

Ashton cleared his throat, took a drink from his cup and sat back. Cyril immediately noted his body language and it demonstrated, from his experience, a degree of guilt.

"I'm as guilty as any of my staff, that I must concede. I hold my hands up. The garage is always empty and I allow the storage of any excess stock or the occasional vehicle. Sometimes we hold cars away from either a workshop or showroom, usually for a day or two and the lock-up garage is perfect. Sadly, Lattimer was asked to collect a van from there a while ago. This was before we knew of his background. It was a cock-up of the highest order."

"And what do you think?" Cyril clasped his hands to stop them from fidgeting and leaned on the table.

Ashton shifted uneasily. "Probably the same as you're thinking Detective Inspector. He had a key cut and was using the lock-up at will and continued to do so after he was sent packing. Had the incident not occurred—"

"Murder, Mr Ashton. Let's not downgrade the criminality," Cyril swiftly interrupted.

"Yes, of course. Had the murder not happened then we'd have been none the wiser."

Cyril said nothing for a few moments as he fiddled with

the spoon that had been in the saucer. For Ashton the gap in conversation hung like lead.

"From our records you had a partner. We'll need the names and contact details of every employee. Every." The repeated word was emphasised.

"I bought my partner out and to keep everything transparent, she's my ex-wife. She was having financial difficulties. It meant taking out a business loan but I have the collateral to support that and business is good at the moment."

"When was this?" Cyril replaced the spoon exchanging it for his pen.

"At the moment, the second tranche of the financial settlement is being sorted. These things work through the proper channels, take a while and are costly. I always do things by the book."

"Unless those things involve certain people washing and driving your cars." Cyril looked up and then back at his notes. "I want details of any properties you lease or rent out. By tomorrow at the latest. I'd be grateful if you could drop everything in to the police station. Ask for me."

"I could send it all electronically. It would be much easier and quicker."

"Tomorrow, at the station. You're familiar with our location? At or just before noon." Cyril stood, collected his pad, pen and the photograph. "Until tomorrow, Mr Ashton. Thanks for the coffee."

On leaving, Cyril telephoned the station requesting that details be collated on Paul Lattimer. He also requested any information on anyone of the name Paul Latham living within a fifty-mile radius of Harrogate. He photographed the image and sent that too. On crossing Tower Street, he looked at the Coach and Horses. The skeleton riding the penny farthing that had hung from the corner for as long as he could remember had been removed. It did not bode well for his favourite hostelry and he wondered what fate was in store. He would enjoy a beer at home.

As he turned to pass through the passageway his phone rang. Cyril was going to ignore the ringing phone and check the caller's ID once home but a ringing phone always got the better of him.

"Bennett."

"Thought you needed to know. We have the latest from Forensics. Beggar's belief too. A key discovered in a bowl in Tom Craig's flat opens the lock-up where Coffrey was found and the key found at Coffrey's nan's garage is also a match. They believe they were cut at the same time. They've checked each and believe neither has been used much," Smirthwaite revealed.

"Do they, by Jove!" He looked up at the darkened sky, never truly surprised at what science could discover at a crime scene. "Any news on Ian Tempest seeing we are in the land of Zeus and Jupiter?"

The comment was lost on Smirthwaite. "Sorry, land, sir? Ian Tempest, not as yet."

"Never mind. I'll explain in the morning if I remember." He hung up and called Ashton's hotel.

"How may I help you?"

"Please put me through to Philip Ashton's room."

Ashton was quick to pick up.

"It's DCI Bennett. Can you confirm in the next five minutes that you have every known key to the lock-up? I'll call back in ten."

Cyril had reached his front door when the information was received. All the official keys had been accounted for.

***

The house always looked the same. The garden, even in the lowering light seemed immaculate, although not at its best owing to the time of year. Looking down the driveway Stephen Firth could see the lights were on in the double garage and the doors closed. He was late and tapped gingerly on the metal door.

"Use the side door." The words echoed in the quiet of the early evening.

Adrian was leaning against a work bench, mug in hand. The strip lights illuminated every corner of the garage. The car was positioned centrally and sitting on a red, metal dolly. The small metal wheels looked incongruous against the size of the car. The aluminium bodywork of the low drag racing version of the E-type held a matt sheen but it was now straight. There was nothing to see other than the main structure. It contained no engine, gearbox, axles, lights, glass or interior.

Firth whistled. "Bloody hell!" He continued to inspect the vehicle. Adrian just sipped his tea. "That, my friend, is a true transformation."

"You're late. Thought you were coming at five. My tea is sitting in the oven. The old bus has been damaged before and repaired. Did you know that?"

"Sorry, yes. Did I not say? I'm sure it was mentioned. Serious crash just outside town." He checked his watch and quickly changed the subject. "Ashton rang wanting me to check we had the key to his lock-up, the one where they

147

found the lad."

"And?"

"I told him we did but he insisted I check. Got a right bollocking too for letting a temp we employed have the key. Official business and legitimate use as directed by the man himself but that made no difference. Don't ever say you've used it otherwise I'm down the road."

"Lips are sealed. There's no reason to, I'll never need it again."

The subject quickly changed as Firth moved away bringing the conversation back to the Jaguar.

"I'm sure I mentioned that it was damaged the day before Ashton got the car. Driver went through here." He pointed to the gap where the windscreen should be. "Ashton had it repaired and he raced it for quite a number of years but lost interest when he crashed it at the Harewood Hill climb a while back. I made a silly offer and he took it. He'd just bought the home in France, the divorce was pending and he had the apartment. He let me store it in the lock-up until I found somewhere."

"That was here!" Adrian mumbled. "I've organised it to be collected tomorrow afternoon. The paint shop is ready and the interior trim is being finalised not that there's much. Engine, gearbox and drivetrain are perfect and looking like new." He pointed out the objects covered at the back of the garage. "A month and we'll see it completely rebuilt and in time for the auction."

"Its value?" Finch asked running his hand on the car's covering.

"You're the car dealer. It's one of the earliest flat floor E-Types but as it didn't start life as a lightweight and is a bit of a mongrel to boot, I think the term is replica, I'll be happy with anything over seventy grand."

"Even with its racing pedigree?" Firth pulled his face into a sarcastic grin but seemed relatively happy with the answer. "You're a pessimist if ever I heard one. My car and cash and your skill. If I do get the boot from Ashton, I'll have this to fall back on."

"It won't get you too far! My glass is always half empty, Stephen, that's me. It's not what it looks like. It's a fraud, a bit like its owners, but I agree it has been raced. Now bugger off as I'm done and my tea's calling." Adrian carefully removed his overalls and gloves and methodically placed them over the seat of the chair before moving to the door. He checked the de-humidifier was on before his hand flicked the light switch and the garage fell into darkness.

"You never told me, Adrian, why you needed to use the lock-up." Firth announced.

Adrian just nodded. "No, true. As I said, my tea's calling."

***

Whittle was propped against the chair. His head was down and blood had flushed over the front of his shirt. A gloved hand gently stroked his thinning hair. "Recognition, we all need it. A wave, now what does that cost anyone?"

A groan burbled from Whittle's lips and more red froth foamed along the semi open mouth. His right leg twitched. It was clear that his breathing was laboured as the airways were partially blocked through blood or swelling.

"Still with us. That's what matters. You see, I've always liked happy faces, laughter, but you seemed so miserable." He lowered the body and put him in a recovery position.

149

"That should help you until a friend comes. Do you have friends? Somehow, I doubt it. That's sad. We all need friends with happy faces. Leave them laughing, that's my motto. You will be my last for some time. Too much of a good thing is bad for anyone and besides people are beginning to search for me. We can't have that." He stood and glanced out through the net curtains. There was an orange glow and the room was now quite dark. "I'm going to leave you now. I'll take my things with me."

The box was still positioned in the hallway at the bottom of the stairs, the 'Fragile' lettering facing uppermost. He opened the flap slightly and slipped in the hammer. Leaving the house, the front door was left wide open and the hall light on. The breeze that now entered made the light shade pendulum gently as if it were counting time.

"Parting is such sweet sorrow." The voice of Olivia Hussey was carried down the hallway.

As on arrival, he met no one in the street and it was only on walking onto Mornington Crescent and Skipton Road did he see traffic and the occasional pedestrian. Now it was dark the make-up could not be seen as readily. He walked on until reaching Regent Parade. It was then he had an idea.

Chapter Nineteen

The official investigations between the police and the college had seen surprising co-operation and the full details of the two junior soldiers excluded from their courses were now held. The police officer had made the mistake of referring to the youths as cadets and had been quickly corrected. Within the hour, Stuart Park would contact both sets of parents and if possible, the youths, one of whom was a Felicity Winters. Park had been amazed that thirteen hundred young people attended the courses at the college, a good percentage female. Within three hours the details had been fed into the system and were ready and waiting for Cyril's arrival in the morning.

***

None of the shops were open as he approached the building housing Stephen King Autos. The huge grey shutter to the left was securely locked. With a degree of reverence, he placed the box in the doorway and stood back. "A gift for the maestro. Maybe it will be here in the morning, maybe not. Whatever will be ..." He broke into song trying to emulate Doris Day – *Que Sera, Sera* but it was quickly halted as someone approached and walked past giving him an extra wide berth. He turned and moved in the opposite direction and began to whistle the tune cheerfully. As to the box, he was fatalistic as to the outcome.

***

Cyril's phone brought him to his senses. His immediate thought was that the alarm had beaten him. Julie lifted her head, mumbled and then pulled the quilt over her head. Cyril looked at the clock. It was 1.47. The ringing continued.

"Bennett."

"Sorry to disturb but I knew you would want to know immediately. We've found the weapon we believe was used in all three attacks."

Cyril sat up and rubbed his eyes. "Three? Go on, Brian."

"We have another attack victim, a Peter Whittle. The hammer was left in a box in front of Stephen King Autos on Regent Parade and the victim lived just round the corner."

He flicked the phone to speaker as he climbed out of bed and stumbled towards the kitchen. He needed tea.

"Hammer with a small ball-shaped end. Blood both on it and the box in which it was found."

"And the victim?"

"Like the other two, only the face was targeted. This one has been mumbling about waving and voices but the strangest comments which he repeated several times since he was found, were, *penny, waving, make-up* and *woman man*. The words *woman* and *man* were always separated. It's all very confused and he's since been sedated. The specialist believes the damage is not as severe as the other victims but bad enough. SOCO are at the premises and they've been secured. We again have the body cam footage from the first responder." The sound of a kettle coming to the boil was all that could be heard. "Sir, do you want me to send a car?"

"Fifteen minutes. Organise house to house starting with any neighbours who are out spectating. Who found him?"

"Earlier in the evening a neighbour had noticed that the front door was open. He checked again before bed. It was the same. He looked out again at just before twelve-thirty and it was still open so he went over. Leaving an open door was so out of character for Whittle. He called the emergency services."

"Make sure he gives a full statement."

Cyril quickly shaved whilst he dressed. The sound of the shaver made only a faint buzz but it still disturbed Julie. Her head appeared from beneath the covers.

"Another victim?"

Cyril nodded as the shaver ran over his upper lip. "The weapon's been found. Can you believe it's linked with a Stephen King?"

Julie frowned. "Sorry?"

"Left outside Stephen King Autos, small workshop on Regent Parade of all places. In plain sight, on the pavement too!" He turned and shrugged his shoulders. "This victim's not as badly injured as the other two by all accounts but is still serious. He mumbled to the paramedic who arrived first something about *waving, penny* and *make-up, woman man.*"

"Pennywise!" Julie sat upright without thinking. "Erm. Stephen King. First thing that came to mind when you said Stephen King and penny – Pennywise. He's the character in the King film. He's a white-faced creepy clown who uses charm to attract you before snatching you to his underground lair. Have you seen the film or read the book?"

"Sorry to disappoint. Besides, nobody's been snatched,

just had their faces destroyed." Cyril moved to the bed and kissed her. "Pennywise. Right! I knew I kept you for something! I'll ring you later. The car's here. You can have my tea. A reward for your ... information. If anything else should come to mind, please shout." He handed her the cup and saucer.

"For a man who's dressed in ten minutes you are impressive. Even the tie is straight." She blew him a kiss.

***

The driver parked at the end of the terrace and the usual scene greeted Cyril. The official vehicles, each with the odd blue strobe, illuminated the house walls intermittently. The officer standing by the tape immediately raised a hand. The front door to Whittle's property was still open and the light diffused from the hallway flushed pale white onto the front pathway and road. There was only one street light along the road and that was further up near a junction. It was now clear how the neighbour would see the anomaly. There appeared to be no other lights on in the house. Cyril checked his watch. It was 2.18. A number of the lights were visible in neighbouring houses. The first response vehicle, the police and the ambulance had brought a great deal of noise and disturbance to the quiet terrace. Some neighbours, wrapped in dressing gowns, were standing collectively in the small front gardens. Cyril could only imagine the speculative chatter that various theories had created. As they all watched the toing and froing from Whittle's home, no one noticed the figure watching at the far end of the terrace as the ambulance took away the victim. No one saw his wave. He left soon afterwards.

Not far away, the SOCO team quickly removed the

police tape and opened the pavement area where the box had been discovered. The only evidence that anything had occurred was a remnant of blue and white tape carelessly torn and left hanging limply around the bough of a tree.

***

It was neither sensible nor would it have been profitable to go back home. Cyril was now wide awake. He needed to trawl though the incoming intelligence received to date. He was conscious of the error he had made over the warrant and could not afford to make another.

The latest toxicology results for Tom Craig showed no evidence of drug use. A contrast from Coffrey's post-mortem. There the evidence suggested major ingestion and incapacitation. He pondered the finding. *So, there was one with and one without. What will yours tell us Peter Whittle?* He tapped the table top with his fingers before looking at the information on the latest victim. The file had already been started:

Peter Francis Whittle. Born 01/04/1956. Cyril scribbled a subtraction and arrived at 65 years of age. *Lived in Harrogate all of his life, married and moved to the house in 1981. No children. A shop manager, men's clothing in the town until retirement two years ago. Wife died last year. Hobbies include walking, bird watching, amateur dramatics and reading.*

Hospital condition – stable. Next of kin – to be established.

"Amateur dramatics. Is that a link? Make sure it's added and investigate further," he instructed himself whilst speaking out loud. "I wonder if that's how he knew the voice?" He quickly Googled 'Pennywise' and found some clips on YouTube. He watched briefly. DS Dan Grimshaw's head popped round his door.

"Sir, Whittle's blood is on the hammer, also found traces within the box. Worth noting too that something's been removed from the shaft; shaved from one side. Possibly a name or initials. There are no fingerprints on the box's internal or external surfaces so completely wiped clean. However, they have found a hair and fabric fibres and they're being analysed."

"And Whittle's condition, Dan?"

"They've sedated him but he's not like the others. He's not been placed in an induced coma. Some facial fractures but not at all like Coffrey. With each attack the severity of the damage seems to have diminished. Still not what you want to wake up to."

Cyril frowned. "The three victims are disparate. The evidence is beginning to weigh towards random acts rather than targeted. It's looking unlikely to be drugs-related as at present we have only one connected." He checked the references to the Scarborough murders. "Interesting! There was a greater degree of injury with the first than the second victim so we have a pattern."

"It's coming together, sir. Dan seemed unconvinced. "Can I get you a brew?"

"Perfect. You wouldn't have a mint, would you? Seem to have run out."

"I'll see what I can do. I'll check Owen's pot."

Cyril returned to his search of the latest evidence. Shane Coffrey's mother was believed to be still prostituting herself to support her drink habit although, according to the Spanish police, no formal complaints or arrests had been made. A warning has been issued. There was nothing recorded to say if she had been informed of her son's plight. Cyril felt as though he were plaiting soot. What drew his attention and caused his heart to sink was the list of people linked to the theatres, both amateur and professional, male and female within the boundaries of the North Yorkshire force. The number of theatres within the area, amateur dramatic venues, drama teachers, children's entertainers and shops selling theatrical items from costumes to props seemed never-ending. Names were categorised depending on the particular skill and repertoire.

The tea arrived along with two mints. "You're a life saver. Have you seen this lot, Dan? Christ, it'll take weeks to plough through." He unwrapped a mint and immediately felt himself relax.

"I'd concentrate on the impressionists, sir. I'm aware most actors can mimic accents and the like, but real impressionists have a much broader repertoire, that's the nature of the beast we seek. The victims clearly identified a familiar voice even though they couldn't necessarily put a finger on who it was or who they were meant to be. Also, in my opinion, there's a reason someone does this and that might even mean giving us clues. I can't see it being anyone in regular employment. Someone who's self-employed maybe? A job where they can pick and choose. Maybe lost their job so a case of revenge."

Cyril was not convinced. "To kill or maim? Don't forget that the Yorkshire Ripper never stopped working, drove wagons and still managed to leave a trail of death. The key element in that case was a voice, a north eastern accent, Wearside Jack, that made them take their eye off the ball.

No there's more. Maybe losing employment is a link. Lattimer lost two jobs in quick succession. Maybe he lashed out at the person who supplied the drugs."

"And the link with him to the two others?"

Cyril rubbed his face. He was beginning to feel the effects of the early start. "Have we tracked Ian Tempest, the scrap man who's friends with Fletcher?"

"Fletcher's been co-operative and is bringing him to the station today." Dan stood. "Arranged for him to be here at ten. I believe you're seeing Ashton at noon."

"If Tempest isn't involved, Dan, as I've already said, I have a feeling this person just strikes at random. A flash in the pan. Maybe they've just upset him for some reason and he seeks retribution. We know all too well that fights start for the smallest and most insignificant of reasons when fuelled by alcohol. Maybe our woman man is taking it to the next level."

"When I was studying for promotion, this was called thrill killing or hedonistic murder. According to findings, they were usually carried out by young males who felt inadequate and were driven by a need to feel powerful. It's certainly true that such killers make the victim suffer in order to feel good and sadism, if I remember correctly, is a key link."

"That category, *youth*, would put Lattimer in the frame. However, we have one small problem. This individual doesn't kill and according to the medical professionals the damage was controlled. Killers tend not to be controlled unless, as you say, some kind of torture predeath is planned. There's no evidence of rape or of their being sexually attacked other than Coffrey being found naked but no evidence of sexual activity. Their faces are attacked. To some extent destroying key senses of sight, speech and maybe hearing is the motive. This person also uses a specialist tool. We now believe they might wear make-up and we do know they mimic people or characters made famous through films. In a nutshell, Dan, we must pick the bones from what we have."

"From all of that, should be easy to find." Dan could not help but chuckle.

"Male or female? Let's try to answer that before we do anything else. We also have a link with the garage key. It seems the person has had the key for a period of time and from what we know has copies. Two have already been left and does he have more?"

"Made enquiries at the regular places but then you're into needle in a haystack territory. There are also the machines in supermarkets and B&Q. Three keys for a tenner and cut in the same number of minutes!"

"Okay. I'm ready to organise interviews and do basic checks once we have Ashton's staffing lists. It should be straightforward, particularly if any are known to us."

"According to Firth and Ashton the original lock-up key is secured within a key safe at the main office and Firth controls that. Ashton has two duplicates and they are always with him. They were in France when the first and second attacks took place."

"What about Ashton's wife?"

"Ex-wife. Divorce is through, I believe. They haven't lived together for years. When they separated, he moved into the flat briefly before going to France. He'd owned the flat for some time, initially rented it but from what he said there was some trouble with a tenant who caused extensive damage and now it's left empty in case he returns. She – her name is here somewhere – Bingo. Constance Hartley-Lowe. Reverted to her maiden name. She had little to do with the business in a professional sense. A lady of substance. He married well. Let's put it that way, although recently she needed to raise funds due to the taxman after her father's death. She faced a huge inheritance tax bill and had money outstanding for work on the family home. Taken to court too."

"All that glitters, sir."

"Get April to pay her a visit as soon as. It's highly unlikely there's anything untoward but you just never know."

Dan was just about to leave when he turned at the door. "On a positive note, we may be in a position to interview Tom Craig tomorrow if he continues to make progress. Also, the details of the youths excluded from the college are now logged. They come to Harrogate from afar. Stuart has organised the local forces to interview the parents. You're aware one of the junior soldiers is female?"

"Indeed. Mobile phones, Dan? We have neither Coffrey's nor Craig's. Have we received the records from the phone companies?"

"No phone registered to Coffrey and only a work phone for Craig. We applied through RIPA. The numbers have been checked but there's nothing we weren't aware of. I'll now check on Peter Whittle."

"We know Coffrey had one. What about Northwind Legal?" Cyril asked as he drained his cup.

"Miss Gail Wilson-North has an appointment later today. She's been through his files and wants to call in. She sounded anxious."

Cyril collected the remaining mint and followed Dan but left him in the corridor to move through to the Incident Room. Much of the new intelligence had or was in the process of being added or uplifted. As he studied the boards briefly before logging in to one of the computers his thoughts turned to the latest victim, Peter Whittle. There it was, the information from Stuart Park regarding the young soldiers. Lattimer was from Skelmersdale and Winters was from Hexham. Their applications were also included within the file. Winters had the better qualifications. Neither had been previously known to the police but that was to be expected having successfully been accepted into the start of their forces careers.

The list of loose ends was steadily growing but at least the staff working on the case had increased proportionately.

Chapter Twenty

Gail Wilson-North was in her office early. She could not sleep knowing she was about to be interviewed formally by the police. The anomaly she had found in Tom's records had nagged her. Initially, she had decided to keep the issue quiet until she had time to discuss it with him as it could well have been a legitimate error. *Why would a man of integrity, a man who followed the rules sensitively and rigorously not fulfil his professional obligation?* The thought tumbled through her head. She walked down to the lower floor. Mike Stockwell had just arrived.

"And I thought I was early!" He glanced at the clock on the wall. "How's Tom?" His voice and expression demonstrated his obvious concern.

"It's positive. He's out of the coma but for the moment he's being kept in a semi-conscious state. I'm hoping to pop in today but they're still keeping a police presence. I think they want to know what he remembers whereas I want him to know we are there for him."

"The mental healing process is going to take time, Gail. I couldn't remember much after this." He tapped his leg. "It was just a blur, as if it hadn't happened. I can remember up to leaving the base but everything else … He'll be the same but it does return and that can be bloody scary."

"Can we talk in confidence? I'd love your opinion on

something and it might put my mind at rest."

"Your office?"

Gail smiled. "Thanks. Let's hope it's a simple error."

Mike had settled in the chair opposite her desk. There was one of Tom's files spread open over the surface. He waited until she was ready.

"Imagine you have a warrant for nonpayment of a rather large bill exacerbated by the addition of legal costs ... let's say thirty grand for round figures. It's all gone through the courts, settlement has to be arranged and a warrant for goods to that value must be collected."

Mike nodded trying to keep up with the scenario.

"Certain items of property, the cars for example, are leased but the house, probably even just one of the rooms contains assets at least to that value. What happens next?"

"Officially? I'd take control of goods to an approximate value of the debt, make a controlled goods agreement and then support the person in looking at ways of meeting the debt. I would advise that the goods should go to auction but that they might not realise their true value once the auctioneer's fees have been added to the equation. If I had a warrant I would act upon it and if needs be, seek police support to fulfil my role in serving the court warrant."

"So why didn't he do that? The preliminary procedures were followed, I've checked. It's what's missing from his file that concerns me. His bodycam wasn't activated for the latter part of the meeting and neither was that of his colleague. I've had words with him but he just tells me it was Tom's call. The warrant he had with him was returned. That, Mike, is the first time he's acted in this way. It's a strange case as her lawyer only requested an independent

163

survey on the building work done after his visit. He presented evidence of poor workmanship at appeal that wasn't forthcoming at the original court hearing. The revised judgement was found in her favour."

"So, what you're saying is that Tom's unusual and uncharacteristic action was in a way positive for her and turned out to be the right call?"

"The builder lost out and had to pick up his tools again. There was also compensation to be paid for internal damage to the property. It was a complete reverse judgement. If Tom did interfere then he overstepped his professional responsibility. There's something not quite right here. Let's say it's woman's intuition. I don't like the smell I'm getting."

"You think there's a link to the attack and this judgement?"

"The note he received, they knew his name. Disgruntled builders have hammers, especially those who work on the lead flashing to roofs."

Mike pulled a face. "Hell, Gail, isn't that stretching the imagination a little too far?"

***

April Richmond had admired the pinkish brick façade of the impressive house as she approached. The noise of the tyres on gravel announced her arrival. She had telephoned earlier to make the appointment. She had only seen the gates and entrance to the driveway after checking *Street View,* the house was not visible, but in all honesty, she was not expecting such a property. Even with the scaffolding and sheeting to the rear of the structure, it was still beautiful. Two builder's vans were positioned nearby. The inside was equally as striking. She took a moment to absorb the general décor. Constance Hartley-Lowe brought in a tray. April immediately thought of Cyril as the tea from the matching pot was poured into cups sitting on matching floral saucers. The sugar tongs and cubes brought back memories of her childhood and tea at her grandmother's.

"I saw the local news and recognised the address. Who could do such a thing? My ex-husband's place too. He always kept that garage empty after he sold his old Jag – he thought more about that car than he did of me!" She chuckled. "Boys and their toys. The same with the apartment, he never rented that again after the difficulties he faced with the last tenant."

"For how long were you partners in the business?"

"When we married, my father invested in his first venture, a petrol station on Ripon Road. Then, unlike today, there were many small stations, usually with a garage repair workshop attached. People once served you, you didn't have to get out of the car can you believe, still like that in Barbados." She paused. "Milk? Help yourself to sugar. Where was I?"

"Barbados."

She chuckled. "I wish. We always used to go there for Christmas. No, the petrol stations. As rulings changed in accordance with European laws, these smaller stations closed down. Many are now car wash places. Philip was clever in moving with the times and he converted the garages to petrol stations and shops and expanded the business by adding more. If he could, he'd lease other areas of the business premises to specialist firms, body shops, mechanics and posh car washes, valet services I think they're called. He's always been into car sales starting with second hand stuff and then the Mazda franchise came along. That did so well he took on other makes. Land Rover-Jaguar was his favourite. These all proved profitable too but not so much now. Daddy did well from his investment but since his passing it comes to the estate. We receive an annual dividend. Daddy was in finance and that was the main issue when he died, inheritance tax. Thought we might have to sell the house to clear it or at least some of the land."

"You divorced when?"

"Three years ago." Constance looked through the window. "Where has that time gone? I hadn't inherited this then; I'm an only child and Mummy died a few years ago. I came back here to be with him. I expected my father to live much longer than he did. He suffered a sudden heart attack. He also had diabetes and seemed to be a creaking gate for a number of years. We managed to pay the tax and also to keep the four staff on but I was in dispute with this builder. I refused to pay for some shoddy roof replacement and they took me to court. Dreadful mess but let's not dwell on that as some personal good came from it. Every cloud as they say. Part of the divorce settlement has helped give me a financial buffer and I still receive annual payments from various investments from my father's legacy. It's not been an easy time as you can imagine."

"Was your divorce amicable?"

"Is this relevant? I thought you were here to discuss the incident at the lock-up and the business partnership."

"From where I'm sitting that seems to be one and the same thing. Everyone linked to the firm directly and indirectly will be scrutinised as the lock-up door was not forced. A key was used. According to Mr Ashton the only key was held by the business."

"I can say that I only go if I'm passing one of the garages for fuel and to collect the cars I lease every two years. Usually, a four by four and a sport's model only because I get a very favourable deal. Leasing is another area in which Philip has moved with the times even though he's no longer there. Stephen Firth, as I'm sure you know, is his number one. He's the business manager so he runs it all. He would know more about the business than Philip now."

"You reverted to your maiden name?"

"Have you ever been disappointed, Inspector Richmond?"

April nodded. "In a relationship, yes."

"Need I say any more?"

April swiftly changed the subject. "I believe some time back you were visited by enforcement agents. Can you tell me more?"

"No! I don't see the relevance."

"It's all about coincidences. You may know there have been two attacks. The first you are aware of and the second victim is a young man who works as a bailiff, an enforcement agent, who was working for the company employed by the court to collect the money owed. Enforcement agents work for private firms as you may well by now know. Strangely, the one who called here on that occasion is the man who suffered a similar fate to the youth found in your husband's garage."

Constance moved a hand to her mouth clearly shocked

by the revelation.

"I'm sorry if that's brought concern. It's the reason for my intrusive questions. Lightning rarely strikes twice in the same spot but we have two similar crimes and both link to you and your ex-husband indirectly."

Constance noted the sudden change in April's questioning. There was now an edge. April too noticed a similar change. There was a sudden flush, almost a panic.

"How is Tom?"

"You know him personally?"

There was a long silence as Constance stared into her cup. "How is he? I wondered why he sounded agitated and why he hadn't called."

***

Regent Parade seemed different. The rain had grown heavier as the day progressed. After a late night, there was no urgency to get up other than a nagging curiosity. The box was gone, he was aware of that and he knew the police had found it. The dangling piece of blue and white police tape was still present and it brought a smile. He glanced at the large *Stephen King Autos* sign. It could not have been a more perfect spot. A car horn sounded lower down on Skipton Road. "Beep, beep to you too." The voice and laugh of Pennywise returned briefly. The police had not caught him the last time he was forced to do these things so there was no reason that he should be caught now, even with the foolish clues he seemed to feed them with. He could never understand why he did that. It was like him, out of control. He popped up the hood of his jacket, turned and glanced at the CCTV camera knowing it was facing down the road. "Lights, camera, action!" Within a minute he was heading back in the direction in which he had come. Like the times before, a feeling of disgust flushed through him.

***

It was clear from Ian Tempest's body language as he entered Harrogate police station that he was neither comfortable nor relaxed, despite the encouraging hand of his friend, Fletcher, at his elbow. Even the truck, positioned in the car park, looked awkward; already half full of domestic detritus, it presented a ménage of tumble dryers, fridges, corrugated iron sheeting and cycles.

Tempest's hair was long and he wore a gold earring in both lobes. Expensive tattoos sleeved both hands and arms. Observing the shape of his nose, he had received a few blows in his time.

Owen had been awaiting the call from the front desk to indicate they had arrived and he went down to meet them. Owen and Tempest were of similar build and they stood facing each other until Owen smiled. That simple act brought a smile from Fletcher and a visible relaxation to Tempest's shoulders. Wasting no time, Owen ushered them through to Interview Room Four. An officer was already stationed by the door.

Cyril entered a few minutes later. As he approached, Fletcher helped his friend to his feet as he whispered in his ear.

"Thank you for your kindness, gentlemen. How are you, Mr Fletcher and how are your good lady and the kids?"

The polite informalities made Tempest frown. He was expecting the usual police interview, cold and direct. He had experienced a few in his time but none like this.

"Well, thank you. This is Steptoe." He laughed and

169

patted his friend's shoulder. "Ian Tempest. This is DCI Bennett."

As he pushed a pamphlet giving details across the table, Bennett informed them about the recording and the data protection policy the police followed. "It's all in there, Mr Tempest. I'm aware you are here voluntarily and we thank you for your co-operation. Now, to begin can you give us your fixed address?"

Tempest gave the full address and post code. "I rent it. Have done for two years. Before that I travelled a bit, tinkers, gypsies, travellers and even worked on the travelling fairs. You'll have that on record."

Cyril nodded. "We do. That, however, is in the past."

"Mr Fletcher tells us that you also have temporary accommodation I believe?"

Fletcher told him that Bennett meant his caravan.

"Right, yes. South Shore Park. Used to be me dad's until he kicked it, like. He was a scrappy too. He rented a smallholding, kept horses and the like. Now me and my brother have the van although he seldom uses it. Me girlfriend loves the sea, so we try to go as often as possible. Also use it if I'm collecting in the area."

"We have it from police records but can you confirm your date of birth?"

"March 26th 1990."

"So, you're thirty-one."

"Getting bloody old. Trying to settle down. Fletch has been a great mate. We help each other out as mates do."

Cyril detected a developing anxiety, not only was he beginning to sweat but his voice grew more high pitched.

"Why do you need to see me?"

"You're not in any kind of trouble, Mr Tempest. May I get you some water?"

Tempest shook his head.

"When did you leave Scarborough?"

"As soon as I bloody could. Worked with me dad but I earned nowt and what I did earn I pissed up the wall. Always fighting and getting into trouble. I used to smack folk if they called me Steptoe." He laughed. "Now I like it!" He looked at Fletcher and then back at Cyril unsure as to where the questioning was leading

***

April sipped more tea.

"Tom was very kind when he came. You expect bailiffs to be officious, obnoxious as well as intimidating. Seeing them appear was really the last straw, I'd had enough, what with paying the inheritance tax, then the court case and fighting to get the job on the roof done properly. I was up to there." She put her hand just above her eyebrows. "Builders, when dealing with a woman, think they can take advantage. The bloody roof still leaked and not where it did before he started. He became quite aggressive until I threatened him with the police. I called Stephen Firth and he came to liaise with the builder – man to man. Stephen has a wicked temper when riled and I knew he'd hold his own in any argument. They seemed to listen to him whereas they were trying to pull the wool over my eyes constantly. I couldn't go up on the scaffolding to look at their work as I suffer from vertigo. Before you ask, it's not a listed building and so the work is not controlled. I only wish it were. I made Stephen promise not to tell Philip about the mess I was in as I knew he'd come over from France and

171

try to take control. Stephen suggested I refuse to pay until certain things were put right. It went on for too long with solicitors being the only winners and eventually the court found in the builder's favour. That's the reason for the debt collectors, the bailiffs."

"Tom Craig?"

"Although he had a warrant and should have taken goods to the value of the debt he didn't. Even more strange to me is that he called later, came to the house informally. He said it was off the record. It was maybe only a couple of days later, if my memory serves me well. He was kind and offered advice to buy me some time and he suggested ways I could settle the payments over a period rather than as one lump sum. He also said that the loss of my father and the trauma of the inheritance tax could be seen as extenuating circumstances that might allow delaying payment. He was the one who advised getting an independent assessment of the building work."

"Why would he do that? Collecting debt is his job!" April enquired.

"He told me he was concerned about me. It wasn't in a creepy or salacious way either. He could see I was at the limit, likening it to PTSD. He'd experienced others in the forces with the same symptoms; on the edge. To be honest, I think he was talking about himself. He was so kind, so much so, I invited him for a drink and a meal."

"Did he accept?"

She nodded.

April could interpret the rest. "Did a relationship develop?"

"Platonic at first but … I know, I know but …"

"Are you still seeing him?"

"Not as regularly as I should like, but yes."

"Did Stephen Firth know about this?" April leaned forward and watched her expression with interest.

"Not in that sense. They met once. It was on the last occasion Stephen had dealings with the builders. Tom arrived as Stephen was leaving. I introduced him as a friend."

"Do you have Tom Craig's mobile number?" April knew from the information already held there had been no telephone records linking him to her other than those calls directly connected through Northwind Legal.

"Funny thing with the phone, Inspector. He always rang me, stressed quite strongly for me not to call owing to the nature of his job."

April frowned. "Was that not strange?"

"No, to be honest with you. I thought he might be married and phone calls from me might have put him in a compromising position. You hear of these things happening more and more these days."

From initially feeling sorry for the woman, April immediately felt a strong disdain. She had discovered enough.

***

"So, Mr Tempest, tell us in your own words what happened on leaving home as a youth."

Tempest tentatively went through his story mentioning the number of times he had appeared in court and his custodial sentence, but also enforcing the fact that he had changed. It was almost a repeat of Fletcher's protestations as if he had been coached. Cyril knew that neither man's

DNA had been found at either site but the links to the two past murders had to be investigated. Whereas he had hoped to come away feeling neither man had any involvement he did not. There was a physical discomfort brought about through suspicion. He was certain Fletcher had been straight and honest throughout their dealings but the same could not be said for Tempest. It was as if he were hiding elements of his past. Cyril also knew this was neither the time nor the place to dig more deeply. He thanked the men and wished them both well.

Checking his watch, he was relieved to note that he had time to get the information he had just received collated and filed as well as seek further information about Tempest's past. He also needed to organise a press release. A talk to camera about the latest attack might just jog someone's attention but there was CCTV footage he needed to assess.

***

Philip Ashton arrived, shook his umbrella at the door before dropping the files onto the desk in the entrance of Harrogate police station. He looked across the desk into what appeared to be the end of an open-plan office space towards an incongruous, old-fashioned wooden coat stand positioned a few metres away; it was full. A number of people were chatting. The sudden, occasional ringing phone drowned out everything until answered. He pressed the bell for assistance. Within a few seconds an officer appeared.

"Mr Philip Ashton. I have an appointment with DCI Bennett at twelve. I'm early."

"Only twenty minutes, sir. Take a seat and I'll see if the Chief Inspector is free. You can leave your brolly in that bin." He pointed to a corner near the entrance. "It'll be safe there."

Philip sat, the files on his knee. There was something clinical about such places and it reminded him of the waiting room at his own MOT testing station; a notice board that nobody looked at, the dual painted walls, the obligatory dado rail to prevent chairs damaging the walls and then there were the lights; no matter what time of day or night they were always on. Within ten minutes, Cyril appeared.

"Mr Ashton, please come this way." He opened the door to a room normally used by duty solicitors. "This is free for an hour and it's more comfortable."

The word 'hour' brought a sinking feeling to Ashton's stomach.

"They're all here as you requested, Chief Inspector. I had one of the secretaries add them to this file in chronological order based on the length of time the staff have worked in the business. Thought that might help. Those with least time, and the ones I don't know all that well, are at the top and then going down to the longest and most loyal employees, many of whom I'd trust with … I was going to say my life but maybe that's a bit of an exaggeration." He grinned but received nothing by way of a response. "In the separate file are the names of individuals who lease my property. Obviously, I don't have a list of their employees."

Cyril flicked through the files. "Thank you for your co-operation. I'll make sure these are copied and returned to you. The officer at the desk will issue you with a receipt."

"I don't see why I couldn't have sent those through electronically."

"You, and more importantly I, know they are here at a set time on a set day and not inconveniently lost in the ether. If we have any queries we'll call. I take it you will be remaining in the UK for a few more days?"

Ashton's frown accompanied by the rolling of his eyes contradicted the forced smile and words. "Happy to co-operate, Chief Inspector."

They stood and Cyril held open the door. "One more question if I may. Why did Firth's marriage break down?"

"You'll need to ask Stephen that question."

Chapter Twenty-One

The names from Ashton's files had been entered into the system and the magic had happened within the blink of an eye. Two employees were shown to have previous convictions. They would be seen first. Interviews were organised to take place at the company's main office and a timetable was drawn up with Firth's co-operation.

April finished chatting to Owen. She had regaled him about the young man seducing the property rich, mature woman. "They have ways, Owen, strange ways. Thankfully our Lothario isn't married." She winked. "I now find I'm interviewing his boss, a Gail Wilson-North in an hour. I hope to goodness she's not a victim of his charms as well. That would make the chat untenable."

"Maybe if he has, it's the double-barrelled names that attract him!"

She glanced at the clock. It was already 13.30.

***

There was something about performing to young children in a Primary school that evoked mixed emotions. His love of the theatre, particularly pantomime, resurrected the excited nervousness all such performances wrought to the pit of his stomach. They also dislodged memories that stood in stark contrast and reinforced the reasons he no longer would tread those particular professional boards again.

Working within a school rather than a child's home also brought advantages. A room would be provided where he could prepare for the performance and that meant neither travelling to nor from the venue in costume and make-up.

Today would be a magic show to one hundred infants. Prestidigitation, as he would announce. He would always include the voices of the characters from the Harry Potter films within the show. They always liked that. The special magic wands were a firm favourite too.

"Sleight of hand, dear boy, sleight of hand," he said to himself as he stared at the face he had just made up. The voice of Jimmy Durante was accurate and clear. "'You can fool all of the people some of the time; you can fool some of the people all of the time, but you can't fool all of the people all of the time.' You even look like Lincoln until you do this." He stuck a huge white moustache, curled and shaped into points at the ends to his upper lip; it complemented the eye make-up and the upturned white eyebrows. "Very Victorian." The tails on his coat curled upwards too as if caught in the wind and his oversized flat shoes brought a degree of the clown to his appearance, deliberately softening his now stern look. The long, white wig beneath the crooked top hat completed the costume.

He knew there would be a degree of unease amongst many of the kids as he made his appearance. It happened when he was in panto too but experience had taught him that impersonating the voice of Albus Dumbledore usually brought looks of incredulity followed by smiles. The character was perfect for a school setting. It did not matter that he was more wizard than magician, he was an immediate and identifiable character.

The props were positioned on the low stage – all stars and sparkles as the children filed into the hall to sit cross-legged. The teachers positioned themselves on the chairs located at the end of the rows. He stared out from the gap in the curtains. It was their faces he loved to see, their excitement, the laughter and the expectancy in their eyes. Some children, and not necessarily the youngest, sat with a finger over their lips, their backs straight, occasionally looking at their teacher for a smile of recognition. *Why did children do that?* he thought. *What were they trying to show? Conditioning, that's what it was. Compliance.* He remembered his own childhood and how he performed to invite his parents' pride and pleasure and he resented it.

"Good afternoon, children."

"Good afternoon, Mrs Shackerly. Good afternoon everybody." The words were robotic and carried no sincerity.

"We have a special guest for you this afternoon, a man with special powers. What might those be? Don't call out, Jonny! Hands up!" She pointed to one child straining as if to burst. "Sarah."

"A wizard, miss."

"Mmm. Well done. What about you, Carl?"

"A magic trick man."

"A magician, yes. We have with us Mr Simulacrum. Can we say that?" She pronounced every syllable and after a few attempts the response was close enough. "Mr Simulacrum is a magician who will mesmerise us all with his magic tricks. Let's all wish him a warm St John's Infant School welcome. Mr ..." she stretched out the introduction, "... Simulacrum."

The theme from the Harry Potter films started to fill the hall as children, apart from two who had anxiously gone to sit next to their teachers, clapped enthusiastically. He waited, allowing the music to build before fading. The curtains parted. The dark suited figure emerged. He swiftly produced a bunch of flowers from his jacket sleeve and this simple trick immediately captured the children's attention but it was his voice that made some of the older children smile and point; he was now instantly recognisable. He saw many a child mouth the name, *Dumbledore*. The nerves he carried quickly evaporated.

As the show progressed, the response from both children and staff filled him with encouragement. He was suddenly trapped within the pleasure of live performance, of laughter, or screams of amazement. His voice too changed, he introduced characters from *Toy Story*, *Frozen* and *The Incredibles.* Each time a new voice was added there was a spontaneous buzz from the audience. To finish, he brought a live, white rabbit from his top hat. Bugs Bunny thanked the audience for their kindness and both the talking rabbit and Mr Simulacrum left to disappear behind the curtains. His head reappeared and the words "That's all Folks!" brought an end to the show. The applause slowly died away and silence surrounded him as it always had done from the first occasion, the day of the car crash. On that day it was all revs and screaming tyres, but then silence, the process continuing whenever he performed.

He left a number of flyers, one for each child. Successful school performances were always good for business. The image of the white rabbit and a magic wand were displayed above the words 'Children's Entertainer'.

Within forty minutes the car had been packed, he had enjoyed tea with the headteacher and had been paid. It had been a busy forty-eight hours.

***

April had concluded the interview with Gail Wilson-North but had discovered nothing that she did not know already. They had a list of addresses Tom Craig had visited and the names of the people he had dealt with over the last six months, including Constance Hartley-Lowe. April had also received the envelope Tom had found on his desk that morning. She had placed it into an evidence bag still wrapped in the piece of A4 paper. She had said nothing to Wilson-North about the information she had received whilst interviewing Hartley-Lowe.

As she entered the Incident Room, Cyril, Owen and Smirthwaite were huddled watching CCTV footage on the large wall mounted screen.

"There, sir. That's looking down Skipton Road. It's a fixed camera. Keep your eyes on the grassed area." They watched as the man in a red anorak type coat crossed and proceeded in a direction taking him away from the camera. Smirthwaite paused the image. "The coat is a match for one found at Whittle's house. That's not all." He restarted the footage. Another man crossed the grassed area at almost the same spot and followed Whittle. "They both walk down Mornington Crescent and then turn off the road to the left." The video was wound on. "Here we are twenty-two minutes later. That same person who was following the man in red we now believe to be Whittle, can be seen returning, but unfortunately, he turns right and away from the camera. I've tried to enhance these images but these you see are at the limit."

Cyril looked at the date and times Smirthwaite had jotted on a handout. "That's the day before he was attacked, the very afternoon."

"As you see from the handout there's more."

April pulled up a chair as Smirthwaite slid across an information sheet. The same camera showed the lights from the cars travelling along the road. It was dark but the streets lights and the technical enhancements had brought a degree of clarity.

"You need to look to the left of the image. You can just see the edge of the pavement. Most of the buildings' façades beyond Westmoreland Street are visible. Stephen King Autos is just out of shot." The video was paused as soon as the figure appeared. "You can see the box, when enlarged it matches that found containing the hammer. You'll also see this same person returning."

Cyril checked the times again. There was a two and a half hours difference.

"We believe the person waited for the area to quieten, speculative, I know but we've not finished. This is CCTV footage taken in the area not far from Tom Craig's apartment. It was brought to light when this character was first identified."

The town has a thousand eyes, Cyril thought to himself but did not reference them as he knew Harrogate only had 212 cameras and any images requested had to be paid for. "That's the same man. You can tell by the way he walks. Compared to the height of the lamp posts he's about the same height too."

Owen had leaned forward.

"The boffins think so too. They've an expert in gait analysis taking a look but they're pretty sure. They should also be able to identify the gender," announced Smirthwaite.

"I believe there are more than two genders these days … I've read there's as many as fifty-two give or take so that should prove of interest. The latest fashion is to be gender nonconforming!" Cyril failed to keep the incredulity and cynicism from his voice. "I despair and feel more like an alien than …" His voice faded in pure frustration. "Do you know, lady and gentlemen, if I'm still allowed to address you as such, we are going to vanish up our own backsides trying to please all of these woke folk."

Owen stood and walked over to the screen. "If we just consider those identifying as either male or female for this exercise, a tenner says male, Smirthwaite. Following on from your thoughts, sir, we're going to need a lot of different prisons to house these individuals or do we just abuse their human rights."

Cyril deliberately said nothing.

Smirthwaite chuckled. "Male? If you say so. I'll await the expert view. Twenty-six to two are strange odds! There's another thing, going back to the cardboard box. There's a logo, hand drawn on the box we found, but it's not visible on any of the video footage. The Amazon smile I call it, looks like a smiling mouth with an arrowhead shape to one side. Originally it was placed under the name 'Amazon' and pointed to the first and fourth letter to show they sold everything from A to Z but now you just see the smile. Eyes and a nose have been added to that logo, in other words …"

"A face," April interjected.

"He's the man we need to find." Those words were so easy for Cyril to say but they all knew that there was a good deal more to discover before they would find this person. April spent a further ten minutes with Cyril and he inspected a copy of the note she had been handed by Wilson-North.

***

Cyril parked in the hospital car park. The sound of the siren from an approaching ambulance reverberated from the walls of the building. He watched as it approached and it made him think of how fickle life could be. *One minute you could be fine and the next …*

He knew where Tom Craig was but he showed his ID at reception and received directions.

As he approached, an officer seated outside the room stood. Cyril had a brief word.

Having been instructed that the patient was still sedated, he had only been allotted five minutes. He was not to expect much clarity. Apart from severe bruising, swelling and nasal cannulas, Tom Craig looked in better shape than he had envisaged considering the images he had seen of the damage inflicted a day or so previously. He was expecting a face swathed in bandages, numerous pipes and tubes running to and from the victim and machines monitoring every life function. That was not the case. There was only a single monitor that continued to signal that he was breathing and that his heart rate was steady and there was a drip of some kind. Cyril even received a weak hand shake. However, owing to the wired structure to the lower jaw there would be no verbal communication. The small white board would have to suffice. After exchanging brief pleasantries, Craig would respond in writing. Cyril's main line of questioning centred on the voice that he had heard in the morning. Cyril read the response Tom Craig had scribbled on the whiteboard. 'James Earl Jones.'

"You're sure it was his voice?"

Tom nodded. The movement was clearly painful.

Cyril had to check the internet to seek clarification. "Was it Darth Vader's voice you heard?" Cyril prompted.

Tom shook his head gently knowing it would bring discomfort. *It was another film but I can't remember which,* he wrote.

Cyril quickly retrieved his phone and looked at Jones's film history. There were forty-five films listed. Cyril handed Tom the phone. "You've enough to choose from there."

Flicking the screen, he stopped at only the fourth and showed Cyril.

"*Field of Dreams*?" Cyril offered.

Tom nodded and handed back the phone.

The words *they will come*, entered Cyril's head but he was unsure as to the actual dialogue. He put the actor's name into YouTube alongside the film's title. There were a few film clips. He played the first clip and impatiently waited for the accompanying advert to end. They both watched. Cyril took the white board and made notes.

People will come – they will arrive at your door – as innocent as children – longing for the past – magic waters – part of our past.

It made no sense to either man. Tom closed his eyes. He was tired and even though Cyril had more questions, the sudden attendance of a doctor was all the hint he needed that his time was up. Taking his phone, he photographed the whiteboard notes and then wiped it clean.

It had given serious food for further thought.

Chapter Twenty-Two

Owen felt decidedly uneasy. Even the word antenatal sounded worrying. For some reason in his own mind, it had a military connotation that he could not grasp. A promise to Hannah, however, was a promise. They had just over ten weeks to go before the due date, a date he had ringed in thick red felt pen on the calendar. He had also scribbled it in large letters on a sheet of paper placed within the pages of the book Julie had given to him. It still felt unreal. He was going to be a father, David Owen, Detective Inspector, was going to be a parent.

This was not the first visit, that occurred at six weeks. The midwife was jovial, a direct contrast to both Hannah and Owen. It was still bizarre but the new baby was clearly visible and growing weekly. It amazed Owen how many pregnant women he now encountered. He had noticed none before receiving the news and then suddenly he seemed surrounded by them. Cyril had told him it was the Baader- Meinhof effect and he took his word for it.

He realised there would be more visits to comply with strict guidelines and he had written the dates in the diary. It was important they worked to the EDD. This rigour gave him a degree of confidence. He was also learning what he should expect at the various stages. The one thing they were certain of was that they wanted the birth at home and he was surprised at the midwife endorsing their choice.

"Hannah's as fit as a butcher's dog, David. The hospital encourages home births. You'll need to hire a birthing pool but that can be sorted nearer the time." She launched into the full details.

It had sounded perfect when they had first considered the option, but the more he thought about it the less enthusiastic he became. Even the idea of a trial run brought a tingle of trepidation. The size and the weight of the thing alone once water was added disturbed him. The pipes, constantly maintaining a temperature of 37 degrees as well as the fact that he would be allowed to share the pool during the birth, brought images of a tsunami flooding the flat at the critical moment. He was also relieved to hear swimwear was compulsory. They were the things nightmares were made of. Hannah, however, was as determined as ever. She had found the address of a doula and grew ever more excited. Owen switched off when she started regaling him about the health and healing properties of the placenta. He doubted he would drink a smoothie again.

***

The briefing room was buzzing with a concentration of conversation. People huddled in small groups, some around the wall boards but others perched on tables. Each had files or handouts. Owen was regaling two people with his experience at the antenatal visit, his hand gestures and facial expressions conveying as much as his words. Both encouraged a degree of spontaneous laughter.

"I kid you not. A smoothie. The pool has to be a certain temperature too. I know I'll get in the way. They have a

188

sieve just in case ..." He paused as if embarrassed to say. "To fish out turds. She might pass one in all the excitement."

"I don't think excitement is the correct medical term, Owen."

"No but she wants a doula too. To you innocents that's a birthing partner, someone who's there to support. I'll be in the way I know! It's all one hell of a learning curve. I'm getting more and more nervous."

Nixon joined in the conversation. "I knew someone who had a birthing pool and the weight of the water and the occupants caused the floor to give way and they dropped into the flat below."

The laughter resumed.

April entered before Cyril and immediately the chatter subsided. Cyril smiled as he made his way to the front, an area behind which was the large wall screen. Placing his files on the desk, he watched as others found a seat. It never ceased to amaze him how his colleagues were creatures of habit and usually positioned themselves in the same places; there was a security in their action, an innocence. Maybe we were descended from migratory creatures after all. The words he had jotted on the whiteboard in the hospital came immediately to mind – *as innocent as children* – people needed the security of place.

Cyril spoke of his visit to Tom Craig and the photograph of the small whiteboard containing key parts of the narrative were shown behind him on screen. They had the identity of their first voice. The next image was that of the note Tom had received earlier on the day he had been attacked. *The town has a thousand eyes.* "Let's also not forget that there's a chance that Whittle might and I stress might, have heard the voice of Pennywise. The links with Stephen King where the box was left, his constant repetition of the words, 'penny', 'make-up', 'woman man' and 'voice'. I have to admit that it was Julie who linked it to the King film. These ideas are now in the hands of our Criminal Intelligence Analyst." He looked up to see if anyone had been inspired to offer any thoughts on the whiteboard scribbles. He watched as a hand was raised.

"I know that song so well it's my father's favourite and I'm sure that you've read the lyrics. There's an amendment. One word. Town has replaced night."

Cyril had not. He said nothing but smiled, encouraging the officer to continue.

"It's about lies, white lies. It suggests the liar will be sorry and that whilst telling the lies, the night has a thousand eyes. So, we now have the replacement *town* ... meaning CCTV? Or could it be reminding Tom Craig about his past when we look at elements from the film – *longing for the past* and *part of our past*? Just thinking out loud. We all know what white lies are."

Owen glanced at April who immediately added to the discussion. "Harmless lies usually told to avoid hurting someone's feelings." She turned back towards Owen. "My colleague here whispered that to me," she lied and a flash of understanding appeared on his face as he nudged her arm.

"Anyway, let's see what comes from our expert, but keep them in mind. What about your visit, April?"

"Our Mr Craig, as you've seen from your notes – M2 in your files – has been blending business with pleasure. One can argue about his professionalism but I believe his heart was in the right place. Whereas he didn't specifically tell any white lies to his employer regarding the meeting with Constance Hartley-Lowe, neither did he employ the full power of his legal authority when dealing with the task in hand. You have to ask whether he was being an opportunist or a Samaritan. This is, of course, the second link we have to Philip Ashton but as yet we've not traced any link from the third attack to him in any way. This again reinforces your hypothesis that they are random acts and not dissimilar from those in Scarborough. We are looking for connections that may not be there or if they are, they are more subtle. It's likely to be coincidence. I'm also assured Ashton knew nothing of the affair and neither did Stephen Firth although Craig did meet Firth by chance. You've seen the note and the images delivered to Craig by hand. The perpetrator knew him by name and also his place of work. In fact, they walked in there as bold as brass and delivered it. Forensics have traced nothing but the graphologist suggests right-handed, artistic and male." She nodded at Cyril who immediately turned to Grimshaw.

Dan Grimshaw stood and went over to a whiteboard. "We've been breaking down the number of theatrical folk on the list and focusing primarily on impressionists owing to the voices mentioned by the first two victims." He tapped the board with his finger indicating the names that had been struck through with a line. "I'm aware that Donald Duck, the Joker and the chap you mentioned from *Field of Dreams* are so different that it would need a good impressionist with such a varied range. They'd more than likely have a well-practised repertoire using those specific voices within their act. I did check for Joker quotes on the net after remembering the T-shirt that was found at the lock-up garage. A key to the garage was also found in both Craig's flat and at Coffrey's nan's. How they got there we're unsure. For Craig, we also have no idea how someone entered his flat if he didn't let them in. We don't know whether our attacker was taken to it, invited in or if, and it's looking possible, he had his keys. This one Joker quote suddenly seemed more relevant than most. 'Never put your key to happiness in someone else's pocket.'"

A number of faces looked back as if to confirm that there was little relevance. Maybe Dan was grasping at straws, looking for something that was not there. It did, however, strike a chord with Cyril. Unperturbed, Dan continued.

"Could our impressionist also be an illusionist? Someone who can take things without people realising. We've all seen them remove watches and wallets without the person or the audience knowing. I wondered if the runner who crashed into Tom that morning could have taken, pickpocketed, the flat keys during their coming together? It's a theory. Although the handling time was limited, a pocket search takes seconds and the guy may have been wearing gloves as runners do. I got the pockets of Tom Craig's coat checked. Forensics apparently use tape and cut to extract touch evidence. Touch DNA traces that were not Tom's were found that match a separate DNA profile left in his flat. However, nothing matched in the garage. They've been put through the NDNAD but nothing has come up as yet. The sample could be from our runner and it will be followed up."

The mood changed quickly and more positive voices could be heard even though there was nothing positive to report. Cyril looked across at Dan and nodded.

The DNA evidence could be from our Constance, thought April. She made a note to check that.

"Also, one more thought regarding Whittle's repetition of the words 'woman man'. It immediately reinforced the word make-up, Pennywise was a clown but in the confusion of the attack it could be interpreted as make-up." Dan turned to Cyril. "Maybe it's worth a public social media posting to see if someone saw anyone made up as a clown or a man in make-up walking the streets on that day?"

Cyril was always prepared to listen to the broadest of ideas and, if needs be, filter them until they brought something to the investigation. It was his belief that openly accepting the most bizarre of ideas helped rid officers, particularly those who were inexperienced, of the fear of saying the wrong thing in briefings. Anything, no matter how off the wall it seemed, was given time and thought. As he always insisted, they must all keep an open mind.

"I'll sort that, Dan. Good point and worth further thought. So, from what you've said, Craig could have been deliberately targeted the same morning Coffrey was discovered. For it to work, if that was the way the attacker got the keys, then there had to be contact. There was an initial theory that these attacks were classed as *kill thrill*, indiscriminate targeting of innocent victims but your idea and the evidence offered may well contradict this." Cyril made a note on the cover of the file before him. "Go on Dan."

"Maybe not. I was researching the condition Intermittent

Explosive Disorder. Maybe things trigger his aggression, even the most insignificant of things. It's all to do with stressors, and who knows what they might be." He paused briefly. "I now have a list of eight theatrical people I feel fit the profile from the many we have within a thirty-mile radius of Harrogate – illusionists, impressionists, I've factored in their age; the person committing these crimes will have to be relatively fit and also be local. They will all be contacted and questioned within the next twenty-four hours. I'll split the names and delegate, some will be interviewed by neighbouring forces."

"What news on Whittle?" someone asked.

"He's making good progress. He'll not be talking any time soon but he's alive and will have to have some reconstructive work. There's every chance we can interview him," Smirthwaite answered. "I'll check and arrange a time that's convenient."

Owen looked across at Cyril. "Sir, might be something or nothing. Is it worth seeing if the victims kept films, DVDs or streamed, any films that were linked to the voice they heard? Was Whittle a Stephen King fan and did Craig own a copy of *Field of Dreams*? We know from Fletcher that Coffrey loved Donald Duck and Batman and that links to the unworn T-shirt found within the lock-up."

"It's worth a look. Whittle is certainly the odd one out. Could he have been targeted accidentally? Right, let's move." Cyril stood and collected his files.

It took a phone call to start the investigative process. The police would hold the keys to both properties until they had been declassified as scenes of crime.

***

Adrian had been up early and the Jaguar's bodyshell had been wrapped in an industrial cling film to protect it from the elements. The extended curves, bulges and coupé roof were almost camouflaged. Firth appeared at the door as the transporter drew up outside.

"It will be back in four days, resplendent in a metallic silver paintwork unless you've had a change of heart."

Both men watched as the car shell secured on the dolly was winched up the ramps and into the container. As the doors closed, they both breathed a sigh of relief.

"The real anxiety will come when it's back and the rebuild takes place. We have to execute that without marking the paint," Adrian commented as he wrapped up the tools he would be taking back to work.

***

Cyril stopped in front of Owen's desk and let two fingers search the sweet mug. Owen said nothing as four empty wrappers landed in front of him before Cyril tracked down a complete mint ball, allowing now a fifth wrapper to join the others. Cyril popped the mint in his mouth and Owen noticed his shoulders relax. It was then he noticed the orange plastic duck that had been sitting on the book Julie had bought him.

"Thermometer, for the birthing pool. These guys don't mess about." He slid open his drawer and he brought out two more, one was a banana and the other the shape of poo. "All anonymous. Even these." He held up a pair of Speedo trunks with budgerigar motifs.

"Smugglers, Owen. What a first sight for any newborn to witness." Cyril grinned.

"I feel this is only the start. I should have kept my mouth

shut."

"On a professional note, you were right about the films. Whittle had an extensive collection of films even in VHS format but you'd know nothing of those, too old tech. They were stored along with his wife's clothing, apart from the King film that was found in his computer drive. There's no cover for it as far as we know. Craig's also had the film relevant to him on DVD. That too was in his laptop disk drive. Now what do you make of that Detective Inspector?" The mint, pushed into his cheek as he spoke, was quickly released.

"Could whoever's responsible for the attacks have placed the DVDs as a sick joke or clue?"

Cyril sucked on the mint. "Are we being led down a dark alley, Owen? Are they leading us astray?"

"Pissing us about I'd say! Speaking of leading, the analysis of the gait of the person in the CCTV concludes it's definitely male."

***

The interviews of Ashton's staff had been completed and the reports were being collated and referenced but without success. Ashton's employees were hard-working and loyal and many spoke highly of both Ashton and Firth. There were five companies who leased property connected to his sites or on land he owned and they would be questioned next. Like all police investigations, it was a monotonous, mind-numbing task but essential. Modern technology had helped alleviate much of the mundane but interviews were still a vital element. Face to face and eye to eye often brought results. Long Valley Restorations was the first to receive a visit. Greg had called Adrian during his absence and had managed to postpone the visit until he was back in work.

The Ferrari Dino was finished. The two police officers arrived as the final inspection was taking place. Adrian wiped his hands on a cloth from the pocket of the grey lab coat he wore during these inspections; the coats were designed without buttons to prevent accidental marking of the paintwork. The introductions were brief. The initial questions were mainly linked to Ashton's businesses and the lock-up. Adrian felt uncomfortable as he knew he could not admit to using the garage on occasion and so he quickly denied any knowledge. Lying did not come easily and he felt himself flush, especially when he also noticed the officer linger on his answer, his eyes firmly fixed on his. It was the next question that caused even greater discomfort.

***

The small, independent book shop was positioned along a narrow street in Ripon. Shakti watched from the opposite pavement as the person in the window displayed a selection of books. DC Harry Nixon finished the last mouthful of the Appleton's pork pie he had nipped to buy after parking on the market square.

"Not bad," he mumbled, the last vestiges of pastry on his lower lip. "Bennett and Owen always say how good they are so had to try."

She pointed to the side of his mouth. "Keeping that for later?"

He withdrew a handkerchief and wiped his mouth. "Thanks."

As they entered, the small bell above the door signalled

a customer and the person she had seen contorted in the window appeared. The smile was welcoming.

"Mr Slingsby? I believe you're expecting us." She held out her ID. "DS Misra and this is DC Nixon."

"Ha, yes, indeed I am. Happy to help. Please come through to the back. We'll not be centre stage there." He chuckled pointing at the windows.

Shakti checked his details and was slightly confused as she looked at a sprightly, quite agile man in his fifties. For some reason she had expected more the librarian type whose age might render him to be too old and unfit for the runner for whom they were searching. "We believe you are an impressionist?"

"My name is Hercule Poirot and I am the greatest detective in the world." The words slipped out on cue. It was the voice of David Suchet's Poirot.

Nixon laughed. "Very good indeed. My mother used to love Poirot."

Shakti immediately asked his whereabouts on the night Coffrey had been attacked. He pointed to the ceiling.

"My home is my shop. I live in the apartment upstairs, have done since I bought the shop; it was then empty and next door was a gallery. I used to act, did a bit of TV and radio when I was younger but it's a cut-throat game. You need a good agent. Reverted to amateur dramatics when I realised that I wasn't going to make a living. It was always the thrill of performance I loved entertaining. It wasn't for fame you understand. Did a bit of kids' entertainment but that wasn't really for me but I do like reading to the kiddies' group we have here in the shop. Their faces are a picture. I can use my many voices." He placed his hands on his knees. "To answer your question, officer, I was here. I no longer have a car but I do have an electric bicycle."

"When was the last time you performed in public?"

"Christmas in the cathedral."

"What impression are you famous for, Mr Slingsby?"

Slingsby pondered the question for a few moments. "The usual I'm afraid, Caine, Bogart, Connery and of course, Poirot. It's keeping up with the trends that's difficult and to be honest I lost interest a while back. They want politicians and modern pop stars, that's not for me. Give me a good book and I'm happy."

"Thank you. We'll take no more of your time." Shakti and Nixon left. Slingsby watched as they passed the window and raised a hand in farewell. Poirot's voice returned, "Not too many little grey cells, Hastings, n'est ce pas!"

***

The noise in the workshop was constant.

"Could you take a look at this picture please?"

Adrian studied the photograph of the hammer before walking over to the tool rack. He pointed to a selection of hammers. "It's one of many. But this," he tapped the photograph, "is a small ball pein. They're used by metal workers the world over. We have a few. Some are heavier and others are for finer work. Did you know that these hammers have a long association with Hell's Angels as they were always carried for self-defence and not so self-defence if you get my meaning!"

Both officers glanced at each other before Adrian picked two hammers from the rack. "I've had these for some years, right through my apprenticeship, in fact. Lost a couple on the journey but I've added to the collection as work demanded."

"Do you always add your name to the shaft?"

He nodded and let his fingers run down the deeply stencilled letters. "More tools are nicked at places of work than you'd think. Some are borrowed permanently even though they are the way a man feeds his family. No honour amongst thieves but then you'd know that. It's not your workmates who are the culprits, it's those who come into the workshop, delivery men, customers and the like. I've been guilty of leaving some small pieces of equipment inside the car's bodywork – you get distracted and then you don't notice it's gone until you next need it. That's why I put things back into their correct place before shutting shop. I encourage it of the apprentice too."

"Have you had one go missing recently, Mr Lovelady?"

Adrian shook his head. "Not one of mine and not that one in the photograph. You can pick these up at any general auction or from car boot sales. Old tools are generally worthless as it's the skill to use them that's key." He handed back the photograph.

The two officers looked at each other thinking about the skill used with this specific tool.

"People nick them and move them on."

The officers chatted briefly with the others in the workshop but soon left.

Chapter Twenty-Three

Three of the listed impressionists had been interviewed. None of them they felt was worthy of further investigation. The possibility of Hell's Angels involvement had not gone unnoticed and a check with DVLA cross-referencing the names linked to the case had been completed. Five more people, four owning a motorcycle and with an acting background were added to the interview list.

April Richmond checked the address on her electronic tablet as she approached the door. Owen was completing a phone call by the gate. She rang the bell realising that it was also a camera. She smiled.

The door opened fully and a woman greeted her. She held up her ID.

"We're looking for a Trevor Jones?"

"You've come to the right place. I'm Trevor. Would you like to come in?" His voice was soft and feminine.

April turned, looking at Owen as she stepped over the threshold. "My colleague will only be a moment."

They were shown through to the lounge. April noted the elegant framed theatrical posters that were displayed. They were set amongst the more traditional posters advertising pantomimes. She paused at one.

"I had these painted, a friend of a friend shall we say. I used them for advertising. There's something about that era, don't you think, Inspector Richmond?"

"They are beautiful." She pointed to the figure in top hat and tails.

"Yes, you can see the likeness. Well done, you!"

She had not, but said nothing.

April sat and Owen entered. "Sorry, I had to take that call. Inspector Owen."

"Two for the price of one. You're welcome Inspector. How may I help?"

"This seems indelicate but your appearance, Mr Jones."

"If you'd called yesterday, it would have been somewhat different. I choose when I wake. I now only perform as a man, The Amazing Crysto. My feminine side I must blame on the years of playing dames in panto and I've done my fair share. There's something about make-up, Inspector Richmond. Don't get me wrong, I'm as straight as the next man. Funny that. It's only been the last few years too. It now seems far more acceptable. No harm done, though."

April and Owen, particularly Owen, seemed even more confused. The interview continued but it soon became evident there was little chance of Trevor Jones being involved in any of the crimes even though there were factors that could not be ignored. He had an alibi for the whole day Coffrey had been hurt.

"When I was in Panto in Bridlington, Bloody Brid we called it, draughty theatre and poor digs, I was an ugly sister alongside a chap called Robin." He paused. "The last name escapes me ... It might come back. He was a fabulous mimic with a staggering repertoire of voices both male and female. If you closed your eyes you'd swear" – a little shake of his head – "Anyhow, he, Robin, started off well and was quite the star but about two weeks in he suddenly seemed to become distracted, he was not himself. I believe he was originally from Harrogate if my memory serves me well. Didn't stay locally when he was with us, stayed in Scarborough of all places for reasons we could never understand. He was a bit of a loner with a strong sense of right and wrong and he didn't suffer fools. Some in the cast said overzealous. I thought him sensitive. He started to have dreadful rows with the director but then she could be an arrogant bitch. After one public dressing down, a matinee performance, he stormed out. Some kid had upset him at the beginning of the show and he lost confidence and that resulted in a humiliating dressing room bollocking. That was the straw that broke the camel's back. He didn't come back. Funny thing was he still added voices during the row, they provided a shield. He seemed to gain strength from the imaginary characters he created on the spot."

"Did you see him again?" Owen asked as he made notes.

Jones slowly shook his head. "No. Strangely, I remember that there were a couple of murders in Scarborough not long afterwards and some wag suggested he was taking it out on his new audiences if they criticised his performance." Trevor smiled at both officers but received nothing in return. Owen wanted to shout, *Oh no he didn't!* in true pantomime form but thought better of it.

"In all seriousness, do you feel from knowing him professionally and socially he was capable of harming someone, whether hiding behind his made-up character or not?" April asked first looking at Owen and then back to

Jones.

"I worked with him and if you believe changing into costumes before and after performances is socialising, then no. He was genuinely funny and kind. Maybe I could use the term normal but he had his moments, as I've said ... he could change in the blink of an eye and suddenly fly off the handle. The sudden mood swings were almost hormonal. If you've worked with women ..." He stopped as he turned to April. "Maybe that was the problem with the director that day. She was well out of order." Jones pulled a face. "Theatrical types. Some can be real prima donnas; pains in the butt. She was one. Only lasted that season and she was gone. To answer your question Inspector are we all not capable of doing something out of character when push comes to shove? After all, more normal people can suddenly become heroes and in contrast, strong men have been seen to cry."

He was right. April had to change tack. "Have you met with them since?"

"The director or Robin?"

"Robin, sorry."

Jones shook his head. "No, I went south, the lights of London were calling. I was much older than most and was desperate for one last chance at fame. As you can see, it didn't work out, I'm now retired. Occasionally, and only occasionally I cover the odd children's party or school event but the real theatre is now part of the past ... Apart from this." He corrected himself whilst pointing to the make-up. "Let's say I entertain myself."

"Did you keep in touch with anyone else from that season who may know Robin?"

There was an extended pause. He stood and went over to a cupboard, retrieved an address book before looking down the index. "Only Charlie Chortle," he chuckled. "We chat on occasion, usually about old times. I know him as Charlie but I'm aware it's not his birth name. He moved with the fairs after that year and I only have a mobile number and that's changed three times!" He showed the crossings out on the page. "I can ring and ask if he minds my giving it to you."

Owen nodded. "Thanks."

There was no answer. "I'll keep trying."

Owen and April left with the understanding he would contact them as soon as he had spoken to Charlie. Neither held out much hope.

"Wonderful pictures and beautifully presented, Owen." It was if she had cast a pearl before his feet. He pulled a face.

"The coloured ones were alright but that one made of sharp cut triangles of brown cardboard was weird. In art speak it would be classed as a card collage. It was like a five-year-old had done it." He held the car door. "You obviously missed that! What's with the idea that some days you can be male and the next ..." He did not finish the sentence but the words 'gender non-conforming' came to mind. He started the car. "Let's imagine he's guilty, he's the man with the hammer. Do we have a prison that could cater for him and his capricious whims?"

April had switched off and was thinking about Robin. From where she was sitting, he had all the attributes to at least make him worthy of further investigation to locate him quickly. Suddenly, she felt the tug of her copper's nag. Alibi or not, there was something about Jones that rankled.

Underlining his name, she added the word 'Robin' immediately after it adding the word 'sisters'. She had some investigating to do.

***

A number of calls had brought April more information than she could have anticipated. She had a list of the cast and crew of the Bridlington pantomime season which had opened just prior to the double murders in Scarborough. Cinderella had proved popular. There was a Trevor Jones and a Robin Collier, both listed as the Ugly Sisters but there was also an addendum clearly marked with a date. Robin Collier's name had been struck through and in its place the name Norman Stansfield had been added. It was evident from the list that Stansfield had been the primary understudy. She checked the poster that had come through with the list. It was probable that one of the faces looking at her was that of Robin Collier.

April listed the names including those of the crew and the general sponsors of the production and correlated their then contact details before delegating them for further investigation and uplifting. It was hoped that something of relevance would quickly follow.

Turning to the whiteboard she read the names and the details of the two people murdered in Scarborough. Like the latest deaths they were connected merely by coincidences. Neither had links to the theatre in any shape nor form. She even doubted, considering their backgrounds, whether they had ever seen a pantomime.

Chapter Twenty-Four

It was still dark when April slipped the lead onto Ralph's collar. She had been awake since five. The ever-growing facts collected in the case seemed to carousel in her mind, bringing more than a little uncertainty and therefore little respite. There were certain elements that just did not seem to connect. There were coincidences, yes, but the more she investigated and slotted the evidence together the more she felt they were likely looking for an extremely focused thriller killer or someone driven by circumstance or situation. The previous evening, she had investigated previous cold cases. In many there were trigger moments that gave them some bizarre permission to act, whether that action be the process of torture or just simply to identify a victim and to kill.

Ralph had been her companion for some time. She had adopted him after his owner had been murdered and in some ways that case bore some similarity to the one that was now their main challenge. There was a definite pattern but not necessarily a reason.

The Stray was quite deserted. The road side and pathway lights flushed a degree of visibility along the periphery leaving the central area still dark as Ralph, now released, sniffed and wandered happily. She had deposited the parcel he always donated twice daily into the bin and she could now relax. Only recently he had taken to retrieving a ball and it never ceased to surprise her how often, even in the dark, he could retrieve it. Settling on a bench, April watched as Ralph came to her, dropped the soggy ball at her feet and rested his chin on her knee. As she stroked the gentle giant, she planned the early part of her day and prayed that she could wrap up one or two loose ends. Since the hammer had been found there had been no other attacks and she hoped that was a sign, like in some of the cases she had read about, the person had moved on. It would give them time.

***

"Early kick off?" Smirthwaite appeared at Cyril's office. "Jupiter and Zeus, sir. The penny's finally bloody dropped. Remember when you said, 'By Jove'?" Smirthwaite grinned. "I did some digging."

Cyril looked up from the document he was reading and slipped his glasses onto his head. There was a look of expectancy on his face.

"Jove is another name for Jupiter and Zeus, I feel, was in reference to Ian Tempest. Thunder and lightning and all that." He cocked his head waiting for a response.

"In one, Brian, in one. Hope you didn't lose too much sleep."

"Once I start, I find the search fascinating. It got me thinking that you might have been close to the truth when you were talking about Fletcher and company as Jove is a fallen angel in Milton's Paradise Lost. I wonder who is tempting whom to sin?" Brian pulled a quick grin and a wink and was about to leave.

"They make viable suspects, all the correct history and

208

attributes, but alas, I think on this occasion, we can look elsewhere." He paused and began to spin his glasses in restless hands. "Who interviewed Stephen Firth during the investigation of the garage staff? I can't see a reference in the files." He dropped his glasses before allowing the papers to flick through his fingers.

"I believe he was interviewed initially before Ashton returned. It's there."

"That was cursory and predominantly about the key and the lock-up. What about the man himself?"

"Do you want him in?"

"I'd like to interview him at home, away from work. There are some personal matters I want to discuss. Please set that up and let me know the details."

Brian Smirthwaite raised a thumb and left.

April sat in the Incident Room, pencil in mouth, pondering the details now spread in multi-coloured ink on numerous boards. Even with modern technology there had been nothing found to replace this simple process of correlating information. It allowed time to contemplate and if you stared long enough, something, it was hoped, would jump out at you. It had a well-proven record and Cyril and the team were never going to dispose of something that was so successful. Every few minutes she would swivel on her chair to peruse the next board's contents whilst intermittently scribbling notes onto a pad. There was a general thrum of work from the collective of staff in the background. That noise comprised telephone calls, chatter and the sound from the keyboards all blending to become one, the monotonous and laborious side of a police investigation, a process that continually filtered the finer details of information from various interviews and agencies. It was a reassuring noise that signalled work was continuing at a pace.

To her police work was like fishing. She had baited a number of hooks and cast them. She needed to be patient. Policing was certainly a game for the stoical.

It was the meeting with Trevor Jones that had sparked the nag and it had not subsided. She noted that one of the voices heard by a victim was an actor also named Jones. Was this co-incidental or even relevant? "Who is and where is Robin Collier?" The pencil rattled against her teeth. After working in the pantomime with Jones he could have gone anywhere. They were already searching National Insurance details and tax records. Everyone paid tax or claimed benefits and therefore they would leave a trail that could be easily traced.

Leaning for the phone, she scribbled a note as it rang. "Hi, yes. Collier, families within the Harrogate area in the last sixty years. Also, if you can, the names within those households. We're looking for a Robin Collier. No age known but an estimate is he's now in his forties. Addresses and any other details you can trawl, please. As soon as, yes. Top of the list if you can. Thank you."

This was fairly basic information to retrieve but there was a fear that it would throw up too many Colliers. Having the name Robin would close down the search considerably.

April turned her attention to the interview with Constance Hartley-Lowe. She moved over to the board detailing the lock-up and added the words – *his old Jag* and *trouble with the last tenant.* Who were you? She reached for the phone again and called the Hotel du Vin. She was soon put through to Ashton's room.

"Ashton." There was a lilt in the voice and she was taken aback.

"Mr Ashton, DI Richmond. Sorry to disturb you. Two things if I may. Can you furnish me with the details of the last tenant who rented your apartment?"

"Harold Broadstairs. How could I forget that bastard? Please excuse my French! He left the place like a bomb site. Cost me a lot in repairs and he simply did a bloody flit. Like all things, even when your lot found him, they did nothing. Never again."

"What about the Jaguar you stored there in the lock-up?"

"My wife's big mouth again. I bet she told you I thought more about that car than I did of her." He paused waiting for an answer but none came. "I might have known, you ladies always stick together. Crashed it racing up the hill at Harewood. Look, I was about to go live in France, the divorce was being settled, we were in the process of selling the family home. It had to go. Sold it to Stephen, my manager. He'd always lusted after the old girl. Needed a lot of work to get it back to anything like and I had neither the cash, time nor the inclination. He kept it in the lock-up with my permission for a few months and then ... I believe a friend of his who's a good hammer man is in the process of making the bent bits straight again."

The words *hammer man* hit her like sharp blows. "Do you know the name of this friend?"

"Sorry, wrong way to describe him considering the reason we're having this chat. Lovely man whom I'm sure you've already interviewed. Works for Long Valley

211

Restorations, they lease the building. He worked on it when I kissed the odd straw bale."

"Do we have a name?"

"Yes, Adrian Lovelady. How does one forget a name like that? He's at Long Valley Restorations as I said. What day is it? He'll be there now until four or five."

April put down the phone and as soon as she did it rang. It was the information she had requested. Leaning over she added her password to the computer, searched for the file whilst still in conversation. There were five Colliers listed but positioned at the top of that list was the most promising. The name Robin Collier was clear to see. It was tagged along with the names of his parents and the address. "Thanks." April printed it off. Frazer Collier married Margaret Jenson in 1978, Robin born in 1980. She made a quick calculation. Robin Collier would be forty-one.

Picking up the phone again she rang Constance Hartley-Lowe's number. It was answered by a male voice.

"May I speak to Constance?" April used her Christian name, an informality that she thought might help.

"May I ask who's calling?"

"DI Richmond." There was a long pause until she heard the familiar voice. "Sorry to bother you. You mentioned your husband's car, the racing Jaguar."

"The love of his life, you mean. Yes, but forgive me, I don't understand your fascination with the stupid car, Inspector."

"You know Stephen Firth bought it?"

"Yes, I suggested it. He'd always coveted it. Whether he'll ever get it back to its former glory is another thing. I don't think he has the necessary funds if I know Stephen."

"Did your husband have the car a long time?"

"The second year we were married. It was offered as a trade-in against a Porsche Boxster. I know that, as Philip had promised that car to me when it came in. It was in red but then a customer came offering the Jaguar. There was instant Karma, however." Constance chuckled loudly. "Sorry, I shouldn't laugh. The day the car was due in the owner crashed it quite badly. He was seriously hurt but fortunately, his son, who was having his final ride, was unhurt. The driver wasn't wearing his belts and according to the police report, was travelling at a speed well above the legal limit."

"Your husband still bought the car?" April was growing ever more confused and was beginning to doubt her reasons for asking. It was getting her nowhere.

"A different deal was done with Margaret, his wife."

A cold shiver ran down April's spine as she stared at the name she had just received and printed on the paper before her. "Could you please repeat that name."

"Margaret, can't recall the surname. I used to joke she had taken my car when I saw her and the car on the odd occasion I was in town."

"Her surname wouldn't be Collier, would it?" April's voice was tentative.

"I think it may well have been. How did you know?"

"I'd be grateful if you could share any information about them."

***

Cyril checked his tie in the mirror and ran his fingers through his hair. He hated press calls but he had made the request. The information he would give would be shared on all platforms, giving the broadest sweep. The room had been set aside. Already a number of journalists were present. They chatted and as Cyril entered there was a steady decline in the noise level. He knew many of the journalists and greeted some by name.

The talk to camera followed standard procedure with a request for help from the public. Places and dates were given and details of whom to contact. The words 'clown' and 'man wearing make-up' were constantly repeated. He also mentioned the name, Robin Collier, last seen in the Scarborough area and he gave the date. The video detailing the possible suspect following the man in the red coat was shown as well as still shots of the man with the box. Other close-up images of the box were shown. Cyril knew how important and effective appeals could be. He rounded up by answering questions. On leaving the room he could feel the sweat beneath his armpits. Thinking of the possible suspects in the case, he realised that he would never have made an actor.

Chapter Twenty-Five

April watched as her boss removed his jacket and stopped by the water dispenser. He collected a small paper cup and flicked the tap. The bubbles churned the water within the transparent bottle.

"All go well, sir?"

"My stomach feels like that." He nodded towards the settling bubbles. "It's done. Just need to keep our fingers crossed."

"I've tracked a Robin Collier. Lived in Harrogate as a youth. We have school details and his parents' address. Organised someone to call and chat. We also now know that he travelled to Bradford to work at the Playhouse. He'd been a member of the green room for a couple of years, it's a bit like a training ground for promising child actors. He was always into theatricals at school ever since he was a youngster. Looking at exam results he wasn't too academic. Anyway, he was cast at sixteen in a minor role in J B Priestley's, *An Inspector Calls*."

Cyril turned and raised an eyebrow. "Let's hope he calls again and pronto! Just a minute, I believe the Playhouse suffered a number of fires."

"It did but as they say, the show must go on and it did. Even more interesting is a car that belonged to Ashton was bought from Collier's father, swopped to be accurate. It's now in the hands of Stephen Firth. There's an awful lot of coincidental connections if you ask me." She handed him some notes. "I believe you're seeing Firth today. It might be nothing but there's something ringing an alarm bell in my head. One other thing, whilst checking back on the notes after the interview with Constance Hartley-Lowe, I noticed that she'd asked Firth to deal with the builder as he was messing her around, bullying her really. She mentioned that he'd a bit of a temper and he would hold his own with the man if push came to shove. Anger, sir, is never good especially when you're linked in a case such as this."

Cyril finished the drink and tossed the cup towards the bin. He missed! "Are you seeing Peter Whittle today?"

"Let's hope he's as helpful as Tom Craig."

***

Cyril could not remember the first time he had been to the village of Burnt Yates but he knew the name had always fascinated him. It conjured in his mind a paint pigment but the exact colour escaped him. He parked outside the cottage and checked his notes again. A thin veil of drizzle swept across the road bringing an opacity to his windscreen. It had been threatening most of the day and the clouds had finally surrendered. Firth's car, clearly marked as belonging to Ashton's Garage, was parked to the side of the property.

Cyril saw Firth look through the house window and raise a hand before disappearing. Within seconds the front door opened and Cyril was shown in.

"Not a kind day, Chief Inspector."

"Thanks for seeing me. I know it's your day off." Cyril sat in the seat proffered.

"You've just been on the local news. It's true what they say about the television adding weight to the human form. They say as much as a stone!"

Cyril instinctively breathed in. He was not pleased to hear this. "It's a strange case, Mr Firth. Having the public involved, we find, can bring interesting results. It can also generate the odd crank call but we know how to deal with those; it's about finding a balance. In some way we're trying to formulate a picture of those connected to the attacks even if they are, like yourself, merely coincidental. Being responsible for a key that was found at the places linked with two of the victims puts you squarely within that frame but I know you appreciate that." Cyril saw a frown appear. "We, and I'm sure too your boss, know that the key you hold has been copied. We've made a log of all those who have had it in their possession over the last twelve months. I'm aware you'll not keep a detailed record but you and certain members of your staff will be able to make up an approximate list."

"I believe this has already been done." Firth shuffled uneasily in his chair.

"Indeed." From his inner jacket pocket, Cyril pulled a sheet of paper on which several names were itemised. "Your name is understandably at the very top as you have signed it out the most. However, we also see here the people who signed out the key and returned it. Those people, however, may not give us the whole picture and might not necessarily be the people who, let's say, put the key into the lock. As we know, you gave Paul Lattimer the key so how many others have been off site with it?"

"There's no way I can answer that and you know it."

Firth raised his voice but brought his emotions back in check. "Only those I handed it to."

"You can try by speaking with each one of these people on the list and add any names they are prepared to include. I'll expect your list by the end of the day. Now, we need a few more facts about you, Mr Firth, before we can remove your name from the frame of which we spoke. I'm sure, like us, you would want that. The fewer, the better for all concerned." Cyril saw his head nod. He knew the next question would not be well received. "Why did you leave your wife?"

***

Stuart Park monitored the public's input after the appeal had been released. As expected, one of the first calls was someone admitting to being the person in the video. After a number of pre-planned questions were answered he was considered to be a crank. The number was still stored. Another of the contacts was more positive. They had seen a character laughing whilst standing in front of Stephen King Autos. They wore make-up that gave the impression of being female and yet the clothing was definitely that of a man. An officer had been sent to interview the person further.

***

Firth looked down at the carpet, his hands clasped before him. "I had an affair. Philip offered some staff the opportunity to visit the motor show as a reward for their hard work over the year, hotel, meal and a day at the show. Someone from the group had a bigger mouth than they should have. Philip's secretary ... It just happened and only the once. I guess I took advantage of her having one over

218

the eight."

Cyril said nothing. His patience was rewarded.

"I've not admitted this to anyone but as I didn't have anything to do with the attacks you're investigating, I'm going to tell you something which Ashton's not aware of. Everyone believes Mary, that's my wife, and I parted owing to my infidelity but that's not the case although it was certainly instrumental ... I'm not proud of this you understand ... I used to beat her."

Cyril did not change his facial expression. "Go on."

Firth nodded. "I deeply regret what I did, Chief Inspector. It seemed somehow instinctive and happened since we were first married. If she did anything that upset or embarrassed me, I'd lash out. I know this is no excuse but my father was the same with my own mother. It's what I grew up with. It was the norm, although I knew other kids whose parents didn't fight. Like my dad, I wouldn't mark her. I was careful not to do that. When the one-night stand happened she went back home. It was a mirror of my own upbringing and parents as they eventually separated. The solicitor's letter arrived and a threat of a restraining order soon followed. I was an arrogant bastard then. I don't know, people might think I still am. Philip nearly sacked me. It wasn't the behaviour he expected from his manager but I had the feeling he thought I'd suffered enough with Mary leaving and a lesson had been learned. I never married again and I've patched things up with Mary. She took the house and I had to start all over again."

Cyril wanted to tell him that's how it should be after his own childhood experience but he was not there to judge. "Philip's wife asked you to help with a problem she was having with her builders. Why did she approach you?"

"Because I will not take crap from men who try to bully and hoodwink women."

"Really! You preferred to strike them."

"I told you'd I'd learned a lesson. I don't have to discuss this with you." Firth's raised voice was immediately intimidating. "I can come to the station with a solicitor and your questioning would certainly take a different and less judgemental tone."

"You are controlling this, Mr Firth. What you decide to divulge is your choice. You're not under caution. You are, I hope, trying to aid an investigation into three cruel attacks that resulted in the murder of a young man by being totally open and honest with me."

There was another pause.

"Sometimes you have to go head-to-head and nose-to-nose with some folk. He who can shout the louder often wins with bullies and the builder was certainly that. His workmanship left much to be desired too. Once the court ruled in Constance's favour when the case went to appeal, he changed his tune."

"Did you ever have an affair with Philip's wife?"

"No, I bloody well didn't." Firth quickly brought his emotions under control.

Jekyll and Hyde came to Cyril's mind. It was as if he were moderating his persona, afraid that his true self would show. Cyril believed that he was beginning to understand who Firth really was and he did not relish what he was witnessing.

"We were good friends and when their marriage was failing, I tried to give support. After all, I'd been there and I

220

know she leaned on me for friendship."

"You were also close to Philip and so you had a foot in both camps. She knew that."

"I was loyal to both. It wasn't easy, believe me!"

"This is another area of our investigation. You bought his car, the Jaguar." Cyril leaned back hoping his open body language would help ease the developing tension and allow Firth to relax.

"The one generous thing he did for me. I'd wanted that car since he first got it sorted."

"What can you tell me about a Mr Frazer Collier?"

Firth's jaw dropped. "Is there anything you don't know? Bloody hell, we're going back a lot of years. I remember Collier came with his wife to look at a Porsche we had in the showroom. Strangely, Philip had promised it to his wife but when he saw the Jaguar E-type Collier was offering to trade, his promise evaporated. I had to tell Constance, let's call it a little white lie. I admitted that I'd sold it. Unusually, the paperwork was finalised a couple of days before it was due in at the garage. Collier had a serious crash in the Jag that next morning. I believe they were coming to the garage in the afternoon to carry out the exchange. Philip still took it and Collier's wife received the Boxster. Collier's medical condition had something to do with Philip's out of character and very generous decision. I told Constance another contract was drawn up to compensate for the damage but that wasn't the case. I think it made her feel better about not getting the car. Good publicity for the business, Philip had suggested to everyone else."

"Another white lie. Did you lie often for your boss? Do you still?" Cyril watched as Firth's fists clenched and could hear as he controlled his breathing.

"It saved trouble and sometimes they are necessary. I do as I'm requested providing no law is broken."

"Right! Go on. Tell me about Collier."

"Collier needed a lot of time to recover. Going through a windscreen does not do much for your facial features as I'm sure you're aware. There was some spinal damage but the doctors believed the paralysis would be temporary and they were right in their prognosis. He sold the house in Harrogate and moved with his family to Pool. It was closer to his business. Sadly, from what I heard he was never the same after the crash. I'm sure if you knew about him then you're aware of this."

"Go on, please."

"There was some rumour about his son leaving home a few years later but I never found out the reason. Their address will be on file at the garage as we serviced her car until she got rid of it."

Chapter Twenty-Six

After chatting to Cyril about the physical damage Tom Craig had suffered, particularly to his jaw, it was with a degree of trepidation that April approached the task of meeting with and interviewing Peter Whittle. It was clear after speaking with one of his specialist team, that the facial damage, although considerable, was not as severe as in the two previous cases. However, considering his age, the psychological damage was their main area of concern. She showed the doctors the list of questions she hoped to ask and assured them that the interview would be undertaken with the utmost sensitivity.

Whittle, although bruised extensively around the eyes, looked better than she had expected. There was no wiring to the jaw but the dental damage and swelling to the lips made communicating with any degree of clarity difficult. She had been warned about the subconjunctival haemorrhages to both eyes and that they looked far worse than they were.

"I remember it all as if it happened a moment ago. I'd seen him before you know. I didn't then see the make-up and I hadn't heard his voice." The pronunciation was as expected and he had difficulty controlling the saliva that dribbled from the corners of his mouth but he calmly talked her through the first sighting of his assailant and the initial part of the attack. His memory failed at the point he had felt the first strike.

"The lunatic said, and he was definitely male of that I have no doubt, that he had done this because I didn't wave back to him on that initial meeting. Can you believe that?" Whittle began to sob and he brought the handkerchief he had earlier removed from within his pyjama sleeve to his eyes. "In my job I was dealing with the public on a daily basis, but never have I witnessed what I saw when he came to my door. It was like he was acting, the face and the voice. In my mind it was clearly Pennywise."

"Had you been watching the film that day, Mr Whittle?"

"My wife had an extensive collection of films but no. I was the reader, she loved her films."

"Did you have a copy of the film in DVD in the house?"

Whittle shook his head and winced. "Not that I'm aware of but as I've said my wife had quite a collection. When in the shop … You know I managed a shop in town?"

April smiled and nodded.

"Well, you could have really quiet days and a good book was just perfect. I'd read King's book, borrowed it from the library. It was one of those novels that stays with you long after you've read it. When I see a balloon or a storm drain cover it brings back parts of the novel. Great writer, Stephen King."

"So how did you know it was the character if you haven't seen the film and heard the voice?" April leaned closer.

"The intonation." Saliva shot from his lips towards April. "Sorry, some words are more difficult to manage. My teeth were knocked out but I don't remember when. They were my own too! When I read, I hear the voices of the book's characters. It was in a way, just how I imagined he would speak."

"Did he demand anything?"

"A wave." Whittle raised his hand and demonstrated. "That was it!"

April placed a hand on his. "You've done well, Mr Whittle. If anything comes to you that might help identify your attacker then please get someone to call me." She placed a card containing her number on the bedside cabinet. He began to cry again.

As she left the hospital her phone rang.

"A bit of a breakthrough." It was Stuart Park. "Robert Colliers," he paused. "A call came in following the appeal. Someone knew a Robert Colliers in Scarborough at about the time Robin Collier was kicked out of the pantomime. If you're going to change your name for whatever reason then you could be a bit more imaginative. Apparently, according to the witness, a Jennifer Brown, he was always changing his voice, he was quite the mimic. They had a relationship for about a month and then he just took off. She never saw him again."

"Can she give a description?"

Park chuckled. "Better than that, she's sent a photograph of them together. It's being enhanced. Hopefully, I'm going over to interview her tomorrow. There's no certainty it's Collier but it's the closest we've got."

***

By the end of the day Cyril had the list of those who had used the key to the lock-up. If they were still employed, they had been cross-referenced with information from their earlier interviews. It left two, both signed out by Firth. One was Lattimer, whom they knew but the other was a customer by the name of Wilks. A note was attached explaining the reason. Cyril felt as though he were no further forward.

Owen popped his head round the office door. "Penny for them?"

"Not worth that, Owen. There's something Firth's not telling me but I can't yet fathom it. I will though, you can bet on that."

"No doubt, sir. Sun's well past the yardarm. Pint?"

Owen drove and found a parking spot on Cheltenham Crescent and they went into The Little Ale House.

"I'll get these. You sit. The window seats are empty."

Cyril moved as instructed and Owen soon followed.

"Never tried this but it's local. Cheers!" Their glasses touched. "Missing The Coach, I bet." Owen drank more. "Thanks for coming. We've known for a while, and apart from Hannah's family I wanted you to be the first to know we are going to have a boy. I've been bursting to tell you for a while. Hannah's telling Julie today too. According to the midwife she's doing really well." Owen seemed to glow with pride as he passed on the news.

Cyril put down his pint. "Stand up, Owen."

Owen frowned but did as requested. Out of the blue and certainly out of character, Cyril placed his arms around him and drew him close.

"That's wonderful news, my friend, such wonderful news. My sincere congratulations. Snips and snails. I somehow knew." Taking Owen by the shoulders he moved him away and grabbed his hand. "You don't know just how happy your news has made me."

Looking at Cyril, Owen was convinced he saw a tear in his boss's eye.

"Just brilliant, Owen. You must excuse me. I need the loo."

On his return he placed a bottle of Champagne on the table. "For you and Hannah. I know she's not drinking but when you meet with her mum and dad she might just take a small taste."

Within half an hour Cyril arrived back home. Julie's car was in the usual place. When he opened the front door the smell of cooking drifted along the hallway. "Coming cold out there and just started to rain. Something smells good." There was an ice bucket on the table and two Champagne flutes. He moved to her side as she checked the food in the wok. He kissed her.

"Cupboard love, Bennett. It'll be fifteen minutes."

The smirk on his face said everything. "I believe Hannah gave you the fantastic news."

She nodded. "We were hoping for one made of sugar and spice and all things nice but I guess you know the reality!"

"Sorry, yes. Snips and snails and puppy dogs' tails. Goodness I'm so pleased for them." The mini explosion from the released Champagne cork made them both laugh. "I couldn't be happier if Owen were my son, Julie. How that man has changed during our time together."

Cyril handed her a glass. "To Snip and his two wonderful parents."

This time there was a definite ring as the two flutes touched.

"Julie. I'm not sure as to how you'll take this but I'd like to discuss an idea with you." Cyril sipped more from the glass.

"Don't you dare get bloody broody on me Bennett!"

Chapter Twenty-Seven

The dawn seemed to be coming early as he approached the coast but the town's lights suggested otherwise. Stuart Park had liaised with the area policing team and they knew he would be on their patch. He would be accompanied by a local female police officer for the interview. It was remarkably quiet, other than the banshee screams from the gulls that swooped and dived, often their shadows from the street lights exaggerating their size. He lowered the window and inhaled. There was a freshness, and to him a salt laden flavour but that, he knew, was probably the psychology of expectation. He checked his watch. He was too early. He had calculated the drive would take just over two hours but there was less traffic than anticipated. Grabbing his notes from the passenger seat he worked through the questions he had prepared.

The evening before he had received full details from Government records of a Robert Colliers living in Scarborough at the time he had disappeared. He had been collecting benefits for two months prior to his disappearance. He had not lived there long. Previously, records supported that he had worked at the holiday amusements arcades but only on a temporary basis. No driver's licence details nor passport details were shared; it was assumed he had neither.

"Morning. DC Park?" A short woman in uniform stood by the open window. At that same moment a gull deposited a stream of shit across the bonnet and windscreen of the car. The sound was startling. She leapt back. "Shit!"

It had also made Park jump. The glutinous stream ran down the screen in two rivulets, the white contrasting sharply against the screen. "That's definitely shit! What the hell did that bugger eat?" He turned to look at the officer who was checking her uniform.

"Lucky escape. I'd do the lottery today if I were you, DC Park. Pauline Shirley." She smiled, put out her hand through the open window and waited. Park shook it. Her face registered disappointment. "Most people ask me to repeat it as I have two Christian names."

"I work for an Inspector called David Owen and he's known as Owen. And you?"

She smiled, knowing this would surprise him. "Crab." She raised her eyebrows.

"Crab?" Park climbed from the car. "Because of the sea, like?"

"No, because of Shirley Crabtree, the wrestler. Big Daddy was his ring name. Don't remember when it started but it's stuck."

Within ten minutes they were sitting in the upper flat with Jennifer Brown. The perception he had formed of her from the photograph and the conversation between them was in stark contrast to the woman sitting before them.

"He was great fun to be with. He was working at the arcade on the front and I'd gone after work with a friend. He was standing by the door and we heard Russell Crowe's voice. He did the bit from *The Gladiator,* 'my name is

230

Maximus' and all that. My friend and I couldn't stop laughing. He invited us for a drink when he'd finished. He did all sorts of tricks, took my watch without my knowing and he was a brilliant pickpocket. That's it. Within a week he had moved in. Good guys were hard to find."

"What do you know of his past?" Pauline asked.

"Seriously? Nothing. I didn't ask. Rob told me he was a resting actor. That was fine by me. He'd clean the place when I was at work and then he'd work late afternoon and evening. It was flexible. The cash helped with the rent for a while."

"Rob. You knew him as Rob or Robert?"

"Rob, only Rob. I assumed Robert." She frowned realising for the first time she considered she did not truly know. "How weird is that? I lived with a guy for a month or so and didn't ask that basic question."

"When was this?" Park was beginning to feel a mixture of excitement and caution.

"A few years ago. I moved here maybe 2008 so, 2010. Don't hold me to that." She grinned. "You people need coffee?"

Both rejected the offer. "Tell us about Rob."

She paused, suddenly feeling self-conscious. "Like what? Okay. Good looking, good in bed." She smiled at Pauline. "Really funny with his voices. Amazingly tidy, kind and a good cleaner." She paused briefly and her facial expression reflected concern. "I remember he had an aversion to flashing lights. You'd see his mood change. That's why he left the amusement arcade, the intermittent flashes from some of the machines disturbed him. They had those rotating ones once used on police cars."

"Did he ever become aggressive during this mood change?" Park looked down to desensitise the question.

"He'd go off on his own, tell me he'd see me back here. He needed space. I wondered if he had some kind of epilepsy. He smoked weed and took other things but I didn't push too much. He was a good guy to hang with."

"Other things? Like what?"

"Coke. He loved cocaine."

"Did you too, Jennifer?" Pauline leaned forward. "Don't worry. For us right now what was in your past stays there. We need to find Rob."

"Bits. Just to be sociable."

"Did you know if he dealt drugs at the arcade or around the arcade?"

Jennifer shrugged her shoulders. "I was teaching then and I grew scared I'd be found out and lose my job if he were caught with drugs and living here. I told him that and I didn't want to see drugs in the flat again. As I said, he was kind and complied."

"So why did it end?" Park asked.

Shaking her head, Jennifer explained. "I came home from work and he'd gone, only left a note and a small present." She pointed to the toy rabbit on the chair at the far end of the room.

"I don't suppose you kept the note?" Pauline stood to pick up the rabbit. "May I?"

"Please do and yes. I did keep it, even had it laminated. It was so beautiful."

***

The house set a short way from the road was beautifully traditional. The stone had an aged patina that

232

complemented the mullioned windows along with the moss-speckled stone roof. Owen parked the car on the cobbled drive.

His first impression of Margaret Collier was that she was a perfect match for the house. The pearls, the cashmere cardigan and the tweed skirt made him think of Cordings, a country clothing shop that once graced the entrance of the Westminster Arcade in Harrogate. She proffered no smile, just a stone hard façade, but the welcoming words conveyed a degree more warmth that he did not expect.

"Inspector? It must be serious." She looked at his shoes as he stepped over the threshold. She was not impressed. She directed him through to the conservatory.

"Thanks for seeing me. We're trying to locate your son, Robin."

"Is he in trouble? Would you like tea?"

Why was it when people are faced with difficulties, the first thing they think about is tea? Owen would never understand. "No, thanks. When did you last see Robin, Mrs Collier?"

"Maybe eight years ago but it could be longer. He called here. His father wasn't well. He never fully recovered from a car accident when Robin was young. We managed to keep the business running but only just. My husband changed, Inspector. He was a tough man, hard on Robin. I remember once when a light bulb went at a key moment, he threw it against the wall. He didn't allow me to clean it up even though there were pieces of glass everywhere. He could be totally irrational, a bully some would say. When we were entertaining, he only expected the very best from Robin and from me. He had pushed himself and become quite well off

233

and believed what was good for him was good for all. He never understood why Robin wanted to go into the theatre. He used to say it was for girls and poofs and his son was not going to be seen as either. I knew then they were growing apart. The final straw came when he promised Robin that when he was older, if he were successful at school and attained a higher academic standard, he would give him the car he raced. He did work hard and he did succeed for him. He was never academic. He was blessed with other skills, I felt, but Frazer even broke that promise. He told him it was because I wanted a car that I'd seen in a local garage but that wasn't the truth and Robin knew it. He was heartbroken when he told him over breakfast."

"Was this the Jaguar, the one he crashed?"

"It was like divine retribution. Robin never spoke of it. He was so lucky, unlike his father who sustained severe injuries. We believe he was driving far too fast for the road conditions. Robin could never speak of the accident. They put it down to psychological trauma." She paused as if to reflect on the day of the accident. "Robin had started attending the Bradford Playhouse, their green room and he was successful. They said he was like a duck in water. Did you know he was a natural mimic?"

Owen nodded.

"Stephen Firth, he was the manager of the garage where I bought the car, became a good family friend. He would often drive Frazer to appointments and Robin when he needed to be at the theatre. I'd go too when he was performing. I shouldn't say this but I think Robin thought more of Stephen than he did of his own father."

"Did his father not object?"

"He needed the support and the friendship. He didn't have many friends, Inspector Owen. When Robin turned sixteen or seventeen, he was bigger and stronger than his dad. As I've said, Frazer was half the man and none of the bully he once was."

"I'm sorry to ask this but it is important. How close were you to Stephen Firth?"

Margaret Collier's features demonstrated the full gamut of expressions before settling on one that showed defeat. "Very close indeed for quite a while and that's all I'm saying."

"Did that affect Robin?"

"By eighteen he'd flit the nest. He had a flat in Bradford. I supported him. Later he upped sticks and left. He was taking acting parts wherever he could find them which meant a lot of travelling. I hadn't seen him until he came for a couple of weeks all that time ago. He'd changed. He was always good looking but there was something about him that made me happy he'd come home, but also so pleased when he left. He was like a chameleon, a different voice, a different mood every day. Quite unnerving. I suppose that was the actor in him."

***

Park took the note.

Dearest Jen,

It's the end of the show and I'm afraid there'll be no encore. It's been great, you've been a total star and I'll never forget your warmth and kindness. I can't seem to put down roots and a couple of things have happened that I need to forget. I can't afford to fall in love.

Keep strong. Think of me from time to time.
Much love.
Maximus Decimus Meridius
Usually known as Rob. Xx

"Makes me cry when I read it. He even remembered how we met."

"I need to take this as evidence but it will be returned. I suggest you photograph it and I'll issue a receipt. We'll need the rabbit too as we may be able to check for DNA. We're grateful for your support. Maybe Pauline here can pay you a call if we need further information."

"Will you let me know if you find him?"

Park nodded and smiled but said nothing.

***

Owen continued. "This may come as a shock but we believe your son has committed a number of serious attacks, one of which resulted in death. These were in the Harrogate area, so you may have heard or read about them. We have some DNA traces we're trying to identify and I would like to ask you to provide a DNA sample. It will either clear your son of blame or ..."

Margaret Collier sat for quite some time. She knew in her heart of hearts that Robin had something to do with his father's accident but she was not sure what. She knew for certain the experience had brought about a significant change in him.

"I will, Inspector, providing I can do it here in my own home."

Chapter Twenty-Eight

Cyril stood before the window. Ogden's was the oldest jewellers in Harrogate. He often put his nose against the glass particularly to peruse the pre-owned watches. He could not see what he was looking for. He entered.

***

Cyril was late into the office. Shopping had taken much longer and was not as successful as he had hoped but he was, after receiving assurances from the manager, at least optimistic.

Owen was at his desk, as his boss passed through having recently returned from his visit. He mentioned the interview.

"She said what?" Cyril uncharacteristically tossed his coat onto the chair. "Someone is blowing smoke ..." he didn't finish the sentence. "I want Firth in here as soon as. I want a priority on the DNA sample too."

"Robin's mother believed that he might have had something to do with the accident."

"Like he was driving the car illegally?" Cyril interjected.

"No, looking at the report the father went through the driver's side of the windscreen. She didn't know why but she believed something had occurred, Mother's intuition, maybe. The lad wasn't the same afterwards. Maybe, it's as she thought, it was the burden of guilt."

Cyril lifted his coat and took a seat. Park came in holding the two items, now secured within evidence bags.

"Worth the early start. He was never known to her as Robert, that was presumed because he called himself Rob and the s added to Collier could also be down to a presumption. He fits the bill. Enjoyed drugs, coke and weed. She also believed he might have had epilepsy but she never witnessed a fit of any kind. He'd just upped and left one day when she came home from work."

Cyril looked at the note. "What's with the signing at the end?"

Park explained.

"Get those tested and get it done with some urgency. I want a briefing at …" he looked at his watch, shook his wrist and checked again. "14.30. Incident Room. And Owen …"

"Sir?"

"Bring your mints."

***

The children were back in class when Lee Burrows, the school caretaker tapped on the Headteacher's office door. Karen Shackerly was just eating her lunch after having supervised the dining hall and the playground.

"Sorry to interrupt your lunch but to find you in one place for a few moments is a rarity," he grinned. "You might not have seen the appeal on the local news about the attacks. Murder, one of the victims has succumbed to his injuries. Only nineteen too."

"Don't stand at the door, come in. I've nearly finished. I hadn't seen the report."

"They're looking for someone whose known for his impressions, also on the latest attack he might have worn make-up, possibly made up as a clown. Got me thinking about the entertainer we had in school."

She smiled. Lee could natter for England if she let him but she had much to do and she was teaching in twenty minutes. "Mr Simulacrum? He was good." She opened her top drawer and withdrew the flyer he had given to her. She pushed it across the table. "Children's entertainer."

"I'm not too bright, Karen, but when I saw the police appeal it came to me in a flash. The make-up, the voices and he was good but it was his stage name if I remember it correctly, Mr Simulacrum. I wrote it down that afternoon as I thought he was marvellous and as my kid's birthday's next month I thought I'd book him."

"Good idea, Lee. Now I must finish this before" – she looked at the clock – "2 and I'm taking Year Six."

"It's just that the victims, see, had their faces damaged and nothing else. The police didn't tell us that but a mate of mine did who cleans at the hospital. Anyway, you know what the meaning of simulacrum is?"

She shook her head.

"I checked it online. It's a representation or imitation of someone of something – even a face." He paused hoping that she would see the same lightbulb moment he had but she did not.

"I don't think that's truly accurate ... Another Headteacher recommended him to me and when he was at his school, he was Mr Whizzo. He has different personas for different performances, then he was dressed in a one-piece sparkly space uniform."

The school secretary knocked. "Sorry! Lee, a girl in Year Four has been violently sick in the corridor and we need it sorting."

"May I keep this?" He held up the flyer and received a nod.

Lee left and Karen looked up with a degree of relief. *There is a God after all,* she thought. *Thank you, Year Four.*

***

Cyril was not in the best of moods as he entered the Incident Room. Those who needed to attend were there. April was finalising the addition of some details to one of the boards.

"Right! Let's go through this in turn and share not only what we've discovered but our thoughts on that information. I feel as though we're getting warm and what makes me confident of that is the fact that we're now seeing that one or two of the people involved are not telling the truth, the whole truth and nothing but. One is a certain Stephen Firth. It's clear that he was carrying on with Robin's mother after the accident. Robin took quite a liking to him but that may be understandable considering the bullying he suffered at his father's hands. Firth's coming in this afternoon to chat. April if you'll join us?"

She smiled. "My pleasure." She flicked through her notes. "Trevor Jones is a bit of an anomaly too and I felt very uncomfortable when we interviewed him. Child entertainer. His details are in your files. Clearly linked with Robin Collier in the past or shall we call him Robert Colliers? Can we take it they might well have been the same person? Supported the link with drugs there too as we also discovered from his then girlfriend. That addiction may have encouraged some strange and aggressive behaviour. According to Jones, he didn't suffer fools although acted the fool socially and professionally. Jones was the other ugly sister. He suggested they were not that close but my instincts contradict that."

Owen chipped in. "He now changes his appearance and sexuality depending on his morning mood but protests he's straight."

April nodded. "According to Jones, Collier suffered serious hormonal mood swings too and could be aggressive."

"When did they last meet?" Cyril asked.

"Not for some time if he's to be believed." April closed her file.

"Do you want him in for further questions?" Cyril enquired whilst twiddling with his pencil.

"Maybe interview him again at home if he doesn't get back to me with the contact details he promised."

"We have a definite DNA link with Constance from Tom Craig's flat but that's hardly surprising considering their relationship. According to his neighbours, a posh lady with a fancy car stayed over on occasion."

Those present went through their findings and a prolonged discussion followed. The two recent DNA samples would, they hoped, steer the direction of the investigation.

Chapter Twenty-Nine

Cyril and April were already in the Interview Room when Firth was shown in. He was immediately cautioned but informed that he was not under arrest. If he wanted a solicitor present then it could be arranged. He declined.

"I've nothing to hide. I've been fully co-operative." There was an air of arrogance about his defensive tone linked to that of his body language that both Cyril and April noted.

"So why did you not tell us the whole truth?" April was the first to probe his defences.

Cyril followed in quick succession. "It's been evident throughout this case that a number of people involved may not have had the best start in life. We understand, Mr Firth, that we cannot control the cards we are dealt at birth. We can only play the best hand we can from the cards we have. Would you agree?"

"Couldn't argue with that. I don't see what that has to do with me." Firth looked puzzled but also flustered and his discomfort was clearly visible. This was not the questioning he had anticipated.

"So, if we're metaphorically showing our hand, then my first card for you to counter is ..." he paused for maximum impact. "Mrs Margaret Collier." Cyril immediately sat back and refused to take his eyes from Firth.

"Collier? Margaret? I told you. The Colliers traded in the

Jaguar and she got the Porsche."

"But she received much more than that didn't she, Mr Firth." April's gentle voice contrasted with that of Cyril. "When did the affair or, to make it sound more respectable considering her husband's condition, your liaison begin?"

"I demonstrated the car to her. One thing led to another. That's not against the law as far as I'm aware. I met Robin, their son, at their home. She'd invited me to call if I were passing. Frazer was still in hospital. Robin wasn't interested in the Porsche which I thought was unusual for a lad of his age. At first, I anticipated he might put two and two together but I don't think he did. Margaret and I were very subtle." The speech was rushed and rambling.

"First the secretary and then a client. This infidelity happen often, Mr Firth?" Cyril fiddled with his pen.

"I tried very hard to help the family." His voice tried to convey a degree of innocence and benevolence but it was clearly swathed within a cloak of guilty body language.

"Yes, I believe you helped Robin and Frazer? Took Robin to the theatre and Frazer to his numerous appointments when they needed support? It says that here in the report."

"As I said, and you'll not believe this, I liked the lad and Frazer was now meek in comparison to his old self. When Robin left, I realised she couldn't and wouldn't leave her husband. She no longer needed me and I knew that there was little hope."

"You saw the house and the relative wealth and played a game of chance?"

"Not exactly. Things just developed the way they did. I've no regrets. It was good whilst it lasted for the four of us."

"Have you seen Robin since that time?" April stood and leaned against the far wall. Firth's lips moved as if they were trying to formulate the words he wanted to express, but knew the ones he should not utter.

"A couple of times, yes, but goodness, I've not seen him in the last few years."

"I wish you'd mentioned this at the start." Cyril shuffled the papers in front of him and looked up at April before nodding as if giving her a cue.

"Mr Firth, I'd also like to ask you to take a drug test and I'd like a DNA swab too. The swab will allow us to eliminate you from samples discovered at two of the crime scenes. After all, as you said, you're innocent so that shouldn't be an issue."

"So why drugs?" Firth's body stiffened.

"We believe you are or were a drug user. Is that true? Remember, Mr Firth, you've been cautioned."

"How do I answer this?"

"Honestly, I would say," April advised. "We know you drove here but we can turn a blind eye to that. If you're driving today under the influence we'll ensure you get home."

He nodded. "Only occasionally, now. When I split from my wife I did quite a lot. I soon realised I was going down the pan and pulled myself together. Occasional weed now and I mean occasional."

"We'll spare you the test." Cyril glanced across at April. "Owing to your honesty. Please sort the DNA, April."

***

The forensic results from the note examined by the graphologist clearly demonstrated certain character traits of its author. Brian Smirthwaite jotted down notes as she spoke on the phone. He had a copy of the note left in the Scarborough flat and also that left with Tom Craig.

"Forensic analysis of the style confirms them to be likely by one and the same hand. Considering the time difference between their writing, it demonstrates convincing similarities. The earlier Scarborough note tells us a good deal about the author. We can be sure that we have an insecure, fragile, revengeful, cold male with an inability to form friendships freely. The writing is in short, staccato sentences, the theatrical terms mixed with the occasional attempt at a compliment tell us there is no love conveyed in the epistle. However, there is clearly envy, uncertainty and guilt. He references two incidents. I suggest they are the beatings that killed the youths and those actions which have evidently brought regret and confusion to his existence that may well have been the catalyst for the swift departure. The character he portrayed from *Gladiator* when he met the recipient, then in his final communication with her, reveals he's a man who has, in the past, been betrayed and is seeking some kind of revenge and retribution. By signing it with that name he is clearly acting out the part, and this is my professional hypothesis based on my years of working within this field; I believe that something triggers his actions and I hazard, and this I cannot substantiate, puts himself in harm's way to trigger it. He's a masochist."

"Are you saying he knows what triggers his aggression and he searches it out?"

"He also regrets his actions once they've been committed. He hides behind characters. He's not committing the act of aggression himself, the character is."

"And the trigger?"

"I interpret the content and try to find answers. As I've said, it's only my thoughts based on years of experience. I have no idea what the trigger is. To some it's watching pornography, others certain pieces of music even colours but I cannot say. I've a full report ready to send but wanted you to have a preview, a heads-up as they say on police television shows." She giggled. "You have my number."

**

The results of Margaret Collier's DNA test demonstrated a mitochondrial DNA connection with the samples found at the crime scenes. Robin Collier had at some time been at all three sites. Cyril waltzed into the Incident Room holding the printed evidence but it was not fresh news. Those there had also seen it.

"We're bloody well closing in on this bastard. I'm certain the note and toy rabbit will release their secrets too."

"Just need to find a Robert Colliers," Park said with little enthusiasm in his voice.

"'Chameleon,' that's what his mother said. He hid behind different faces and voices from one day to the next. He's changed his name and probably continues to do so as he moves around," Owen pointed out.

"Not easy. You need a National Insurance number and references, driver's licence and stuff," a voice to the side added.

"How many fake doctors are found? Paid by the NHS. Some arriving here on false passports and with false papers. It's easy. There are many still to be discovered. To get the stuff you just need to know where to look and trust the people from whom you make the purchase," Grimshaw announced, a degree of frustration in his answer.

"Adrian Lovelady has been working for Firth rebuilding the Jaguar. Works from home in his spare time. He will be paid when the car is sold at auction. Known Firth and Ashton a number of years, the restoration workshop is leased from Ashton's company. I've no reason to believe there's any involvement other than professional." Shakti added.

"Could the hammer have come from there?"

"Check. Show him. He'd know. Do it today," Cyril instructed, frustration clear within the demand.

"Sir." April raised a hand to her mouth and then spoke thoughtfully as if she were thinking as she spoke. "We need to be careful we're not putting a square peg into a round hole. We have too many pieces falling suddenly into place and yet the main suspect, Collier, cannot be traced. We showed his mother the photograph Jennifer Brown gave us. It was definitely her son. However, Jones was there, in Scarborough and Bridlington at that time too. From our interview with Jones, I believe he knew more about Collier than he should considering the short time they worked together. I have a feeling that they were closer than he was making out. Maybe he's concealing something. Maybe he knows more about Collier than we think. Why did he move to Harrogate? Did they move together? He certainly knew about the two murders and made a joke that Collier might have been getting equal with his critics."

Cyril tapped the table. "Dig a little further. Do we have a

photograph of Trevor Jones?"

April nodded. "From his website."

Cyril turned to Stuart Park. "Show the photograph of Jones to Jennifer Brown and see if she remembers him. Do it personally. You'll be returning her property I take it?"

Park agreed.

Chapter Thirty

Lee Burrows picked up the flyer, checked the number and dialled. It rang but quickly went to answerphone.

"Children's entertainer. Thank you for your interest. Sorry I can't get to the phone just now. Please leave your details and I'll get back to you in a flash."

Burrows did as he was requested. He also took the opportunity to mention that he had seen the act at St John's Primary School and how much he had enjoyed it. He wanted to make a booking for his son's birthday. He hung up.

Within ten minutes Lee's phone rang.

"You just called, Mr Burrows. Sorry I missed you. You wish to make a booking?"

Burrows gave the date and apologised for its being imminent. There was a pause whilst the diary was checked. "Yes, I'll have to get back to you. If I can, do you want five until six or earlier?

A time was agreed. "You came to school as Mr Simulacrum, a great show. I must ask, why the name?"

"Curiosity killed the cat, Mr Burrows." The voice of Blofeld from the James Bond films was instantly recognisable. There was a pause followed by a chuckle.

"Very good. I hope you're not stroking a white cat too."

"No, allergic to our feline friends. Simulacrum – it's because I can be me but then also whoever I want to be, a representation of someone else. I can hide my fears behind a vocal or made up mask."

"The police are looking for someone who does just that, but then I guess you've seen the appeal on the news and social media?"

"No. No, I haven't. Checking again, Mr Burrows, I can do that date. Now, I must get on. Let's just confirm the time, date and I'll need your address."

***

Lovelady handled the hammer. He held the head and then the shaft allowing it to balance within his hand. "Bloody hell! You showed me a photograph. Is this the same one?"

Owen nodded.

Holding it to the light he withdrew another slightly larger pein hammer from the rack; his name block printed on the shaft. "It was once mine. This is where the name was. It was replaced by ..." He allowed his finger to run along the line. "That one. It's not the same. I never bought a replacement. I now use these. As I told you last time, if it's not nailed down, someone will nick it."

"Do you ever take it away from here?"

"If working at home, yes but then ..." He paused. "No. I'm careful. It would have come back here to the rack." The thought of the lock-up brought a discomfort to his stomach. "I think we need to talk, officer."

After a few moments it soon became clear.

"So, Stephen Firth let you have the key to the lock-up?" Owen asked.

"Yes, he couldn't really say no as his car was cluttering my garage. I knew about it because I'd been to inspect the Jaguar after Firth bought it years ago. He had it stored until he could afford to get it sorted. I knew Ashton's was empty unless they were storing the odd motor. The Jag eventually ended up at my place. I have a double garage workshop at home, but when mates wanted me to knock the panels of their cars into shape, I needed to borrow the key to the lock-up."

"What you're trying to say is that you could have left the hammer there."

He nodded. "Unlikely, but possibly. Maybe. Yes, I could. It looks to be one of mine."

***

Michael Stockwell had arranged for Tom's flat to be professionally cleaned. The blood on the carpet was now gone. He walked his colleague up the stairs.

"Not going to be easy, buddy, but then life never is." The door was ajar. "You go in. Someone is there."

Tom Craig turned to look at him. "Like this?" He pointed to his damaged face, the dark glasses still protecting his light sensitive eyes.

Michael tapped his metal leg. "A war wound, like mine. It's still you inside. Now go in so I can bugger off. Some of us still have work to do as you will all too soon."

Constance stood at the end of the hallway. "I've missed you, soldier!" Her voice was reassuring. "Thank goodness you're home."

Tears immediately rolled down his cheeks and he sobbed before she moved closer and embraced him. "We're going to mine. There are too many ghosts here."

251

***

On Owen's return to the station, he checked the list of those who had been trusted with the key. Adrian Lovelady's name was not on the list. He moved through to Cyril's office.

"Bloody hell fire! Does Firth do anything but lie?" Cyril stubbed the pencil point into the note pad.

"Probably afraid if Ashton found out, particularly after the debacle with the young soldier, he'd have been down the road."

"Debacle, Owen?" A smile came to Cyril's lips surprised by the vocabulary of his colleague.

"An ignominious failure, sir, some might say fiasco. Is that not what it was?"

"Keen as mustard, Owen, that's all I can say. Whatever you had for breakfast have it tomorrow. Before the first attack our man knew about and used the garage. We need to know the last time Lovelady used the place."

Owen checked the file. "He thought about a month ago. He can't give an exact date."

Chapter Thirty-One

Lee Burrows popped his head round the Headteacher's door. "The entertainer we had is coming on Wednesday. Our lad doesn't know and he's got six friends coming. I'm looking forward to it, hope it's a repeat performance. He was good to do it at such short notice. I told him what I'd heard about the police looking for someone who was an impressionist. He suddenly realised he'd made a mistake with his bookings and was actually free. I'm glad I mentioned the police announcement. He's coming as a clown, popping in my home this afternoon." He checked his watch. "Coming to check the space we have for the party. Must fly."

Mrs Shackerly watched him leave. Something did not sit right. She checked her diary for the date he had performed at school. There was no name just *Children's entertainer* and the fee. She had paid cash and received a receipt. Moving through to the secretary's room she went to the file. The signature was illegible, a squiggle at best.

She checked the police Facebook page requesting information and watched DCI Bennett's appeal. She quickly found the designated details to the link and picking up the phone she dialled 101 and the option number as directed. It was answered and she asked for the officer mentioned in the request for help.

"DC Stuart Park, please." She waited.

"DC Park. Thank you for calling. How may I help?"

She explained her concerns and apologised for not mentioning it on first hearing their appeal. "I foolishly don't know who he is. We knew him as the children's entertainer. I understood he was Garda vetted to work within this authority. I even paid cash which is something I rarely do. Everything now seems so wrong somehow."

"Do you have a contact number?" Park asked.

"Yes, it's a mobile. He's meeting with my caretaker this afternoon at two to organise a children's party for his son." She gave the address.

Park checked the time and immediately called for assistance to be sent before calling Cyril.

"Get a car. I'll be down in two minutes," Cyril instructed as he grabbed his jacket.

On his arrival, an estate car was parked on the road hemmed in by two police vehicles. The flashing blue lights still active. The front door of the house was open. Cyril entered whilst slipping on gloves. Lee Burrows was sitting on a chair in the dining room. The towel wrapped around his head was clearly bloodstained. An officer was with him.

"Made a bolt through the back and probably jumped over the fence. Called it in and we have three in pursuit."

"Send for a dog and I want it urgently."

Burrows looked as Cyril pulled up a chair. Park went outside. He looked at the shed and the fence at the bottom of the garden but then let his eyes search the rest of the space. Large evergreens bordered the sides of the lawn. He paused.

Inside, Lee was speaking. "He was bloody scary. Made up like a clown. He said my name and stepped inside. He suddenly started juggling with three of them." He pointed to the two juggler's clubs on the floor. "It was the laugh. Evil, absolutely bloody evil. He just grabbed two in his left hand and swiped me with the third. Had it not been for the sound of the sirens I think he'd have killed me."

Cyril took out a clean tissue and lifted one of the clubs. It was heavier than he had expected. "That was not his intention but still there would not have been a good outcome. Did he say anything?"

Burrows nodded and immediately regretted his action and pulled a face. "He said that 'I'd made him see red', those were his words but they were mixed with laughs and squeals as if he wasn't in control."

Outside, Park stood. The garden was eerily quiet. He moved to the left of the lawn and crouched down. It was then he heard the faint sound of somebody counting. The dog handler appeared round the side of the house. Park moved away as the dog went straight to the border before growling and barking. The bushes separated and a clown's face appeared. The dog darted forward but was held by the leash.

"I'll kill you all!" The voice of Pennywise broke into a laugh.

The dog strained even harder against the stretched leash.

Park saw him raise the club. The clown's voice changed. "On my signal unleash Hell!" It was clearly the voice of Russell Crowe.

The handler looked at the laughing clown and then at Park. "What the fuck's going on?"

The clown disappeared back into the bushes.

"Release the dog!" Park's voice was calm as the dog leapt forward quickly followed by the handler.

The back end of the police dog was now down as it tugged, pulled and growled before there was a sudden scream. "Stop it! Please!"

The dog pulled the falling figure through the foliage and onto the lawn. The handler grabbed the dog and instructed it to release. It did with only slight reluctance as Park secured the man's hands.

Cyril looked from the kitchen window. The clown stared back, his make-up smudged and tears of black running down his white cheeks.

Chapter Thirty-Two

April, Owen and Cyril looked at the CCTV of the man handcuffed in Interview Room 2. The make-up had run giving him an even more disturbing appearance. All the while he talked to nobody, his voice jumping from one character to another. He would then begin to count, shout and call out colours.

Cyril turned to April. "You had a nag about this character."

"It's Trevor Jones, one of the entertainers we interviewed recently, he worked with Robin Collier in Bridlington. You're right, sir, things didn't sit right with me."

"But is it Jones or is it Collier?" Cyril asked. "The ugly sisters. Maybe one has taken over the other's identity. As you said, April, and correct me if I'm wrong, he knew more than he should have done about Collier considering the time they were working together."

Owen turned to Cyril. "I checked missing persons and neither Robin Collier nor a Trevor Jones were listed. Besides it would have been thrown up on the system had they been. DNA will tell us who he is. The blood the dog drew has been sent for analysis and they took a further sample during the medical intervention. Testing for drugs. When Park showed Jennifer Brown the photograph, she remembered them as mates. They were close."

"The plot thickens. April. You're with me. Let's see what he remembers. I'll call him Jones and you Collier. You watch from here, Owen. We'll call if we need you. Before we do ..." Cyril collected his iPad and found a specific clip from the film *Gladiator*. They entered the room. An officer stood directly behind the suspect.

Cyril played the clip.

"Maximus Decimus ..." Crowe's voice was clear.

"You know my name even when I'm wearing make-up." He turned and leaned towards April. "Inspector Richmond. It's been a while, well a day or so. It's always good to see a pretty face. I like faces. Do you like mine?" He thrust his tongue in and out of his mouth.

She was neither phased nor intimidated and she saw that brought a degree of confusion.

"Different from the last one I saw, Mr Collier or shall I call you Robin?"

He sat back and did not flinch. "You can call me what the fuck you like. Maximus would be good but I can be so many people. I choose. I am who I want to be. Mr Simulacrum, that's me! I can change my identity as easily as you change your clothes."

"How about an Ugly Sister, Mr Jones. You've been there many times. Or may I call you Trevor?"

"Like I told her, Maximus. Did you not listen? Ugly Sisters? The audience have to boo you, hiss and shout dreadful things. Not a part I loved. I could have been anything. I was good too. My father was against my theatrical dreams."

"What was your father's name, Trevor?"

"James."

April chipped in. "What was your father's name Robin?"

"Frank … Frazer. I called him Frank. It was my pet name. Never had a pet. Cats make me come out in a rash and dog's bite." He looked at the bandaged arm.

"What about your father's car, Trevor?"

He shook his head. "My father had a motorbike, cold, wet and totally uncivilised."

"And yours Robin? You loved it and he promised it to you but then …"

"Sold it. It was a racing car."

"What car was it?"

There was a long pause. "I forget. Fast though. He went through the window, my father that is, turned red. It was the flashing light. Just a touch of the wheel and that was that and I could go to the theatre. No more shouting and pointing his finger. Firth helped but he was shagging mum. He didn't think I knew but I did. He'd have been next had the little man from school not twigged. Bastard."

"You can be who you want to be?" April's voice lowered as she asked the question.

"I can. Robin killed two, he told me. He was always so good I admired him, wanted to be him. If he could do that, take life, then so could I but better more subtle. I just wanted to stop them smiling. I could be Robin but also still be me. Robin felt remorse when he had done it. He said he didn't know why. That was a little white lie he told me about the lights, the colours, the red. I admired him when he stood up to that bitch at the panto. I knew I was in control, better." He looked at Cyril for confirmation but none came.

"Lights. Tell me about the lights." April asked.

"You know about the lights. Who told you?" He laughed

bringing his knees up to the edge of the table – a child-like action and pulled a face. "When they flash, they make me so angry. I see red you know. I do things I shouldn't. I hate people with two faces, the Janus figures who live amongst us, those who say one thing and do the opposite. Then there's the people who point. My father used to point when he was angry and then if people don't wave when I wave, I see red. It's my job to change them. I can you know. It's so easy. I make them into someone else, someone good. Dad was good after the accident. He never shouted or wagged his finger."

"But you have more than one face." Cyril leaned back.

"I create them. I bring them from the films to suit my needs. I control them. That's the difference. I'm no Janus."

"What did you do to Robin, Trevor?"

"I worked with Robin, shared a flat in Scarborough for a time until he found a woman, Jennifer Brown. Even she was a colour. She enticed him. He was never happy. He vanished. Did you not know that? Poof and he was gone, like drops of rain. Pure magic! Let's just say he was frozen in time bit by tiny little bit." He brought a fake shiver to his whole body and started to sing a song from the film *Frozen*. "Robin told me that when you are hurting you talk. Once I knew his weakness, the flashing light, it was easy. We met again and he stayed. We talked and talked. He was bitter and confused. I tried the lights, the flashing – lights, camera, action but – I just had to pretend and find the next person in red."

"You came to Harrogate because of Robin?" April quizzed.

"It was where he came from. He liked the idea. He liked

the posters. You liked them too." He leaned towards April. "He's in them with me. We're still together."

"Did you kill Robin?"

There was a pause. Jones placed a finger on his smudged lips as if in thought. He giggled.

"Did I kill cock robin?" His voice became that of Richard Burton. "No. Two ugly sisters just became one. We blended together as if by pure magic."

Cyril had heard enough. "He's a chameleon living in a fantasy world, living Robin's life as well as his own. He thinks he's another person living another life in another place and will, I have no doubt, change that whenever he chooses." He called for a second officer to remain in the room. He and April met Owen in the next room. They stared at the CCTV screen. Jones had spread himself over the table with his hands on his head. Cyril knew that he was looking at Trevor Jones. "Remove the make-up and photograph him. Charge him too. I want a psychological report as soon as. He's clearly delusional."

"What colour jacket was Craig wearing the morning the runner bumped into him? Pound to a penny says it was red." Cyril had answered his own question.

Chapter Thirty-Three

Within three hours Trevor Jones's home had been sealed and a forensic team was methodically working their way through. Cyril sat opposite Stephen Firth. He slid the photograph which had been taken earlier. "Is this Robin Collier?"

"No."

"Seen him before, Mr Firth? Let me remind you that you're still under caution."

"I have. I purchase the occasional drugs from him. I don't know his name or anything about him and to be honest I used to leave money in the lock-up and he'd deposit what I needed. It was private and convenient. I was introduced to him through Latham or as we found out Lattimer. I had the key cut, others I can't say. The lad who was murdered must have been dossing there or taken the money or drugs. I don't know. He gave me the bloody creeps I remember that."

Cyril was neither surprised nor fully convinced. "You know your friend Lovelady used the garage and that's how the hammer was left there, the murder weapon?"

"Shit. Am I in trouble?"

The naivety of Firth's question failed to surprise Cyril. "I believe the lad Coffrey did the drop and collections for our friend here. It was simple. He paid him in small packets of cannabis, maybe even cash. He made a mistake of staying over a couple of nights when he had nowhere else to sleep and it was seen and reported. Was that to you, Stephen, and you passed the message on?"

Firth shook his head. "No!"

"The nights are cold at this time of the year and when you've been thrown out of your temporary accommodation you look for any kind of shelter and the lock-up was perfect, until you upset someone, that is. He broke the rules. So, you want to know if you're in trouble? I think so. Right up to here." Cyril put his hand to his throat.

***

"We have evidence that both Firth and Lovelady were at the lock-up but there's no DNA trace elsewhere. The sample taken from Jones does not match that found at the crime scenes and yet we know he is the perp."

As Cyril was speaking, his mobile phone rang. "Bennett." He listened whilst looking at the group before him. He hung up and placed the phone on the desk. "Forensics have located samples of DNA, probably from scrapings of the inner cheek or saliva, stored within an ice-cube tray within Jones's freezer. They tell me that the solution was slightly saline which is an effective way of storing, transporting and depositing DNA. If the cube were left on the victim's body or a carpet it would melt and you have the same DNA. There were bags of hair too. The mobile phones belonging to the three victims were also located as well as a shoe box containing a news report of the accident and other personal items belonging to Collier."

"Collier's DNA?" April asked what the rest were thinking.

"The reason for doing this is without any certainty," Cyril glanced at the line he had written a number of days before. *The uncertainty of reason!*

"So, the million-dollar question, sir. Where is Collier?" As he spoke, Park leaned over and dropped a packet of extra strong mints next to Cyril's phone. "Reward, sir."

Cyril looked up. The smile not only showed relief but gratitude.

Smirthwaite stood as if taking centre stage. "Here's a scenario for you. Thought about this often when my wife buggered off with my so-called mate. Funny how I suddenly wanted to take a life. There was once an advert showing a dripping tap – bit by bit it disappears was the main idea – you might recall it? There are hundreds of miles of canals, rivers, roads and motorways. If I'd killed her, I thought I could cut her into many pieces, really small pieces and freeze them. I could then pop the bits in a cool box and deposit them in a variety of locations wherever I was travelling. A walk along the canal, down the roadside drain, in a deserted hedgerow, a river or the sea."

"Like drops of rain. If they were small enough, you'd never find them," an officer added with a chuckle.

Cyril popped a mint in his mouth. "This could have been some time ago too and if the person wasn't lost or registered missing, their disappearance would not be investigated."

His phone rang again. He listened. "Body parts have been located in the garden. We'll know once the tests have been done. A neighbour has mentioned that two people were living there twelve months back but one hadn't been seen for some time."

"If it is Collier, I wonder what brought him back to Harrogate." Owen asked.

"Whatever it was, he'd shared much of his life story with Jones. The flashing light trigger was something Collier suffered, I feel sure of that. He probably killed the two in Scarborough. Jones's mental instability allowed him to take it up. Make use of it. Maybe some complex form of hypochondria, who knows. Those who know the human mind better than we do may find the answers."

April popped a photograph in front of Cyril. "The jacket worn by Craig on that morning. You were right. Red." She also had a framed poster. She pointed to the painted figures depicted in a pantomime scene. "Recognise any of these?"

Both men moved over as Cyril dropped his glasses onto his nose. He paused and looked at April before Owen pointed to the largest figure. "That's Jones! Collier?"

April nodded. "Check your files. That's Jennifer Brown and we have Joker and the actor from *Field of Dreams*. There's even Stephen King."

Cyril pointed to the small image of the clown's car, an E-type Jaguar. It's all here. The full story, April."

"Yes, I looked at this in his flat and I didn't see that the whole case was staring me in the face."

Cyril shook his head. "You couldn't make this up! You knew though. You had your nag."

***

Philip Ashton stood looking at the flowerbed at the front of his hotel. The day was bright yet cold. There was still a crispness in the air although no frost was visible on the swathes of grass. The Aston Martin was parked at an angle. He checked his watch and looked up towards the church. Seeing Bennett, he walked to meet him, his hand outstretched.

"Detective Chief Inspector. Thank you for your message. All has been secured with a new garage door and one set of keys." He tapped his pocket. "You've got him I hear?"

Cyril smiled. "And what of your Mr Firth?"

"He's no longer my responsibility. I have to say a number of my employees were rather pleased with the sacking. What will happen to him? I believe he's been bailed."

"9(1)(b) Withholding information. Fine or imprisonment. We will have to see. He could have made our life a lot easier and his reluctance or fear of losing his job might have endangered life. We'll see what the court says. I'd like to thank you for your co-operation." Cyril turned and then paused. "What about the Jaguar? The thing that may have started all of this?"

Ashton laughed. "I'll be paying for the rebuild. I gave Firth what he paid and it will be painted black and auctioned, the proceeds going to the local hospice. At least that way the honest folk don't lose out and maybe we can benefit the community."

Cyril nodded his approval. "Safe travelling."

***

The office seemed quiet. It always did after a case was concluded. It gave Cyril time to reflect. He considered the outcome and contemplated the missed opportunities, opportunities that might have brought a swifter resolution to the case. He thought of the patterns that had been inaccurately assumed, the frailty of the many characters and the lies given in fear. All human traits. He then thought of the positives. They had caught the perpetrator. He had justified the human resources required. April knew first. It was there, she had the nag. That was something you could not be taught. He would be sad to see her move on. All in all, it was a result of creative, solid police work. He had a good team. He smiled and opened his drawer for a mint.

Chapter Thirty-Four

Cyril did not stop and look in Ogden's window but entered the shop. Within thirty minutes he was home.

"What time are we collecting Hannah and Owen?" Julie asked whilst putting the back to an earring. "Dad's driving so we can have a drink. He's coming back for us at ten."

Cyril looked at his watch. It seemed so different. "In twenty minutes."

Owen sat in the front of the old Bentley, Hannah, Julie and Cyril in the back. He looked straight ahead frightened he would turn green before their arrival at Grantley Hall.

"I nearly hired a chauffer's outfit for the evening." Julie's father kissed her on the cheek. "I'll be here at ten. Have a wonderful time and congratulations you two!"

Hannah gave him a hug and whispered her thanks.

The meal had been wonderful and they waited for the cheese to arrive. Cyril swished the wine round in the glass, he needed to move his hand.

"We've chosen a name for the sprog." Owen's eyes glistened with pride. "You tell them, Hannah."

"Christopher after my father, Cyril, after someone Owen works with." She laughed at Owen. "The bump will be christened, Christopher Cyril. Maybe if we marry, we can tag Owen on the end of that!"

Hannah slipped her hand onto his as he saw Cyril begin

to fill up.

"I'm so proud. Thank you. An old-fashioned name but …"

"New watch?" Owen asked pointing to Cyril's wrist trying to make him feel more comfortable.

Cyril looked at Julie and she took a parcel from her bag, leaned over and placed it in front of Owen. He looked at them both.

He unwrapped it slowly to reveal a green box with the word *Rolex* printed in gold letters. He lifted the lid. The Explorer 2 looked brand new. "This was yours, your fortieth present?"

"I bought that the year we started working together. It's a time that has been special. You have been a wonderful colleague and friend. There's a note there too but it's for Christopher."

Owen unfolded the paper. The note was handwritten:

I have given my watch to you and your father, my dearest friend. He will be its custodian to wear throughout your happy childhood. He and your mother will determine the correct time when it will become yours, hopefully to cherish. I pray when you receive this you will feel as proud of your parents as we do and that every occasion you seek the time you will remember with pride and thanks the commitment and love they have given to you.

Cyril Vaughan Bennett
Julie Bennett.

Owen stood and came around the table. Cyril stood. They hugged.

"It's our pleasure to give this to Christopher. You need to wear it."

Owen slipped on the watch. He looked at Julie, then Cyril and then at the watch before shaking his wrist. "Bloody hell, sir, it's got a memory too!"

Featured Artist

Reginald Charles Brundrit R.A.
(1883 – 1960)

Reginald Brundrit was born in Liverpool. He was a painter in both oil and watercolour having been trained at the Bradford School of Art and The Slade School of Fine Art under the animal painter and sculptor John M Swan and Wilson Steer.

He was the founder member of the Wharfdale Group and he specialised in portraits, land and seascapes exhibiting at the Royal Academy, the Royal Institute of Oil Painters, the Walker Gallery, Liverpool, Paris Salon and elsewhere abroad. The National Gallery of New South Wales acquired the painting *A Northern Winter.* He exhibited over two hundred works at the RA becoming a full member in 1938.

Yorkshire was a favourite subject of Brundrit's and he captured its beauty in all its glory throughout the seasons, gaining a reputation as one of the leading landscape artists of North Yorkshire. He was, like many within the Wharfdale Group, keen to promote modern trends in contemporary paintings. His work was admired by many including John Piper and of course, Cyril Bennett.

271

He died in Masham where he had lived for many years.

Acknowledgements

What we call the beginning is often the end. And to make an end is to make a beginning. The end is where we start from.
T.S. Eliot

I do hope this quote is true. It has been a pleasure to write *Uncertainty of Reason*, book eleven in the Harrogate Crime Series, a tale that came about after a chance conversation. One sentence in the chat was enough to kindle the idea and stimulate the itch to write. Thank you, Chris, I'm grateful.

During the writing process I do try to keep a record of those who have helped put the words onto the pages. My wife has been the keystone of this process yet again – Thank you, Debbie, you keep the whole structure standing.

Thanks to Helen Gray who checks every word and offers so many editorial words of wisdom.

There is a small army of people who are key elements within this process – the many Beta readers who have kindly offered their comments – you can never have enough eyes. Sarah Hardy, Donna Morfett, Dee Groocock, Susan

Hunter, Susan Hampson, Kath Middleton, Jane Fowler, Lynda Checkley, Craig Gillan and Gill and Ian Cleverdon.

Before I move forward, I must thank many unknown people for the numerous and various quotes used within the story. I may have adapted and adjusted some of those to work within the tale, so my apologies.

My thanks also to Samuel Taylor Coleridge – *Kubla Khan*

> *'And all should cry, Beware! Beware!*
> *His flashing eyes, his floating hair!*
> *Weave a circle round him thrice,*
> *And close your eyes with holy dread.'*

Quotes from Rudyard Kipling – 'Them that asks no questions' … *The Smugglers*

'If you can meet with Triumph and Disaster And treat those two impostors just the same.' *If.*

I was blessed to discover the smoke photographs taken by Kevin Graham when I republished this series and they have graced every book in the series. A special thank you to Craig Benyon of Create Print, Wigan, for his work with creating a consistent cover design.

Having never had children, writing this part of Hannah and Owen's life would have been impossible without the support from Julie Meyers RGN RM BSc. Thank you.

My thanks, as always, to Caroline Vincent. (GA)

Thank you, Stephen King, for the use of your garage.

Thanks to Donna Morfett for Julie's description of Pennywise. Sorry for putting you on the spot but I needed a spontaneous answer.

Huge thanks to many author friends for their encouragement and support. All writers need their names whispered far and wide. This never happens by magic, even with Mr Simulacrum in the book, but through dedicated readers who turn their reading hobby into a passion, either writing reviews, administering social media sites or reading groups or just by commenting about a book on a social media platform. Each is critical to bringing the authors and their work to the general public. I give sincere thanks to each and every one of you.

Mike Clark – the spark worked.

Finally, as always, last but not least, I mention you, yes you, holding the Kindle or the paperback, the reader, for without you I would not be here. Thank you for continuing to support my writing

If you have enjoyed it, please mention my name to friends and family, as word of mouth is the best way to get more people reading the Harrogate Crime Series.

Until number twelve.

Best wishes,

Malcolm

For more information, please visit my website.
www.malcolmhollingdrakeauthor.co.uk

Printed in Great Britain
by Amazon